FAST FURY

DEA FAST SERIES

KAYLEA CROSS

FAST FURY

Copyright © 2018
by Kaylea Cross

* * * * *

Cover Art & Formatting by
<u>Sweet 'N Spicy Designs</u>

* * * * *

ISBN: 978-1983468995

Dedication

For Pamela Clare, an online friend who became a real life friend. I'll never forget the adventures we had together this year! Thank you for helping me brainstorm for this one, and for braving the helo rides. They were totally worth it, weren't they? xo

Author's Note

Dear readers,

I'm so excited to bring you this next installment of the DEA FAST Series and tell Kai's story. He's such a unique character, who is so proud of his heritage. I have travelled to the Hawaiian Islands every spring break with one side of my family for the past 7 years, and while I've set epilogues to stories there, I've always wanted to set a book there. This was my chance. I hope you enjoy it.

Happy reading!

Kaylea Cross

Chapter One

"Can you see anyone behind you?"

At her best friend's voice coming through the car's Bluetooth system, Abby McKinley checked her rearview mirror a second before making the left-hand turn onto the street her building was on. It was a beautiful, early June evening, the sun still hours from setting, the trees lining the street all lush and green. "No. I know I sound like a paranoid freak, but I swear someone's following me." She'd called Cindy a few blocks from work, wanting to be on the line with someone in case anything happened.

That damn tingling at the back of her neck was still there, so even though Abby didn't see anyone following her, she continued past the building and through the next light. A black sedan stayed on her bumper to get through the yellow light, then slowed, giving her space. And it didn't follow her when she turned right at the next corner.

Abby relaxed a little. Maybe she was wrong about the tail. Maybe it was all in her head.

"How about now?" Cindy asked.

"Still no. I'm going to circle the block one more time, just in case."

Her fingers tightened around the steering wheel. She could *feel* someone watching her, dammit. Why couldn't she see them?

You're acting crazy. Why would anyone want to follow you?

"How long have you felt this way?" Cindy asked in concern.

"Off and on over the past week or so." Being a pharmaceutical rep wouldn't warrant being followed by someone, so this was crazy.

"Has something happened that would make someone follow you?"

"Not that I know of, other than the thing with Kai." Her Polynesian god of a former neighbor—and also a badass DEA agent of some sort. Kai had been forced to move out of his apartment across the hall from her a few weeks ago. A member of the deadly *Veneno* drug cartel had somehow gotten hold of his personal information, including his home address and details about his family. Kai had told her about it the day before moving out.

Scary shit she certainly hadn't expected to hear. She'd been vague with Cindy on the details, for Kai's sake. But if the cartel could stoop to kidnapping and threatening to kill the nine-year-old daughter of Kai's teammate to make a statement, then they were capable of anything.

Including following Abby in hopes of finding a

lead on Kai.

"God, that whole thing just freaks me out," Cindy said.

"Yeah, me too." She might be making something out of nothing, but since Kai had moved out, Abby wasn't taking any chances with her safety. For all she knew, the cartel had someone monitoring the building.

It worried her that Kai might have a target on his back. He was more than just a neighbor to her; he'd become a friend. Someone she trusted, who looked out for her and did repairs around her place when the superintendent wasn't available.

If he hadn't been unavailable the whole time he'd lived across the hall from her, maybe they could have even been more.

With him totally out of your league and both of you with histories of unhealthy relationships? Yeah, that would've worked out well.

Abby shook off the thought and checked her mirror again. She would have talked to him about this situation before now, but he'd been out of town for work until late last night. Maybe now he could put her mind at ease about the cartel casing the building theory, so she could stop looking over her shoulder wherever she went.

She turned right at the next corner. Still nothing behind her that tripped her radar more than it already was. Time to go home. "Okay, I think the coast is clear. I'm heading to my building now." Except the idea that someone might be following her and know where she lived made her skin crawl.

"I'll stay on the line with you until you get inside."

"Thanks. This is why I love you—you care about me even though I'm a paranoid freak."

"That's the part I love most about you," Cindy joked.

Abby laughed. "Thank God for that."

"Are we still getting together tonight?"

"Definitely." On most Friday nights they met up with a larger group but it would be nice to spend some time just the two of them. She pulled into her parking spot. "I'm here." Palming her keys, she grabbed her purse and twisted around to reach into the backseat for her briefcase. "Text you once I'm changed and ready to meet up?"

"Sure. Bye."

Abby climbed out and shut the door, the sound muted by the noise-dampening material sprayed on the concrete ceiling of the parking garage. She rounded the rear bumper and headed for the elevators, then came to an immediate halt when she saw she wasn't alone.

A woman stood between her and the elevators. Disheveled. Wearing pale gray sweats, her dark hair hanging lank around her shoulders. She was visibly distressed, wringing her hands.

The way she stared at Abby sent a cold shiver up her spine. Wary, Abby started to take a step back.

"Hey," the woman said softly in greeting.

Abby froze, shock blasting through her as recognition hit. Holy hell, it was Shelley, Kai's drama-queen ex-girlfriend. Abby's gaze raked over her from head to toe and back again, hardly able to believe what she was seeing.

Shelley had already been thin before, but now

4

she'd lost so much weight that she looked ill, the sweats hanging from her tiny frame. Her gorgeous dark brown hair lay lank and oily-looking around her slumped shoulders, her face pale and without a hint of the perfect, sophisticated makeup she always wore. A shocking change from the polished, supermodel image Abby was used to.

Shelley wrapped her arms around her ribs, the picture of utter misery. "Have you seen Kai?"

It took a second for Abby to get over her shock enough to find her voice. "No."

"Do you know where he is?"

Abby shook her head. "No, I don't." Truth. She hadn't been to Kai's new place, didn't even have his address. "He moved out weeks ago."

Shelley's face fell. "Do you have his number? I've tried calling him so many times. He must have blocked me."

You think? After how you treated him? He'd gotten a new phone and number after the security leak, but Abby wasn't going to tell her that. "Sorry."

When it was clear Abby wasn't going to be forthcoming with any help where Kai was concerned, Shelley made a distressed sound and dragged her hands through her hair, grabbing handfuls of it at the roots, almost as if she was ready to rip it out of her scalp. Then her dark blue gaze locked on Abby and the pure, wretched grief reflected there was so real that Abby couldn't look away. Whatever Shelley's insecurity issues were about, she was in a hell of a lot of emotional pain right now. Adding to her misery would be cruel.

"You don't know what he's like," Shelley rasped

out a moment later, tears gleaming in her eyes. "What it's like to be with him. He's *ruined* me for anyone else." She paused, a sob jerking her too-thin shoulders. "I can't eat. I can't sleep. How am I supposed to get over him? Be without him for the rest of my life?"

Maybe you shoulda thought of that before you ranted and raved and pushed him away with your constant suspicion and insecurity?

Shelley looked so distraught, Abby didn't have the heart to say it aloud, even if it was true. The shocking transformation in the wealthy, high-power ad executive was enough to ignite a spark of sympathy in the hardest heart, and Abby's wasn't nearly as hard as she wanted people to think.

"I'm sorry," she said, meaning it. She might not like Shelley, but seeing her suffer like this was awful.

Shelley sagged, her face crumpling as she dissolved into tears she had valiantly tried to fight. "I need to see him. I can't go on like this, I..." She sucked in a shuddering breath, wiped at her face before meeting Abby's gaze once more, her desperation so strong Abby could all but smell it. "If you see or hear from him, will you tell him I miss him, and that I'm sorry? I want to tell him in person so badly."

Not a chance in hell. As far as Abby was concerned, Shelley didn't deserve Kai. And Kai sure as hell didn't deserve the woman's constant sniping and insecure jealousy.

Abby wasn't going to open herself up to more of this kind of thing in the future, if Shelley and Kai got back together again. Because if they did, they would absolutely break up again, and probably within a week or two.

Abby sighed. She might have judged Kai for staying in such a turbulent relationship for so long, except that would make her the worst kind of hypocrite. She had the real-life equivalent of a PhD in dysfunctional relationships. It had taken her a damn long time to extricate herself from her previous disaster, so she was in no position to throw stones. "Sure," she finally muttered.

Those devastated blue eyes held hers for a long moment, as though Shelley was trying to determine whether the offer was sincere or not. Then she nodded once in acknowledgment. "Thank you. I won't bother you again." She turned and began walking away, arms wrapped around her ribs, shoulders slumped.

Then her words registered. Wait, *again*? "Have you been following me?" she called out.

Shelley stopped and looked back at her in confusion. "What?"

The puzzlement seemed genuine. Abby pressed, wanting an answer. "You didn't follow me in my car on the way here?"

Her dark eyebrows pulled together in a frown, and there was a hint of hurt on her face now. As if she couldn't believe Abby would think such a thing of her. "No. I was already here waiting when you pulled in."

Damn, Abby hadn't even noticed her, she'd been too busy looking over her shoulder and talking to Cindy.

Shelley turned around and walked away.

Abby stayed put until she disappeared from view, the woman's light footsteps fading on the concrete ramp that led to street level. Glancing around the garage once to make sure she really was alone, Abby rushed for the elevator.

Up in the safety of her apartment with the door locked, she hurried past Kai's pet Siamese fighting fish, Goliath, swimming alone in his tricked-out tank next to the window. While she and Kai had lived across the hall from one another she'd looked after his fish and grabbed his mail for him whenever he was away, because Kai had considered her more dependable than Shelley. She'd agreed to keep Goliath here until Kai got back from this latest work trip.

At the front window she pulled the blind aside, spotted Shelley climbing into her white Lexus at the curb. Abby made note of the model, squinted to see the license plate clearly and mumbled it to herself to memorize it.

As soon as the Lexus drove out of sight, she let the blind fall back into place and stepped back from the window. Kai and his team had arrived back in town sometime last night. He needed to know about this, might be able to reassure her that no one was following her.

Her gaze slid to Goliath, drifting without a care in the climate-controlled fishy paradise, his elegant purple fins and tail rippling in the false current along with the fake aquarium plants. "I have to call your dad."

Digging her cell phone out of her purse, she dialed Kai.

****

"You better bring your A-game tonight, man," Prentiss said.

Kai Maka grinned at his teammate's words and kept his phone tucked between his head and shoulder as he carried the bags of groceries into his kitchen. "I always bring my A-game, brother. It's why I'm reigning champ." He loved hanging with his FAST Bravo brothers when they had downtime, doing things that had nothing to do with work. They played every bit as hard as they trained and operated, and it was the reason their bond was so tight.

"Wish we could be there to see it in person, but Autumn's got another decade and then some to go before she can get into a bar."

"Just tell her Uncle Kai's got something special planned for her tonight. I'll have Khan video it and send it to you guys."

A pause. "You're keeping it PG, right? She's only ten."

"G-rated, I promise."

"Even better. All right. Can't wait to see what you come up with. See you Monday."

"Yeah, man. Later."

Kai paused to stretch out his sore lower back, a low groan of pleasure/pain spilling from his lips. His body had taken a beating at the training school down south this past week-and-a-half. Damn, and he was starving, too.

Shoving a handful of roasted nuts into his mouth, he tossed the last of the sad-looking produce he'd found wilted at the back of his fridge. He'd only been gone nine days this time on a recent training event, but the berries and lettuce had long since given up the ghost. No time to put something together now. He'd grab something at the bar later.

As he shut the fridge door he thought of Abby, his former neighbor he'd lived across the hall from for the better part of two years. Most times when he'd come home after being on the road he'd find something she'd whipped up in her kitchen sitting in his fridge or freezer, with a little note welcoming him home and saying what it was.

Since he'd moved in here, he'd missed her like crazy. And not just because of her insanely awesome cooking. Ever since that day when she'd witnessed that final bit of drama between him and Shelley in his apartment and afterward pointed out that he'd been enabling a toxic relationship pattern, the way he viewed her had begun to change. He'd already liked her as a person and thought she was cute, but somehow after that day…his feelings for her weren't neighborly at all anymore.

They texted back and forth and she still looked after Goliath for him when he was away, but it wasn't the same. He hadn't seen her since the day he'd moved out of their building, and while he loved his new place, it was a bit lonely without her across the hall.

In so many ways she was a mystery to him. The entire time he'd known her, he'd never seen her with a guy, though he knew she'd dated here and there. She'd hinted that she'd been in a bad relationship before, but it had been a long time ago and Kai would never understand how someone as hot and together as her was still single. Couldn't be due to lack of male interest. Not with someone like her. Maybe all the guys she'd met since her ex were losers. Or maybe she was super picky since her breakup, and no one had made the cut yet.

Yeah, that had to be it. Made him wonder what it would take to make her cut. And whether or not he might have what it took.

He was in the process of putting boxes of cereal into a cupboard when his cell rang. His heart skipped a beat when he saw Abby's number on the screen. He could picture her so vividly—her piercing blue eyes and that sassy platinum blond pixie cut. The top of her head barely reached his shoulder. And her firm curves had fit against him perfectly when he'd finally given into temptation and pulled her into that hug the day he'd told her he was moving out.

"Hey, we must have a psychic link. I was just thinking about you," he said.

"Yeah? Let me see, it's almost dinnertime. Were you thinking about me, or my lasagna?"

"Both." It was his favorite dish of hers.

She let out a soft, husky laugh, and heat flared in the pit of his stomach. It had been happening more and more often lately whenever he imagined or heard her voice. If he thought for a moment she was interested in him, he'd jump all over the chance to see where things went between them.

"Well at least you're honest," she said.

"Always. So, what's up? Is Goliath giving you a hard time?"

"No, he's been a very good boy." She paused.

"When are you taking him home, anyway?"

"I can pick him up this weekend if you want."

"No, I'll drop him off one night for you, if you're okay giving me your new address. I've got some mail here for you too."

Of course he was okay with her having his address. "You're the best, Ab."

"I know." Another pause. "Hey, can we talk about something?"

She sounded so serious, he stopped what he was doing and straightened. "Sure, what?"

"I'd rather say in person."

He turned away from the cupboard to lean against the counter, not liking the cryptic edge to her words. "Are you okay?"

"Yeah, I'm just a little unnerved, is all."

"Why, what's going on?"

"Tell you when I see you."

He frowned. "Abby, straight up. Are you all right?" Because something was bothering her and she never complained about anything.

"I'm okay. I'll just feel better once I talk to you about a couple things."

Why wouldn't she tell him over the phone? That concerned him. "Okay." He checked his watch. "You eaten yet?"

She huffed out a laugh. "Is food all you ever think about?"

He grinned. He had quite the reputation where food was concerned. "Nah, but I'm just on my way out to meet some of my teammates at a bar about fifteen minutes from you. Can you meet me there? We can grab a bite to eat and talk after."

"After what?"

"After I defend my title."

"What title?"

Anticipation curled inside him. He wanted her to see him in action tonight. Wanted to see her, period, and find out if there was any chance she might view him as more than a friend now that they weren't living across the hall from one another. Either way, whatever was bothering her, he would help. "Just come. You'll see."

Chapter Two

Abby arrived at the bar forty-five minutes later to find Cindy already waiting for her by the front door. The sight of her bestie standing there in skinny jeans and a flowy, pale yellow top made her smile and erased the niggling anxiety inside her.

"Hey," Cindy said, wrapping her up in a big hug. "Good to see you. You look awesome."

"Thanks. You look hot."

Cindy leaned back and grinned, her green eyes sparkling. "I know. So, were your Spidey senses tingling on the way here?"

"Not really." She'd been alert on the drive over here, and hadn't noticed anyone tailing her.

"Good. Now when do I get to meet your hunky neighbor?"

An irrational spark of jealousy sliced through her gut at the thought of watching Cindy and Kai flirting all night. Not that she could blame Cindy, as her friend had no clue about Abby's new feelings toward him. But after witnessing the emotional chaos of his relationship with Shelley, Abby felt irrationally protective of him. Which was stupid, because he could *more* than take care of himself. Just not when it came to the fairer sex, apparently.

Abby frowned at her. "You've never met Kai?" How was that possible, with him living across the hall from her all this time? Surely he and Cindy would have crossed paths at some point?

"Uh, no. So? When?"

"I guess pretty soon." She yanked open the door and was immediately hit by the unmistakable scratchy lyrics to AC/DC's *You Shook Me All Night Long*. The place was packed, even though it was only seven o'clock on a Friday night.

Abby wove through the tables arranged around the periphery and skirted the edge of the crowd, heading toward the stage up front where a big bearded guy wearing jeans and a plaid button-down shirt over a white tank, and a tweed flat cap on his head was lip syncing to the song for all he was worth.

He looked familiar, but it took her a moment to place him. Logan. One of Kai's teammates who had come to help him pack the day he'd moved out. With his reddish beard and that shirt, he reminded her a little of a lumberjack.

"Wow, he's really good," Cindy yelled to her over the music, nodding her head in time to the beat, a wide grin on her face as she took in the show. Cindy loved being wherever the action was.

Abby nodded absently and glanced around,

searching for Kai. He was huge, therefore impossible to miss, and if Logan was here performing, he had to be close by. She couldn't see him though. Defend his title, he'd said. As in, a lip-sync title?

"Hey! Abby!"

She spun around to see a dark-haired man with a bronze complexion waving her down from the edge of the stage. She smiled in greeting. "Zaid, hi." He'd been there to help Kai move too.

The men all worked for the DEA, but she didn't know in what capacity. Other than their job was dangerous enough that it had resulted in the team being targeted by the *Veneno* cartel. She wanted to talk to Kai about his work, find out what he really did and why he was gone so often, but he was private about it and she hadn't wanted to push. Until now, because of the scare with the cartel.

Zaid pushed through the throng of people crowded around the edge of the stage and took her elbow, leaned down so he could talk in her ear and be heard over the music. "You here for the battle?"

"I guess I am."

"Good. Come on up front with us, so you can see better."

She gestured beside her. "I've got my friend Cindy with me too."

Zaid smiled at Cindy. "Nice to meet you. Right this way." He led her by the arm to the front row, where five more huge guys stood drinking beer from the bottle, some solo and others with their arms around a woman. She couldn't help notice that Zaid had a bottle of water instead.

Once they were in place he bent down to speak

next to Abby's ear again. "Granger's giving it all he's got, but I don't know if it'll be enough to unseat the king," he said, shaking his head in amusement as Logan pretended to belt out the chorus. The crowd was totally into it, singing along and cheering, throwing their hands in the air. "You already missed Rodriguez and Colebrook's duet."

She blinked at him. "A duet?"

Zaid nodded, a smirk on his face. "It was epic and romantic. We told 'em to go get a room."

Laughing, Abby turned her attention back to the stage. Logan stalked from one side of the stage to the other in that iconic tweed cap of the AC/DC front man, gesturing with his arms, holding the dead mic out to the crowd during the chorus in a bid for audience participation. The volume in the room immediately doubled, making the air throb and the floor shake.

Wow. This was way more intense than she'd expected.

The song ended in a flourish of drums and electric guitar. Logan held up both arms then lowered them as he bowed, the crowd whistling and cheering, including Cindy and the rest of Kai's teammates.

"All right, people, and now it's time to see what our defending champion has up his sleeve. Please welcome Master Kai to the stage!"

Another raucous cheer went up from the crowd. Two women behind Abby squealed and pushed between her and the bar. Abby exchanged a loaded look with Cindy and bit back a laugh.

But it died in her throat when Kai stepped out of the shadows and onto the stage. The women in front of her screamed and started jumping up and down, waving at him.

Oh my god, he had lip-sync groupies?

Cindy elbowed her sharply in the ribs.

Startled, Abby met her gaze with a scowl. "Ow!"

Cindy jabbed her with a finger this time. "*That's* Kai?"

Abby nudged her friend back with her elbow for good measure. "Yeah, what of it?"

"You lived across the hall from *that* for almost two freaking years, and this is the first time I'm meeting him?" Cindy smacked Abby's arm. "What the hell is wrong with you?"

"I don't know how you never saw him before. And he was taken," she said over the noise, her gaze sliding back to Kai. *But he's not taken now.* Who could blame her for staring?

"Mmm, that is a whole lot of man right there," Cindy added appreciatively.

Don't I know it. Six-foot-four of muscular, Pacific Islander hunk lit up by a spotlight, the ray of light highlighting his short black hair and dark caramel skin.

"You're going down, Maka!" Logan yelled, hands cupped around his mouth where he stood with his teammates at the edge of the stage.

Kai shot him a cocky grin, raised an inky eyebrow. "Lemme show you how it's done, son." He raised the mic, then his expression went all serious and he lowered his head. The lights dimmed. Next to her, Zaid raised his phone to video Kai as the music started.

The instant the first iconic notes hit the air, a roar

of laughter erupted through the room. Abby laughed along with them as Kai raised his head and began lip-syncing to *Let It Go*, from Disney's *Frozen*.

He was damn good, too. Adorable, charming, his willingness to poke fun at himself endearing as he hammed it up, adding dramatic movements and gestures while he pretended to tell Elsa the ice princess's story and belt out the lyrics. Abby shook her head at him.

A bra flew past her head and landed on stage three feet in front of Kai. He grinned and winked at the thoughtful audience member as he continued his performance.

Cindy leaned her head close to Abby's to be heard over the music. "I'd throw mine too, but I need one under this top."

Abby didn't answer, staring at Kai. She couldn't take her eyes off him, he was that magnetic. The entire bar was singing along now, even the guys. How did he even know the lyrics to this?

At the end of a loud, drawn-out note he suddenly stopped, a comical expression on his face, one hand raised in the air, fingers curled upward in a dramatic pose. The song ended abruptly, then the opening bars of Taylor Swift's *Shake It Off* started up.

More laughter swelled around her, the volume becoming almost deafening when Kai started dancing around on stage, his gestures and goofy facial expression priceless. Abby grinned and shook her head, then started clapping along with everyone else.

By the time Kai struck his last pose a couple minutes later, nailing the ending, there were four bras on the stage, and one pair of panties. While he stood there with that killer smile and accepted the adoration of his enthusiastic audience, his teammates were all whistling and yelling *Hana ho*—whatever that meant—as they flashed the ubiquitous Hawaiian *shaka* at him. That, she knew.

"Thank you for that riveting performance, Master Kai," the announcer said. Kai gave him a thumbs up and bent to scoop up the bras and panties, handing them to one of the bouncers before returning to the center of the stage. "And now it's time to find out if the king has fallen. Let's have all the contestants on stage, please."

Six guys lined up with Kai, including Logan and two other guys from the team, Jamie and Easton. All big, good-looking guys.

But none of them even came close to Kai.

The announcer called each performer forward and asked the crowd to rate their act by volume of applause. The first three acts got anemic responses. Jamie and Easton got a slightly less lukewarm reaction. They both stared at the audience with incredulous expressions and raised their hands in a perplexed "what the hell more did you people want from us" gesture.

Logan stepped forward next. Cheers and shouts rang out throughout the room, several women screaming his name. He grinned good-naturedly and put his arms in the air, basking in the praise. Before stepping back into line, he gave Kai a shot in the shoulder with his fist. Arms folded across his massive chest, biceps bulging under the sleeves of his T-shirt, the punch didn't even budge Kai.

Finally, it was his turn. He lowered his arms and stepped forward, unleashing another round of swooning female response.

"And now, for our defending champion. What did you think of Master Kai?"

The audience's reaction nearly shattered Abby's eardrums, but she was too busy whistling and clapping to care. Cindy was hopping up and down as much as the two women in front of them, their shrill screams adding to the din. As for Kai's teammates, they were all booing and giving him the thumbs down.

"And the king keeps his crown!" the announcer shouted. "Congrats to our defending champ." He walked onstage to clasp Kai's hand and raise it in the air victoriously. Kai's smile hit her straight in the gut, and when those dark brown eyes landed on her and held, it felt like her heart stopped beating.

Holding her gaze, he crossed to the front of the stage, the two women there seeming to melt away as he hopped down right in front of her. With his focus entirely on her, for a moment it weirdly felt like they were the only two people in the building.

"Hey, thanks for coming," he said, reaching those long, powerful arms around her back to pull her into a hug.

Unprepared for it, Abby had to lock her knees to keep from melting to the floor. As his clean, spicy scent swirled around her and those warm, steely muscles pressed to her front, every nerve ending in her body seemed to short-circuit. Including the ones in her brain.

She distantly heard someone clear his or her throat

beside her, and remembered Cindy was standing there, waiting for an introduction. "Oh. Um, this is my best friend, Cindy," she said, pulling away. "Cindy, Kai."

Kai offered his hand to her. "Hey. Nice to meet you."

Cindy's smile was full of dazzled female appreciation. "Likewise."

He introduced them to his teammates and significant others, a couple of them new to Abby, then faced her. "You wanna grab a bite now?"

She glanced at Cindy in question before answering. "Sure."

"Actually, I can't stay," her friend said.

Wait, what? They always hung out on Friday night.

"I just came for the show. Gotta meet some other friends across town. See you later, Ab." Cindy hugged her, leaning close to murmur in her ear. "You better call me later and tell me *everything*," she warned, then shot Kai a gorgeous smile and sauntered away.

Abby stared after her. This wasn't part of the plan. *But there's nothing to tell. He's just a friend.*

One that gave her shivers whenever he touched her now. But that was her problem, not his.

"So," Kai said, drawing her attention back to him. "Shall we?" He set a hand on her lower back and gestured toward the rear of the bar where all the tables were set up.

The heat of his palm sank through her leather jacket, igniting heat of another source in her body. She slid into the booth, a bit surprised when he scooted in beside her rather than take the chair opposite her. She didn't consider herself to be a small woman, and years of struggling with body image issues and poor self-esteem made her feel bigger than she actually was, but next to him she felt tiny. In a heightened, ultra-feminine way she liked a whole lot. Not that she'd ever admit it, being a strong, capable and independent woman who could take care of herself.

Kai slid a menu over to her. "Okay, tell me what's bothering you," he said without preamble.

Not seeing the point in dancing around the subject, she simply told him flat out. "Well, for one, Shelley was waiting for me in the parking garage when I got home from work tonight."

AT THE MENTION of his ex, Kai's entire body stiffened.

His attention sharpened on Abby, every single one of his protective instincts bristling. If Shelley had threatened her, Kai would take care of it personally. *No one* was going to bother Abby while he was around, whether it was his ex or a freaking *Veneno* cartel member. "What did she want?"

She shrugged, the scent of her trademark black leather jacket reaching his nose, her cap of pale blonde hair almost glowing in the dim light. "To know where you were and find out whether I'd seen you. I told her I hadn't, which is true. She was really upset, but when I didn't have anything useful to tell her, she left."

Kai absorbed everything and analyzed it. After almost two months apart, he didn't miss Shelley, or the constant exhaustion from having to soothe her ruffled feathers all the time. He'd tried to make it work for way too long, when the truth was, nothing would ever have made it work. He saw that now.

Thanks to Abby.

Sometimes it took another person's perspective, then time and space to give you the distance to look at things with new eyes. He hadn't liked what he'd seen about himself, that he'd been enabling toxic relationships for pretty much his entire adult life. So he'd finally ended it, though Shelley didn't seem to have accepted that they were done.

"I'm sorry she did that," he murmured. Abby had been privy to more than her share of the drama that had played out between he and Shelley. It embarrassed him that she was still dealing with more of it because of him. He wanted that chapter of his life over and done with, so he could move on. To better things.

And hopefully, to Abby.

"It's not your fault. But the thing is..." She hesitated a moment, fiddled with her menu. "Okay, I don't have any proof, but I feel like someone's been following me around lately."

He frowned in concern. "What? For how long?"

"Around a week or so. When I'm driving."

What the hell? "Why didn't you call or text me?"

"Because you were gone, I didn't have any proof, and I thought I was just being paranoid because of the reasons why you had to move so suddenly. When she showed up tonight I thought maybe it might have been her I sensed, but she seemed genuinely stunned that I would think that."

Shelley had her problems, for sure. Insecurity and jealousy being the worst ones. Would she be frantic enough to stalk Abby just to try and get a lead on him? Maybe. She'd said and done a lot of things he wouldn't have thought her capable of during their turbulent relationship. "I can't say for sure that she wouldn't do it."

"I thought so too, but her reaction to my question was real, and believe me when I say she was too upset to be able to make up that convincing a lie so fast. She was in such rough shape I barely recognized her when I first saw her standing there."

Kai covered a wince. He felt badly for Shelley. He might not want to be involved with her anymore, but that didn't mean he wanted her to suffer, either. "I'll contact her and tell her to leave you alone."

"No, that'll just open up a whole new can of worms and she'll keep trying to contact you. Better to leave things the way they are and give her the time and space to get over you."

She was right. Though he felt bad for Shelley, they didn't need to see or talk to each other again. "Even if she was following you, I don't think she's dangerous." Desperate and in need of a healthy dose of self-esteem, maybe, but not dangerous. Not to anyone but herself, anyhow. "Did you ever see someone? Get a vehicle make and model or a plate number?"

"No. It's just a feeling I couldn't shake, and strong enough that I wasn't going to ignore it. Maybe because of everything you told me before you moved out."

Smart. Kai leaned back and regarded her more

closely. How had he lived across the hall from her for so long and not really *seen* her? He'd been fucking blind, it was the only answer. "We did have someone watching the building, just in case, but he was reassigned as of last week."

Abby began perusing her menu. "It could just be my imagination."

Maybe. But maybe not. And that bothered him. "I don't like that you're scared. And I hate that it's because of me."

She turned those vivid blue eyes on him. "No, don't be silly. You said yourself that moving would make everyone safer."

He nodded. "I had to go." After little Autumn Prentiss had been kidnapped on the order of a *Veneno* lieutenant a few weeks ago, Kai and the DEA weren't taking any chances with security. Continuing to live there when the cartel knew his address would have put everyone in the building in possible jeopardy.

"I know." She put down her menu and gave him a wry little smile. "Shelley also made a comment that you ruined her for anyone else."

Kai shook his head, a pang of sympathy slicing through him. He'd been good to Shelley. "That's because she never dated anyone who treated her right before."

Abby's smile disappeared. "And I bet we could say the same about the two of us, too," she murmured.

Her words hit home. "Yeah, probably." Before things could get any heavier, the waitress came and took their orders. When she left, Kai leaned back against the booth and regarded Abby. "So, what's new with you these days? You seeing anyone?"

She made a face and fiddled with the paper napkin rolled around her utensils. "I'm working a lot. Been on a few dates, but not seeing anyone." Her face brightened, light sparking in her pretty blue eyes. "But hey, I might finally get to visit your homeland."

He raised his eyebrows. "You're going to Maui?"

"Maybe. Not sure yet. My boss and his boss are going to a big pharmaceutical convention there, and they want to take a rep with a strong sales record for the last three quarters. It's down to me and one other person. I'll know by Sunday night, hopefully. The convention starts a week this Wednesday."

"That's great."

"If I go, you'll have to tell me all the places to hit up before I leave."

"Might be able to do you one better."

She cocked her head. "Yeah? How?"

"We've got a training thing scheduled for late this coming week, on Oahu. I'm trying to see if I can get some time off after that, maybe a week or so, and go visit my grandma and cousin back home. Been over a year-and-a-half since I've been back. If it works out, I can take you around the island personally for a couple days." He'd freaking love to show her around his home island, get to spend more one-on-one time with her. See if he had a shot with her.

The corners of her lips curved up. "Really? You're serious?"

He was more serious about her than she seemed to realize. He intended to make that clear real soon. "Totally serious. I'd love to show you my island."

"Well then, I accept. If I get the nod and you get

27

the time off, I'm all yours."

The words heated his blood, filled his head with all kinds of things he would do to her if she were his. Hot, dirty things that would leave them both sated and sweaty and craving more of. "Deal."

Getting the time off was going to be a tall order, however, because FAST Bravo was in more demand than ever before. The war on drugs was raging hotter than ever, the body count piling higher with each passing day—and the *Venenos* were right at the epicenter of it.

Chapter Three

I'm not ready.

Unfortunately it didn't matter, because she didn't have a choice about doing this.

Diane followed the coroner down the hallway in a complete daze. Her body moved on autopilot, the rubber soles of her sneakers squeaking against the linoleum. The harsh overhead lights glared off the white walls, hurting her eyes. A stale smell hung in the air. And with every step she took, bringing her closer and closer to the double doors at the end of the hall, the more the bubble of panic burned inside her chest.

The coroner, a young woman in her late-twenties, paused at the doors to look at her, her brown eyes sympathetic behind the lenses of her stylish glasses. "Are you ready?"

Diane stared at her for a moment. *No, I'm not ready. I'll never be ready.* She rubbed her cold, damp palms against her jeans and nodded, her heart thudding painfully against her ribs.

The harsh, stringent scent of chemicals hit her as soon as the door swung open. Everything was eerily quiet, completely sterile. Cold. A stainless steel autopsy table sat empty in the center of the room. In front of her, a wall of stainless steel compartments with handles covered one end of the room.

The soles of her shoes stuck to the floor. She faced that terrible wall, every muscle in her body drawn taut as the pathologist stepped forward to grasp one of the handles. A metallic click echoed in the unnatural stillness of the room, then the door slid open. The woman reached in and began pulling out the refrigerated drawer inside.

Diane took an involuntary step back, terror gripping her. But no matter how afraid she was, she couldn't tear her gaze away from that drawer. Could only stare as the body came out, covered in a pristine white sheet, then the pathologist began to draw it down to reveal the victim.

Dark hair. A ghostly pale face, almost blue.

An inhuman sound ripped free of her chest. One trembling hand went to her mouth, agony and horror knifing through her. *Bailey.*

"Nooooo," she cried, the sound scraping over her raw throat. She wanted to scream it. Prayed for this to be a horrible mistake. A sick joke.

But the irrefutable evidence was right before her.

Her beautiful twenty-two-year-old daughter lay stretched out on that cold steel slab, eyes closed. A bluish tinge surrounded her eyes, mouth and nose, the little star-shaped piercing there glinting in the unforgiving overhead lights.

Diane's legs gave out. Pain shot through her knees, jolted through her entire body as she hit the linoleum floor. The pathologist gasped and lunged forward to grab her. Diane lashed out with her arms, a feral cry of rage and agony emitting from her lips.

Her stomach twisted. She doubled over, gagging. A trashcan appeared in front of her face. She grabbed it blindly, bent over it and retched, until nothing was left and her throat and mouth burned from the bile.

Voices swirled around her, unfamiliar and disembodied. Strong hands reached under her arms. She made a half-hearted attempt at swatting them away, but she was too weak.

Someone lifted her onto her feet. A man. She swayed, the room pitching and spinning around her. Her lungs were on fire, ready to burst.

I can't bear this. Just let me die. Please, God, take me instead. She would trade places with Bailey in an instant if it meant bringing her daughter back.

"Mrs. Whitehead, please come with me out into the hall," the man said.

Panic shot through her. She wrenched her arms free and stumbled forward a step, shaking her head. "*No*. Don't touch me. I'm not leaving my baby." She'd fight them. Fight them all with everything she had. They'd have to bodily drag her out of this room.

The man made a frustrated sound behind her. "Mrs. White—"

"*No*, goddamn it. Just get out!" She lunged for Bailey, afraid they would try and tear her away. She grabbed hold of her daughter's ice-cold hand, and finally the grief broke through the pain. Great sobs wracked her as she stood there staring down at Bailey's frozen features.

Baby, look what they did to you.

Voices murmured behind her. She didn't hear any words. Didn't care what they were saying. Didn't care about anything anymore. Had never known she could hurt like this.

Her daughter was still so damn beautiful. So much potential, wasted. "Bailey," she choked out, shaking all over. She couldn't bring herself to look at Bailey's arms. Didn't want to see the needle tracks she knew she would find there. "Baby, I'm so sorry. So sorry…" *This is partly my fault. I didn't do enough to stop this.* That almost killed her.

It had all started with a bad car accident.

Multiple broken bones and a concussion, whiplash. The doctor had prescribed Bailey Percocet and oxycodone. They'd helped at first. And Diane had missed the signs early on. She hadn't noticed the way Bailey had begun relying on them. Sneaking them when she wasn't looking. Hiding vials of them in various places.

Then the increased dosage had stopped working. So Bailey had begun taking more and more. Seeing a problem in the making, the doctor had cut her off, with Diane's full support. And the unthinkable had happened.

Her sweet, loving and well-adjusted daughter had run away from home and turned to street drugs to feed her addiction.

Diane had found her. Put her directly into rehab. Bailey had left the first time. Relapsed after finishing on the second attempt. So Diane had done what any loving mother would do. She'd pulled up stakes and taken her daughter far away to save her.

Moving to Maui last year was supposed to give them both a fresh start, a new life far away from the toxic environment and people Bailey had been hanging with back in West Virginia. Bailey had completed rehab here. She'd been clean for over nine months.

Until her good-for-nothing ex-boyfriend from back home had destroyed her with a single phone call, derailing her recovery and sending her back to the heroin that had ultimately destroyed her.

Diane gazed down at her baby's horrifyingly still face. The face of her only child and best friend. The only person who had truly understood and loved her on this earth. Now she had nothing and no one. God, she couldn't take this, couldn't bear to continue living in this place that was supposed to have been their island paradise, and instead had become their worst nightmare.

"Mrs. Whitehead, please," the pathologist begged. "Come away now."

"Just leave me alone."

Utter devastation suffused Diane's heart. They'd killed Bailey. The people who had sold her the heroin. The doctor who had prescribed the opioids that had begun this unimaginable tragedy. And all of Diane's efforts to save her had been in vain.

Rage built beneath her ribs, a raging inferno that melted away the ice. Those people had murdered her daughter.

Gripping Bailey's chilled hand tighter, she stared down into her daughter's beloved face, the need for vengeance burning bright as the sun. "I'm going to find the people who did this to you," she whispered. "And when I do, I swear to God I'll make them pay."

****

The familiar smell of stale sweat and hard work hit Kai the moment he opened the gym door. Over the smack of boxing gloves against pads, calls from the trainers rang out as they worked with their clients.

In the closest of the three rings, two guys wearing protective headgear were sparring while the trainers shouted encouragement and instructions. In the far ring, a huge guy worked with someone else. His back was to Kai, the level of his hands at mid-chest height suggesting that whoever was throwing the punches was a lot smaller than him.

Kai headed for the far ring, his attention riveted on the man's invisible partner. He'd come here for one reason and one reason only: to see Abby.

He'd thought about her all last night, couldn't get her out of his mind. Would getting involved be a huge mistake because of their friendship? They weren't neighbors anymore. It's not like they would see each other unless they made plans to meet up. But if shifting their relationship out of the friend zone would make things too weird for her, then he wouldn't pursue anything. He didn't want to lose her.

The trainer turned slightly, revealing a little blonde pixie throwing punches. Abby wore pink boxing gloves, a purple sports bra and a black running skirt. Her platinum bangs were stuck to her forehead, her face glistening with sweat as she threw punch after punch as her trainer called them out, the muscles in her arms and shoulders standing out.

Kai stopped and folded his arms, careful to stay out of her line of sight so he didn't distract her, enjoying watching her. He'd never realized she'd taken up boxing. When she'd started going to the gym religiously a little over a year ago, he'd assumed she did yoga or whatever.

This was unexpected. And surprisingly hot. It suited her, that slight edge she had about her. An outer toughness he saw right through to the softness beneath. The combination was totally endearing.

Abby moved along with her trainer, paused to wipe a forearm across her sweaty forehead as the man stepped back and gave her instructions. She went into a fighting stance, unleashed two jabs, a cross and a hook before executing three roundhouse kicks and finishing with a spinning back kick that resulted in a loud smack and rocked the big guy back on his heels. Her trainer was a freaking monster, around six-six, so Kai knew exactly what kind of force she'd managed to put into that shot. He was impressed.

Abby stopped, panting, bending over to rest her gloved hands on her knees.

"You got an audience," the trainer said, looking over at Kai.

Abby twisted her head around, caught sight of him and shot upright, her eyes widening. "What are you doing here?" she blurted, mopping at her face with the hand towel snatched from the top rope.

"Thought I'd meet you halfway." But mostly he'd been curious about what she did here and wanted to surprise her. The receptionist had let him in for a tour.

She murmured something to her trainer that Kai didn't catch, then bent and climbed through the lower and upper ropes to hop down from the ring. Her face was bright pink, a shade or two darker now than before as she wiped at it. "I'm so embarrassed."

Kai frowned. "Why?" He hadn't meant to embarrass her.

"Look at me, I'm disgusting."

She looked sexy. In an honest, authentic way that was completely opposite of Shelley and all the other women he'd dated. Maybe that's why he found it so appealing. Abby was the exact opposite of his usual type.

Not that his usual type had ever worked out for him.

This wasn't the first time he'd noticed some self-consciousness from her, however. She'd made passing derogatory comments about her body before, and based on previous things she'd mentioned about her ex, Kai laid a good chunk of the blame on that dipshit. The dick had been a controlling asshole, plain and simple, taking shots at Abby's self-esteem because it made him feel better about himself. Fucking disgusting.

"You look great," he said. "And I had no idea you were a kickboxer."

She shrugged. "I'm not. I mean, I don't compete or anything, it's just for fitness."

He ran an appreciative but subtle eye over her body. She was fit, but still had curves a man could hold onto. And with her midriff bare below the sports bra, each breath created a hint of definition on either side of her abs.

Stop staring, dude.

He raised his eyes to her face, took in the bright pink glow in her cheeks. She had gorgeous skin. "Did you bring Goliath?" he asked.

"He's in the backseat of my car, wrapped up all cozy inside his plastic baggy."

Kai should probably just grab him and go, but he didn't want to leave. He wanted to spend more time with Abby, find out if there was any reciprocal attraction on her part. Something told him he had to be careful not to come on too strong or move too fast, or he'd scare her away. "That kind of training sure works up an appetite. Let me make you dinner at my place. As a thank you for looking after my attack fish."

She shot him a frown. "I can't go to your place right now, I'm gross."

"Did you bring a change of clothes with you?"

"Just what I wore to work. I'd need to shower first, and—"

"You can shower at my place." Just the thought of her standing naked in his shower with the water sluicing over her bare body made his blood run hotter.

She lowered the towel and met his gaze. "You don't need to make me dinner. You don't need to pay me back for looking after your fish."

"Abby. Let me cook for you." He wanted her to come to his place, for them to spend time alone together. It had been way too long since they'd shared a meal. He missed her. Way more than he'd expected.

Her expression changed, a hint of surprise lighting the depths of those brilliant blue eyes. She exhaled. "Well then can I at least grab some groceries for us on the way over?"

"No." He reached down and picked up the familiar pink gym bag lying beside the base of the ring, unwilling to take no for an answer. "Come on, I'm starving. You can follow me over."

Tonight he was going to test the waters, and find out if there was enough room for something more than friendship between them. He'd wasted too much time being unhappy in his last relationship, putting up with all kinds of crazy bullshit instead of noticing what was right there in front of him.

No more. It was time to make a move and show Abby how good they could be together.

Chapter Four

When she'd woken up this morning, the last thing Abby had expected to happen was that she would wind up in Kai's shower tonight.

She breathed in deeply as she worked the shampoo into her wet hair, and almost moaned. The clean, spicy fragrance was all Kai, made her imagine him standing in here completely naked with soapsuds trailing over his smooth, deep-caramel skin. And had it been her imagination, or had he kind of checked her out back at the gym?

Granted, she'd been sweaty and disgusting with not even a trace of makeup on. Maybe she'd imagined it. He went for model types, not people like her.

Clean, dry and dressed in dark jeans and three-quarter sleeve faux-wrap top that did wonders for her cleavage, she paused in front of the mirror for a moment to smooth her bangs to the side.

A nervous flutter stirred in the pit of her belly. Weird. This wasn't a date, but it felt entirely different from when they'd shared a meal when they'd been neighbors. More intimate. It was like that parting hug the day before he'd moved out had changed things between them somehow.

Or maybe you're nuts.

Yeah, okay, maybe. Her intensifying crush on him might be clouding her judgment.

She found Kai busy getting things prepped in the kitchen. He stood with his back to her, allowing her a moment's privacy to admire the width of his shoulders, taut waist and the way he filled out those snug jeans.

"Need a hand with anything?" she asked.

She loved food. It was her solace and had been since she was a teenager living in her constantly tension-filled house. She loved to eat it, cook it, and share it with people she cared about. In the kitchen, she was in her element. There, she felt the freest, and in control. It was why she spent so much time there, cooking up big dishes she no longer had anyone across the hall to share them with. Without Kai, her place and life seemed a little empty.

He glanced over one muscular shoulder at her and shot her a smile that made her belly flip. "No, I'm okay. I'm not anywhere as good as you in the kitchen, but this I've got. Want some wine?"

"If you've got some."

"I do, and it's your favorite."

It touched her that he'd remembered her favorite label and bought some for her. "Wow, you're spoiling me."

He tossed her another of those lazy, appreciative grins, and he turned back to pouring her a glass. "You always spoiled me. High time I returned the favor." He handed it to her.

"Thank you." She stood at the island and sipped at it as he got the salad together, savoring the delicate cherry notes to her favorite red wine. God, she'd missed him. "Your place is really great, Kai." A loft-style space, open concept, with lots of old brick and great light. Big step up from the units in the building she lived in.

"You like it?" Kai asked.

"It's gorgeous." Urban without being too modern, masculine, and warm rather than cold the way industrial-style places so often were. "Suits you perfectly."

She wandered into the open-concept living area. Goliath was safely ensconced in his tank in the living room portion of the loft. Framed pictures of Kai and his grandma or teammates lined a long shelf mounted on the brick wall separating the main living area from the master suite. She especially loved the ones of him in his Marine dress uniform. *Hot.*

"I lucked out. It had just come on the market the day before I got the word I needed to move." He picked up the plate holding the steaks. "I'm gonna go grill these outside on the deck, if you wanna join me."

"Sure." She followed him through the far end of the loft and through a large sliding glass door out onto a private balcony, giving them a panoramic view of the city and river. Out here she could breathe easier, that undercurrent of sexual tension simmering between them less prevalent. "Wow, look at that view! No wonder you were so quick to get out of our building," she teased.

He stopped in the process of lifting the lid to the grill, his eyes meeting hers. He had gorgeous eyes. At first glance they seemed dark as espresso. Up close in the light, they were studded with bits of dark amber and chocolate. "It's a great place. But it doesn't feel as homey as when I lived across from you."

Something in his tone and expression gave his words a weight that told her he missed her. "No," she agreed. "It's not the same for me now either. Not gonna lie, I miss having you around. I felt safe with you there, and I liked being able to share my cooking with someone who appreciated it."

"You're still safe," he told her, sliding the steaks onto the hot grill. "I had someone from the agency review the building's security video surveillance. No sign whatsoever of anyone casing the place or following you to or from the building or parking garage."

"When did you do that?"

"Last night. Called in a favor on the way home from the bar."

"Oh." Warmth glowed in her chest that he would go to such trouble, that he cared about her so much. "Well, thank you."

"It's nothing. After what you said about being followed and then Shelley showing up, I wanted to be sure." He stepped back from the grill and leaned against the deck railing to fold his arms, giving her an eyeful of the muscles in his arms and shoulders. The swirling edge of a black tribal tattoo peeked out from beneath the bottom of his left sleeve. So many times she'd wondered where they started and ended, wanted to see the whole design.

And then trace it with her fingers and lips.

"So, any word on Maui yet?" he asked.

She shook away the mental image of her licking Kai's muscular chest. "No. But I keep obsessively checking my phone to make sure I didn't miss a call or message." She took another sip of wine. "You were born in Maui, right? So that makes you a native Hawaiian?"

"Born there, yes, but I'm only half Hawaiian. Other half's a mix of Samoan and a bit of Scottish, but there's bound to be some Tahitian mixed in there as well."

"Scottish? Really?" He looked all Pacific Islander to her.

He lifted a broad shoulder. "That's what I'm told."

"And you were raised by your grandma, I think you told me once?"

"Since I was three. Never knew my dad. He was a rugby player who came to the Islands. He and my mom hooked up during a music festival in Honolulu. Took off when I was a couple months old, never contacted her again."

"Oh." How had she never known this about him? "And so your mom raised you until you were three, and then…?"

"She left for the mainland." He went back to the grill and flipped the steaks. "She always hated living on the island. Felt caged there. So she moved to Cali to look for a better job and sent money home to us. In my junior year of high school, she met a guy and remarried, moved to Nevada. I still see her once or twice a year, but I'm way closer with my grandma."

"Oh. Sorry, I didn't mean to be nosey."

"You're not." He shrugged those broad shoulders, but she sensed an undercurrent of tension beneath the casual façade. "I'm what we call a *hanai* child in my culture. In the old days, and even now, it's not uncommon for a child to be raised by someone other than his or her biological parents. Usually a grandparent." He shifted the steaks to a cooler part of the grill. "My grandma raised two of us, me and my cousin Hani. He's eighteen months younger than me, so we were like brothers."

That made her smile. "I've never heard you talk about him before."

His expression closed up a bit. "Yeah, well, we…aren't in contact anymore."

She wanted to ask what had happened, but held back. She'd pried enough already.

He set down his grill tongs and resumed his spot by the railing, studying her. "You still see your parents? I know they divorced when you were in high school."

Abby sighed. It was a freaking family mystery how they'd ever gotten together in the first place, let alone made it that far together. Looking back, her pattern of tolerating unhealthy relationships had begun with them and their example, then born of her need to avoid conflict.

"It's complicated, I guess you could say. I still see

them both, but not much, and I'm a bit closer with my dad. I had to live with my mom right after they split, until I left for college. Neither of us were happy. They're both remarried, with step kids. We're on a rotating holiday schedule. Gets kind of messy sometimes, but it is what it is, right?"

One corner of his mouth tipped up. "Yeah, true. And what about you? You said you're not seeing anyone right now."

The abrupt change in topic threw her for a moment. "Um, no, not right now. You?" Although how could he be, he'd just broken up with Shelley a few weeks ago and then been away for work most of that time.

"No."

Why had he asked her? "You're not ready to put yourself out there again anyway."

He gave her an enigmatic smile that made her insides curl. "I might be. Depends."

"On what?"

"On whether the right woman was interested."

He can't mean me. But the way he was looking at her made her think that maybe he did.

Unsure how to respond, she averted her gaze and tried to laugh it off. "I know you don't mean me. We'd be a total disaster."

"Why?"

Why? She forced herself to meet his gaze again, her heart beating faster. Part of her was elated that he might be interested in her that way, but the other... Would she risk starting something and maybe lose his friendship if things didn't work out? Because based on their dating histories, the odds weren't in their favor. And she didn't want to get even more attached to him than she already was, only to have her heart broken later.

"Oh, come on," she said with a laugh. "With our track records? Please. Neither one of us would know what a healthy relationship looked like if it hit us between the freaking eyes. And you just got out of a not so awesome long-term one. You need time to get over that before you get involved with anyone else."

"No, I don't. We've been officially split up for a while now, but for me it ended a long time before that day you saw me take my key back from her."

Well, still. "You don't think it would be a bad idea to jump into a new relationship right after getting out of a bad one?"

"Like I said, not if it was with the right woman." That glint in his eyes stirred her insides. "We both know what a bad situation looks like well enough to recognize it. And I've never been friends with someone first. I hear friendship is the best foundation there is for a relationship. Maybe that's what I've been missing."

The unmistakable heat in his eyes shocked her. Made her mouth go dry in a way that had nothing to do with the tannins in her wine. "I…" She trailed off, not knowing what to say without making a fool of herself.

He shut off the grill. "Food's done. You ready to eat?" he asked, changing the subject as though he hadn't just tipped her world on its axis.

She breathed a sigh of relief. "Yes."

He scooped the steaks up onto the platter and carried them back inside. They sat across the table from one another and ate. The salad was light and tangy, the steaks perfectly cooked and seasoned. But throughout the whole meal she couldn't stop thinking about whether he'd been serious about them getting together. It was driving her crazy.

"The steak's perfect," she told him in between bites. And she was a bit of a food snob, so she wouldn't say it if it wasn't true.

"Good." He took a sip of beer, eyeing her. "So I'm curious."

The way he watched her had that stirring sensation starting up in her lower belly again. "About what?"

"*None* of the dates you've been on recently went anywhere?"

She was relieved he'd let the part about them go. "One got a second date. And he shouldn't have."

He winced. "Was it bad?"

"Not terrible. Far from the worst date I've been on. We met through an online site, whereas the others I was set up with. But there was no fire with any of them. I mean, zero, not even a spark. Not that fire is the be all, end all when it comes to a potential relationship. I know it's not that important because it always burns out eventually, but—"

"What are you even saying?"

She stopped, surprised by the vehemence in his tone. "What?"

"Chemistry is *everything*, especially early on."

She shook her head, confused. "No, it's not. Chemistry is like false advertising. It's an illusion, and it doesn't last. Relationships need a hell of a lot more than physical attraction if they're going to get off the ground. Like friendship, as you pointed out. Respect. Trust." Her friendship with him had those things. But they might not last if they muddied the waters with physical things.

"Chemistry is every bit as important as all those things." Kai shook his head at her, almost in disappointment. "What the hell kind of guys have you been with, short stuff?"

Abby blinked at him, at a loss as to how she should answer. He seemed convinced about his opinion, passionate. But he was a guy. They thought differently than women did. Was she missing something? Was there something wrong with her that she'd never experienced that kind of intense chemistry with anyone?

Kai leaned a muscular forearm on the table, a frown drawing his black eyebrows together. "What about the guy you were living with before you moved into your apartment?"

Roger. Even his name made her mentally make a face. "What about him?"

"You must have had great chemistry with him, right? At least in the beginning. I mean, you were with him for years and you guys lived together."

She frowned, thinking about it. "I guess so. I mean, sort of." Not really. "It was more that…"

That he paid attention to me.

She stopped herself before those damning, pathetic words could come out. Looking back on it now, she could see that Roger had dazzled her simply by showing interest and paying attention to her as she'd come out of her awkward teenage years. How sad was that? Even at twenty-two-years-old, she'd still been struggling so much with self-esteem and self-image issues from her teen years that she'd blindly given her heart to a man who hadn't appreciated it, let alone respected it.

Or her. She'd allowed herself to be bullied and emotionally abused simply to have someone to come home to at night.

That still pissed her off. But that was Old Abby, and thankfully she was long gone. She was New Abby now, thanks to a lot of work. Powerful. Confident—mostly. Hear her roar.

She played with the stem of her wineglass, not wanting to look at Kai as she spoke. Her relationship with Roger wasn't something she was proud of. "I should have left him after the second year when things started going downhill, but I kept telling myself things would get better. That he was stressed, that I should try harder, whatever."

"What finally made you leave?" he asked quietly.

"It took me crying myself to sleep on my mom's couch on New Year's Eve after he and I had been in a huge, public fight at a party, to realize it *wasn't* going to get better. If he could treat me like that in front of a big group of people, then he didn't love or respect me. I guess it was like a light bulb went off in my head. It had never occurred to me before then just how bad things had gotten, or that I deserved better. I finally decided I'd rather be alone than feel that lonely in a relationship." She looked up.

Kai's jaw was tight, annoyance stamped all over his face. "I get it."

A measure of relief hit her. Yeah, Kai did get it. He'd been through it himself. "I know you do." She cocked her head. "Why did you hang in there with Shelley for as long as you did?"

He sighed. "She was…fragile, I guess is the right word. I felt protective of her. Kept thinking that once she learned to trust me and our relationship, that she would stop being insecure and things would get better. But no matter how hard I tried to reassure her, it just never happened. If I didn't text her back within thirty minutes she automatically assumed I was pissed at her about something. Or when I was away for work she thought I must be off cheating on her with someone else." He shook his head at himself. "She just flat out didn't trust me, is what it comes down to. Well, not just me. Every guy she's dated."

It was really sad, actually. Looking at her from the outside, Shelley had everything going for her. Looks, brains, a killer body, money, a successful career. Yet she had sabotaged her own happiness with Kai because of her insecurities. "What finally turned the light bulb on for you, if you don't mind me asking?"

"You."

Abby blinked, surprised. "Me?"

"That night when you were at my place and Shelley barged in to throw more drama my way. You saw what it was like—she thought I was cheating on her with you."

Yeah, Abby hadn't appreciated the insult to her integrity, but she'd also felt bad for Kai, who hadn't done anything wrong. It physically hurt to think of Kai being treated that way by someone he loved.

"It was what you said to me after she left. About how you'd enabled a toxic relationship before. I'd never thought about it like that until then, but it's exactly what I'd been doing. What we had was totally dysfunctional, and I'd not only allowed it, I'd willingly participated in it. That hit home hard and woke me up, made me realize she was never going to change, that I had to be the one to end it once and for all. So thank you."

She smiled at him, gratified that she'd been able to help him see all that. "You're welcome. I hated seeing the way she treated you. Reminded me of what I'd gone through." Having your partner chip away at your foundation as a human being until you forgot who you were was a pretty shitty way to live. "So no, in answer to your question, I guess there was never really any fire there at all between my ex and me, even at the start." More like a pilot light instead of flames.

Kai shook his head slowly and set his fork down, staring at her. "Well, you deserve a hell of a lot better. You know that, right?"

"Yes." She reminded herself of it every day. "And so do you."

He nodded. "Yeah. But trust me, heat matters. I don't ever want you to settle for someone without it again." Taking a sip of beer, he lowered the bottle to his lap and regarded her. "You need a guy who will pick you up, pin you to the closest wall and kiss you until you can't even think, because he can't get enough of you."

Abby's fingers tightened around the stem of her wineglass, her mouth going dry. His words resonated in a hidden place inside her, a soft, defenseless spot she'd long ago locked up and fortified with armor that she didn't allow anyone to get close to. And suddenly all she could think about was Kai, his strong hands winding in her hair, one muscled arm wrapping around her hips as he hoisted her in the air and pinned her to the wall with that powerful body, his mouth fused with hers.

Holy. Shit.

There was no way she could pretend to misunderstand his intent this time. She sat up taller, drew in a badly needed breath of air. "Kai, we're friends."

"I know. But we could be more. A lot more." His dark stare never wavered, and the intensity there sent a tendril of heat through her. "All the pieces are there."

There was no denying she wanted him, was insanely attracted to him. But she didn't trust her judgment about men any more than she did his about women. "I value our friendship. And I'm not willing to risk that for the chance to be your rebound girl."

"You wouldn't be, because I know and care about you. I just wasn't sure whether you were attracted to me."

She barked out an incredulous laugh. "Are you insane? You know what you look like. But for me, it's not that simple." Much as the offer tempted her, as much as they liked and respected each other, and both knew what a relationship shouldn't be...

This wasn't as easy as simply making the decision to lower her guard and take a chance on a hook up with him. Because sex always complicated things. At least in her experience. And usually with disastrous consequences.

"I'm not willing to risk losing you if things don't

work out." Even if she was certain she would appreciate him and treat him the way he deserved. Part of her desperately wanted to show him what that looked like.

"And what if it did work out?" he challenged, his dark stare unwavering.

She didn't have an answer to that. Didn't trust that it might be possible. So it was time to leave. "It's getting late. I'd better get going." Standing, she carried her wineglass to the kitchen and put it in the dishwasher.

When she turned around, Kai was standing between the kitchen island and the front door, that deep, dark gaze locked on her. He held out her backpack and keys to her.

"Thanks," she murmured, not meeting his eyes as she took them and slipped her shoes on.

He didn't touch her as he walked her down the hall to the elevator and stepped inside it with her, but the moment those doors slid shut, the invisible tension between them intensified so much she could feel the latent electricity crackling along her skin. He stood at her back, close enough for his body heat to lick at her spine, the back of her neck. And God help her, part of her wondered why the hell she was denying herself. Why she shouldn't just turn around and kiss him the way she was dying to.

Sanity prevailed, and she pulled in a deep breath when the doors opened at the parking garage. "Well, thanks for dinner. I'll let you know if I get the call about Maui—"

She broke off when Kai gripped her upper arm and spun her around. Before she even knew what was happening, he'd pulled the backpack off her shoulder, locked one arm around her hips and hoisted her into the air.

Abby gasped and automatically grabbed his shoulders for balance. A heartbeat later he had her pressed against the concrete wall around the corner from the elevator, one large, strong hand cupping the back of her head.

Unable to breathe at the feel of him plastered against her in such a blatant, possessive hold, she stared helplessly into those molten dark chocolate eyes.

You need a guy who will pick you up, pin you to the wall and kiss you until you can't think, because he can't get enough of you.

His earlier words echoed in her head, unleashing a tidal wave of arousal through her body. She should stop this. Say something. But her mind was utterly blank.

Her breasts tingled, the nipples beading tight, and a hot throb ignited between her legs. He was hot and hard all over, the unmistakable, thick ridge of his erection pressing against the center of her jeans, lighting her up in a single, dizzying rush of need and desire.

And then his mouth came down on hers and she couldn't think at all. Could only feel as he gripped the back of her head and kissed her, a smooth, hungry blend of lips and tongue that turned her body to liquid.

Oh, God, the way he used his mouth…

She sank her fingers deeper into his shoulders, a velvet ripple of heat expanding in her belly as his muscles bunched and flexed beneath her hands. He smelled amazing, clean, masculine spice, and he stroked and caressed the inside of her mouth with such sensual skill that she could only whimper and give him what he wanted.

She was only vaguely aware of the elevator dinging and the doors swishing open somewhere off in the background. Kai broke the kiss but didn't let her go, keeping her pinned to the wall with his body as he stared into her eyes. Breathing hard, Abby gazed back at him in shock, her body on fire, pulse thudding in her ears.

Holy. Shit.

"That's how it should be," he said in a low voice that sent a delicious shiver up her spine. "If a guy doesn't kiss you like that, like he wants to crawl inside you and stay there forever, then he doesn't deserve you."

Unable to form a single coherent thought, much less a response, she could only stare into those dark, intense eyes while her insides quivered and her heart knocked against her ribs. No one had ever made her feel like that. Not ever.

Slowly, Kai eased the pressure of his hips and chest against her, let her slide down the front of his powerful body until her feet touched the ground. She continued to cling to his muscled shoulders a moment, struggling to find her balance, battle the haze of arousal he'd left her in.

Without a word, he turned away and bent to scoop her backpack and keys off the ground. Snagging her hand in his, he led her to her car. By the time he'd unlocked it and she'd slid behind the wheel, her brain was functioning again, only now it was in overdrive.

They'd just crossed so many lines. They couldn't go back to the way it had been before. What did that mean for them?

Kai leaned down to peer at her through the open door, one thick forearm braced against the top of her car, his gaze intent. "You okay to drive?"

She was still dizzy as hell, grappling with this sudden, shocking shift between them. "Yes."

He searched her eyes a moment, then a slight, sexy grin tugged at his mouth. The mouth that had just taught her everything she'd never known about kissing. Shown her the kind of passion she'd been missing out on her entire life.

How much more had she missed out on? She squeezed her thighs together to stem the ache between them, had to bite back a moan at the thought of what else Kai could teach her.

He leaned in, cupping the side of her face with one hand, and kissed her softly before easing away. "Drive carefully, shortcake," he murmured.

She managed a nod, struggling to get her body back under control.

He straightened and shut her door, stepped back while she fired up the engine and reversed out of her spot.

Not short stuff anymore. Shortcake. The significance of the upgrade wasn't lost on her.

Abby didn't even remember the drive home. All she could think about was that kiss and what it had felt like to finally be wrapped up in Kai's arms.

And oh, hell, whether it was crazy or not, she wanted more.

Chapter Five

The number on display was unfamiliar, with a California area code. Hani got into his vehicle before answering his cell phone, looking around to make sure he hadn't attracted any unwanted attention. People around here recognized him, even if they didn't know his name. All his best customers lived in Happy Valley. "Yeah."

"This Hani?" an unfamiliar, Spanish-accented male voice asked.

"Who's this?" he demanded, suspicious.

"Name's Juan."

He didn't know anyone named Juan. "How did you get this number?"

"From Pedro. You heard about him, right?"

Hani set his jaw. Yeah, he'd heard about Pedro. His *Veneno* supplier. Well, former supplier. Pedro had been executed with two bullets to the face sometime last night. Police had found his body floating amongst the rocks this morning at Turtle Town, down in Makena. "What do you want?"

"Calling to tell you there's a new boss in charge. From now on, you answer to me, *cabrón*."

Hani didn't like his tone, or the attitude. "Who's in charge?" Although he was afraid he already knew. With the former lieutenant Ruiz in prison and awaiting trial, it opened a turbulent and dangerous power vacuum back in Mexico.

"Let's just say, the rumors are true."

Nieto. God *damn*... "Since when?"

"Since this morning. I'm flying in tomorrow. I want a face to face meeting."

So "Juan" could have one of his enforcers kill Hani? "I'm busy."

Juan laughed. "Better clear your schedule then. Because you either do business my way, or you don't do business at all."

The implied threat was clear enough, but Hani didn't trust that Juan wasn't simply planning to off him at this meeting anyway.

"And don't bother trying to leave the island. I've got eyes everywhere. You try to run, I'll find you."

Hani itched to hang up on the cocky son of a bitch, but didn't have the guts. "I'll be here," he muttered.

"Good. How's your grandma, by the way? Heard she's been slowing down lately. And any word from your cousin?"

A chill spread through his gut. "Haven't seen him in years. And leave her out of this. She's got nothing to do with my business."

"She'll be fine as long as you play by the rules."

Juan's rules. Whatever they were. Hani would

have to learn them in a hurry.

"As for your cousin, he's made a real name for himself recently."

"What?" Kai had cut contact with him years ago with an invitation back into his life if Hani ever went straight, but last he'd heard, his cousin had gotten out of the Marines and was in some sort of law enforcement job back on the mainland.

"Oh, yeah. He's big time now. With the DEA, on one of its FAST teams."

Hani closed his eyes and cursed silently. He knew what FAST teams did, because it was his industry they went after. The news wasn't welcome, but in some ways it wasn't a complete shock, either. Didn't surprise him that his cousin had made the DEA's tier one unit.

Kai had always excelled at everything he did. He never quit. While Hani had wanted the easy life, the get rich quick life, and been sucked down to the place he found himself now. It hurt like hell to learn that his lifelong idol was now his nemesis.

"Yep," Juan continued in an oily tone. "Ruiz put a bounty on your cousin's head before he was captured. New boss says he'll honor it if any of us takes him out. Had someone staking out his old place for a while, but never saw him. So if you see him, you could wind up a rich man. You can tell me all about him when we meet up. And we *will* meet up in person, Hani."

"I said I'd be here," Hani snapped.

"Yeah, I'm not worried." Juan hung up.

Hani exhaled hard and dragged a hand down his face. This business could make you rich. It could also kill you in the space of a single heartbeat.

There was no point in trying to hide. The island was a small place, and even the most remote places here weren't big enough to allow him to hide for long. Word amongst the locals spread fast, and the place was crawling with tourists. Leaving wasn't an option, because the *Venenos* controlled the ports and had people inside the airports as well.

But he wouldn't run anyhow. Even though he'd chosen this path, chosen to live on the wrong side of the law and make money off others' misery, he would never knowingly jeopardize his *tutu*. His grandmother had raised him and Kai, had sacrificed so much to give them a loving, secure home. The *only* love and security they'd ever known, except for each other. Hani couldn't leave to save his own skin and risk something happening to her in retaliation.

Reaching for the key in the ignition of his brand new F-150, he froze, his pulse stuttering when he caught sight of his grandmother on the sidewalk out in front of the grocery store. It had been weeks since he'd last stopped in to see her at her place in the upcountry. She must be here for her weekly grocery run and to visit friends from the old neighborhood.

Hani sighed, torn. He loved her, and she still loved him, even though his choices had broken her heart. She still refused to give up on him, told him she prayed every night for him to give up the life he'd chosen and be the man she knew he was meant to be.

He didn't deserve her faith. The man she wanted him to be didn't exist. Maybe he never had.

Her wrinkled face brightened when she spotted him, making his heart twist in his chest. She made a beeline for his truck, three bulging grocery bags in each small fist.

Guilt smothering him, Hani got out and rushed to take them from her. "Hi, *Tutu*," he murmured, bending to kiss her papery cheek as she threw her arms around his shoulders.

"Been too long since I saw you," she chided, squeezing him tight. It hurt him, deep inside. She loved him so fiercely, and he didn't understand why.

"I know. Been busy. Come on, I'll drive you home." He hated that she wouldn't drive. He'd offered to buy her a car so many times, but she'd refused unless the money he paid for it with was clean money. So she stubbornly continued to take the bus into Kahului three or four times a week, carrying her groceries and supplies home with her. Today, she'd come to Happy Valley instead.

He put the groceries into the back seat and helped her into the front, lifting her slight frame into the leather seat.

"New ride?" she asked, her tone making him groan inwardly.

"Yeah," he muttered, shutting her door quickly before she could start in on him about where he'd gotten the money. She knew exactly where he got it.

She eyed him with those piercing, dark brown eyes when he slid behind the wheel and started the engine. "I heard they found a local boy down in Makena today. Shot dead by someone. Police say he was a drug dealer."

Hani hid a wince. Pedro. He'd been far more than a simple drug dealer. "I heard that too."

"I don't want it to be you one day, Hani. I couldn't

take that."

The sadness and fear in her voice made him squirm inside. His whole downward spiral had begun with hanging out with the wrong crowd in middle school. They'd shown him how to earn money. Fast money. Lots of it. Stealing stuff, delivering drugs, selling it.

Some had died since then, others moved away or become addicts themselves. While Hani was still here, stuck in the rut he'd created for himself. Sometimes he dreamed about getting out, starting over someplace new. But he couldn't without the cartel coming after him. He was trapped.

"I know. Don't worry, I'll be fine." He cleared his throat, changed the subject before she could continue. "So, what's the latest with you?"

"Kai's coming home."

Hani's entire body stiffened. "What?"

"Called me the other day. He's going to Oahu for something, and then he's coming to spend a few days here after."

Panic burst inside him. "When?"

She shrugged. "He wasn't sure of the dates. Maybe within the next week or so." She shot him a sidelong look. "He'll be staying with me. Would be nice if you would be there too."

Him in the same house with a DEA FAST member who had a bounty on his head? "*Tutu*, I don't know if it's a good idea for him to stay with you."

She frowned. "Why not? I barely ever get to see him anymore."

Because the Venenos *are gunning for him, and he*

could put you in danger.

We both could.

Hani wracked his brain, but couldn't think of a good reason to give her without incriminating himself. Dammit.

"Will you come see him?" she pressed. "You boys were so close for most of your lives. It breaks my heart to see this rift between you." She reached for his hand, pried it from the steering wheel and folded it between hers, her skin papery against his. "Please. For me. I'm getting older. I don't know how many years I have left, and I need to know you boys are both going to be okay after I die. I need to know you'll both look after one another."

The plea undid him. This woman had given him so much, and she'd never asked him for anything, except to turn straight. She was almost eighty. Didn't have much longer on this earth.

His conscience pricked at him like hot needles. He'd denied her everything else. He couldn't deny her this too. "Yeah, all right. I'll come by." He'd figure something out.

Even as he said it, an ominous weight settled in the pit of his stomach. If the cartel found out that Kai was here on Maui, Hani would be put in the position of either watching someone kill his cousin...or becoming a target himself.

****

The boat bobbed gently on the waves, the water beneath it a deep, cobalt blue. In the distance, the shoreline of Lahaina was just visible.

Diane stood at the stern of the charter catamaran with the alabaster urn in her hands, alone as the warm, salt-tinged breeze blew around her. The captain and first mate were both inside the wheelhouse, giving her total privacy.

Bailey had loved the ocean. She'd loved sailing, surfing. Even just sitting on the lanai looking out at the water. Making this her final resting place seemed the most fitting spot.

Diane gazed out over the distant horizon, her heart heavy as lead in her breast. There were no more tears. Her grief was too deep, too terrible. All that was left now was the need for vengeance, and deep, aching emptiness that would never go away.

Taking a deep breath, she lifted the lid off the urn and reached out over the side of the catamaran. "I love you, sweetheart. Sleep well and be at peace." Every time she saw the water from now on, she would think of Bailey.

With trembling hands, she tipped the urn. A stream of white ash spilled from the vessel, falling toward the rippling surface of the water. The wind caught it, spreading it into a fine mist. She reached up and closed the fingers of her right hand around the locket hanging from her neck. The one containing a tiny amount of Bailey's ashes.

Her mind remained blank as she stared at the film of ash while it settled onto the water and vanished. After a respectful amount of time, footsteps approached behind her.

"Mrs. Whitehead?" the captain asked. "Are you ready to go back now?"

She nodded without turning around, her gaze

fixed on the spot where her daughter now rested, mixing with the wind and waves.

The ride back to shore passed in a blur, but as the shoreline became clearer and clearer in front of them, her mind began to whirl. Bailey had been laid to rest. Her suffering was over.

But for the people who had wrought this pain, their suffering was about to begin.

In the parking lot she changed clothes, in the privacy of the shadows alongside the building that the charter boat rides were run out of. There were no security cameras here. The rental car she'd secured under a fake name was nondescript, her outfit of capri jeans and a plain gray T-shirt chosen because they wouldn't draw attention.

Everything else she needed was already in the trunk.

Funny now, to think that the one positive thing from her childhood—her marksman father teaching her how to shoot—would pay off this way. It had been the one thing they had in common, though she'd done it only to spend time with him. Over the years she'd become an expert shot. Today, that same skill would become her weapon in meting out the justice Bailey had been denied in life. She had nothing left to lose. She was willing to go to jail as long as she could kill at least one monster responsible for this.

Diane had failed her daughter while she was alive. She'd be damned if she'd fail her in death too.

Ten minutes later she pulled into the parking lot of the medical building and parked in a spot off in the corner, closest to the exit. There was only one other car there, a silver Mercedes that belonged to her target.

She'd done her homework carefully over the past several days. Doctor Bradshaw's last patient was a seventy-one-year-old woman scheduled for seven o'clock. He generally ran behind at the end of the day. His staff left out the front of the building, and he always came out the back, where his Mercedes was parked beside the steel door.

His parking spot was ideal. The security cameras installed on the building had a view of his car, but only the front of it. The trunk, where he always placed his briefcase before climbing behind the wheel, was out of view. And with the trunk up, it gave her the perfect amount of concealment.

Her hand was damp but steady as she gripped her pistol, hidden in her handbag. The plastic, disposable raincoat she wore would keep her free of any splatter.

Movement in her peripheral vision caught her attention. An elderly woman with white hair came out of the rear entrance, leaning heavily on the cane. Dr. Bradshaw's final patient.

Diane's heartbeat quickened as she waited, her gaze locked on the steel door. She'd killed pheasants before. An occasional deer. But never a person.

Her conscience pricked at her, but she wrestled it back. This man was a monster. There were no real consequences for people like him, for the people who made and sold and prescribed the drugs that destroyed so many lives. The world would be a better place with him gone.

Minutes later the lights on the second floor turned off. She slid out of her car, careful to remain in the shadows and out of view of the camera, or anyone who came out the back door.

It opened. Heart in her throat, she stared at the opening. The good doctor himself emerged, briefcase in one hand. He didn't bother looking around as he locked the door behind him and made for his car.

Diane shoved her nerves back and stalked toward him on silent feet, the pistol grip solid in her hand. She was twenty feet away and Bradshaw still hadn't noticed her. As if in slow motion he hit the button on his keyfob that unlatched the trunk and turned toward it, his back to her.

The moment the trunk swung upward, Diane acted.

"You killed my daughter," she said in a low voice, raising the pistol. It was like an extension of her hand, the weight and feel of it perfect in her grip.

Bradshaw whirled to face her, his startled expression turning to fear when he saw the weapon pointed at his chest. He jerked his eyes to hers.

It was what she had been waiting for. That moment of recognition.

Grip steady, she fired three fast shots. Each bullet hit their mark, dead center in Bradshaw's worthless chest.

She barely saw him hit the ground before she whirled and hurried away in the shadows. The shots had been loud, but necessary. People would come to investigate at any moment.

Pausing at her vehicle only long enough to strip off her plastic raincoat, she stuffed everything in the beach bag and drove out of the lot at an unhurried pace even though she was scared to death of being seen. Of being caught on some security camera she didn't know about.

Her heart hammered in her throat, a queasy sensation roiling in her stomach. If Bradshaw wasn't already dead, he soon would be.

Diane drove through the quiet streets back to the motel she was staying at. She couldn't risk going home yet, in case anyone suspected her. Home was the first place they'd look.

With each passing mile she fought off the instinctive rush of guilt, the terrible knowledge that she'd just taken a human life.

He deserved it. They all did.

One down, so many more to go.

Chapter Six

"You shoot me with that thing, you better be able to outrun me."

Kai smirked at Freeman's stark warning and stroked a hand over the barrel of his modified eight-chamber Nerf gun. She was fully loaded, and ready to play. Since their long day of conducting maritime operation training was done, Kai was ready to play too.

And his trigger finger was damn itchy.

"Why so serious, *brah*? Not butt hurt about being shown up in the water by a Marine, are you?"

The team point man stopped in the middle of peeling off his wetsuit to shoot him a hard look. "In your dreams, jarhead. I'm twice as fast as you on any given day. Everyone knows this except you." Freeman was a former decorated SEAL. Whenever they assaulted a target, he was the first one through the door. Everybody on the team admired his skill as an operator and his steadiness under pressure, including Kai.

That didn't mean he got a free pass on the smack talk Kai loved delivering to each and every one of his teammates, however.

Kai raised an eyebrow, anticipation spreading inside him. They had a long-standing friendly rivalry about this. Maybe it was time to settle this for good. "Oh, it's like that, huh?"

"Yeah, it's like that."

He glanced at Prentiss and Khan, who were both getting out of their own wetsuits across the team room, and grinned. Of all the guys he was closest to them, but got along well with everyone on the team. "All right," he said to Freeman. "Let's put that to the test, so we can settle this once and for all. Like men."

Freeman eyed him, a glint of interest in his dark brown eyes. "I'm listening."

"You and me hit the beach outside right now. There's a three-quarter-mile stretch between the officer's housing and the northeast shore we used to swim all the time, back when I was stationed here in the Corps. First one to make it to the other side is king of the water. Rest of the team will stand witness. You game?"

Freeman stripped the wetsuit off his legs, leaving him in just a pair of swim trunks, his gaze locked on Kai. "Yeah, I'm game. Let's go." He twisted to the side to hang the wetsuit up to dry.

Kai seized upon the juicy opportunity, raising his weapon and squeezing the trigger. But instead of firing one foam dart, his personal modifications turned the single-shot weapon into a fully automatic one.

Freeman bellowed and threw up his hands as dart after dart pelted him in the back of the head. Laughing, Kai dropped his weapon, got up and ran barefoot out of the room while laughter and shouts of encouragement followed him out into the hall.

Hamilton stopped in the middle of the hallway when he saw Kai barreling toward him and stepped aside, raising his eyebrows. "What'd you do now, Maka?"

"Just gettin' my boy motivated," Kai called back as he streaked past his team leader, sprinting for the exit at the far end of the hall. A delighted laugh burst out of him when the team room door exploded open behind him, followed by pounding footsteps in the hall.

"You really did it this time, Maka," Granger called out behind him, his voice full of glee. "Freeman's riled up."

"Good, he's gonna need it if he wants a prayer at staving off total humiliation," Kai called back. He glanced over his shoulder as he neared the door, hooted when he saw Freeman bearing down on him, his face a mask of raw determination, their seven other teammates hot on his heels.

Awesome.

He slammed down on the metal release bar and plunged outside into the warm, tropical sunshine. The salty scent of the ocean hit him, along with the muted roar of the waves curling against the beach up ahead.

His smile widened. God, he'd missed the islands. And in just a couple days he'd be home in Maui.

Hopefully with Abby. He couldn't stop thinking about her, about what they could have together if she was willing to put caution aside and step outside the friend zone with him.

Kai reached the edge of the beach. The feel of the hot sand under his feet was bliss, triggering a thousand memories of him and his cousin Hani spending time at the beach when they were kids. Bittersweet memories now. They were different people now than back then, because they had chosen two completely opposite paths.

"You're getting' slow, big man," Freeman shouted. "You forget, I was a star wide receiver in college."

The voice was way closer than Kai expected it to be. He risked a glance behind him, eyes widening when he saw Freeman fifteen yards away and closing. Kai was fast, but the bastard was faster, his smaller frame an advantage moving over the sand.

Kai ran into the water. Two steps into the surf, calf deep, a heavy weight hit him in the middle of the back and took him down. They hit the water with a huge splash, Freeman on top. Kai rolled, pushed free and surfaced with a laugh just as Freeman popped up too, his grin bright white against his deep brown skin. "Gotcha," he taunted, giving Kai a smug grin.

"You're fast, I'll give you that. On land," Kai added, wiping the water from his face. "But water's what separates the boys from the men."

Freeman nodded, dark brown eyes sparkling with glee. "True. Let's do this."

Enjoying himself immensely, Kai stood and walked back to the edge of the surf. Four of the guys were already there.

"Khan, Granger and Prentiss all headed over to the finish line," Hamilton said, standing on the beach like he owned it, arms folded across his chest. Colebrook and Rodriguez stood on either side of him, both with their phones at the ready, waiting to record the race. Lockhart's eyes were hidden beneath his shades, a big grin on the former sniper's face.

Kai twisted around to see the other three running along the beach to get to the spot that marked the end of the race route. He used arm signals to move them into position, then gave them a raised fist to tell them to stop. "There," he said to Freeman, lining up beside the other man on the strip of wet sand that marked the edge of the water. "From here to there's three-quarters of a mile."

Freeman's gaze was fixed on the end point. "Less talking. More action."

Kai smothered a laugh. "Okay. Cap, you count it down," he said to Hamilton.

"All right. I want a nice, clean swim," Hamilton instructed. "No choking or drowning your opponent. No wedgies or pantsing. And definitely no biting or hair pulling." The others chuckled.

"Well that's no fun," Kai muttered under his breath. He leaned forward slightly, eyes on the finish line, his muscles tensed, ready to go. Before them lay a quarter mile of rolling ocean, and a bitch of a rip current that would try to pull them out to sea. It was one of the reasons his instructors had loved using this stretch, to tire them out.

"Three," Hamilton called out in a deep, authoritative voice. "Two. One...*Go*."

Kai took four running steps into the water, then dove headfirst into an oncoming wave.

The moment the water closed over his head, it was like coming home. The cool water surrounded him, hugged him as he knifed through it.

He kicked hard, feeling the pull of the rip against his body, and came up for air. Stretched out full length at the surface on his belly, he angled his head to take a breath, and began a punishing front crawl stroke. The water deepened, the sand changing to reef before it dropped away.

Waves broke over him. His muscles began to burn a couple minutes in. He savored it, pushed his body to go faster. Harder.

The next time he surfaced he glimpsed Freeman a few yards off to the right, trailing by a body length. The former SEAL was amazing in the water, but he hadn't grown up in it like Kai had, and here, Kai's large size wasn't an impediment. He propelled himself through the water, shut his mind down and focused on the rhythm of his arms and legs.

Beneath him, the water shallowed as reef appeared again. The muscles in his shoulders and legs were burning like fire, his lungs laboring. But he was almost there, and damned if he would lose to a SEAL here in his element.

Using the last of his energy reserves, Kai shut out the physical discomfort and put on a final burst of speed. The coral gave way to sand. When the water was chest deep, he surged to his feet. Freeman was a few yards back, but it was gonna be close.

Panting, he forced his tired legs to push him the last few yards to the beach where all seven of his remaining teammates were waiting. They were all yelling, some cheering and some trash talking, several recording everything with their phones.

Kai splashed through the water and onto the wet sand, running for the line someone had drawn in it. Splashing footsteps signaled that Freeman was right behind him. And the former SEAL moved way faster here than Kai ever could.

With a final lunge, Kai crossed the line a full second before Freeman did.

Yes!

He doubled over, resting his palms on his thighs as he dragged in gulp after gulp of air.

"Just want you to know, my money was on you all along, big man," Khan said, scrubbing a hand over Kai's wet hair affectionately.

"He's totally lying," Prentiss said, tossing Kai a towel.

"Whatever, you owe me five bucks," Khan shot back.

Kai snorted a laugh but couldn't answer, too busy trying to get his breath back. Made him feel better to see Freeman sucking wind as well.

"That was epic," Granger said, grinning as he looked at his phone. "Got it all right here on video, too."

Kai swung his head around to look at Freeman. "For the record, nobody's ever come that close to beating me."

Freeman narrowed his deep brown eyes. "Don't try to make me feel better." He heaved a breath and straightened. "That rip was a bitch, man."

Kai grinned. "She always is." Crossing to

Freeman, he clapped a friendly hand on his buddy's back, then held it out. "Good race."

Freeman clasped it. Hard. "Yeah. And for the record, I've never seen anyone your size as good as you in the water."

"Oh, God," Rodriguez moaned. "Now Maka thinks he's the king of the ocean *and* lip-syncing."

Everyone laughed, then Hamilton clapped him on the back. "Guess that means the beer's on you tonight."

Kai grinned, took the shirt Khan held out for him. "Yeah. Guess it does."

"Here. Brought your phone, too," his friend said. "I recorded it for you. And you got a text when you were about halfway across."

"Thanks." Kai took it, and when he saw Abby's message, he smiled, excitement flooding him.

Guess who's coming to Maui in three days?

He was thrilled at the prospect of getting to see her, spend time with her, but even more so that she'd reached out to tell him. He'd been worried that he'd scared her off, that he'd come on too strong, because after the other night, she'd pulled back. Or seemed to have. Only texting him back in response to something, rather than reaching out to him first. Texting instead of answering his calls.

He could never regret that kiss, though. So many times over the past week he'd replayed it over and over again in his mind, recalling every little detail. The look on her face when he'd picked her up and pinned her to the wall, the feel of him against her.

How soft her heavy-lidded eyes had been as she'd gazed up at him after, her porcelain cheeks flushed and her lips pink and shiny.

"Whatever you're thinking about right now, I don't wanna know," Freeman muttered beside him.

"Hot date with your former neighbor?" Khan asked, a knowing glint in his eye. Both he and Prentiss knew how bad things had been with Shelley.

"Nah," Kai said, downplaying her importance and his eagerness. He wasn't even sure if this was going anywhere yet. He didn't want the guys to know just how amped up he was about it, in case it didn't happen. His relationship with Abby was something to be cherished, and protected.

Looking forward to showing you paradise, he typed back to Abby. In whatever capacity she'd let him.

He couldn't wait to see her. Couldn't wait to show her all the places he loved, introduce her to his grandma. He had all kinds of seduction ideas too, but all that would have to wait until she was ready. Until then he would spend as much time as he could with her, prove to her that it was worth giving them a shot.

"I don't know about you guys, but I'm freaking starving," Colebrook announced as they started back up the beach toward the building they'd vacated earlier.

"I'm more thirsty than anything else," Freeman answered, shooting Kai an evil grin. "After that swim, I figure I can put away a dozen beers, easy."

Kai mentally winced at the damage that was about to be done to his credit card, but smiled. As the others went on ahead, he dialed his grandmother's number and brought the phone to his ear.

"Hey, *Tutu*, it's me," he said in Hawaiian. "Just

calling to let you know I'll be there in time for dinner on Tuesday. And I'm thinking of bringing a friend over on Wednesday night, too."

Except he hoped Abby would be far more than that by the end of their time on Maui together. Which meant he had just over a week to change her mind and make her his.

****

Shown up in front of the whole team by a damn jarhead.

Malcolm Freeman mentally shook his head at himself as he reached for his first beer from Maka. "Thanks." Man, he must be getting old. It was the only explanation. When he'd been in the Teams, no one could touch him in the water.

His teammate pulled the beer out of range, raised a black eyebrow. "No hard feelings?"

"Not if you gimme the damn beer."

"Cool." Maka handed it over and sat his huge frame down on the stool next to Mal's, helping himself to a mouthful of peanuts from a dish on the bar. Guy had a monster appetite, seemed to always be stuffing his face with something, and it usually wasn't all that nutritious. "Did you train in the islands much when you were in the Teams?"

"Not as often as we would have liked." He took a sip, the cold, crisp brew sliding down his throat. "You must miss being here. Pretty great place to call home."

"Yeah. Funny how I didn't appreciate it until after I left."

"That's how it goes." People never appreciated what they had until it was gone. He knew that better than some.

Maka nodded, opened his mouth to say something else then paused as his phone chimed. He checked the screen, grinned, and began typing back a response.

Maka had a fish on the line. And Mal was pretty sure he knew what kind. "So who's this girl? Your old neighbor, the blonde?"

"Abby. It's no big deal. She's coming to Maui for a work conference this week. She's a pharmaceutical rep."

No big deal, huh? Mal had known him for a long while now, and couldn't remember seeing his teammate so amped up about seeing a woman before. Mal had met Abby once, when he'd gone to help Maka move last month. She seemed nice and was a hard worker, ready to help without any expectation of something in return. And sure as hell, Maka deserved someone nice after the shit show he'd stuck through with Shelley for so long.

"I liked her," he said. Not that his opinion mattered, but he wanted Maka to know.

"She's awesome. Been a really great friend to me."

Seemed like Maka was way more into her than he was letting on. Mal hoped it worked out for them. Their job as FAST operators took a toll on them and the people they were close to. And it was a damn lonely life when you had no one special to share it with and continually came back to an empty house when the team was back in Virginia.

Leaving his teammate to his texting, Mal turned his attention to the TV above the bar showing a baseball game back on the mainland, except now his thoughts were on something else entirely. A beautiful face from his past that still haunted his dreams.

Hamilton slid onto the stool on Mal's right, wearing one of his Captain America T-shirts that had earned him the nickname Cap. The rest of the team settled around them, taking up two sides of the bar. "You two friends again, or what?" the team leader asked.

"For now," Mal said with a wry grin. But if Maka shot any more Nerf darts at him, the truce was off.

"Is there still food available, or did Maka empty the kitchen already?"

"You're safe," Maka answered. "Haven't placed my order yet."

"Thank God for that," Hamilton muttered, perusing the menu. "I need to get mine in before you do."

Mal ordered a steak sandwich with fries. Maka ordered two double cheeseburgers with a salad on the side. As if that meager serving of veggies was gonna do anything to save his colon.

Hamilton gave the waitress his order, then took a phone call. A few seconds later, he groaned and sat up straighter. "It's only been a few weeks. She's been through hell, it's no wonder she's refusing to testify against those bastards right now. She needs more time."

Mal hid a wince and tried not to listen in, but it was hard not to with Hamilton sounding so frustrated and borderline angry. Their team leader was as steady and levelheaded as they came. Whatever had him upset must be pretty big.

Hamilton hung up a few minutes later and let out a harsh sigh. "They're pressuring Victoria Gomez to testify against Ruiz and his crew," he said.

The investigative reporter who had been held captive by the former *Veneno* lieutenant Carlos Ruiz. Hamilton and two others had found her in the woods the night they'd gone in to rescue her. Naked, beaten and bleeding, after being held and abused in every possible way for weeks. In the nick of time to save her from being sold into a human trafficking ring.

Hamilton had spent quite a bit of time with her in the past few weeks, sitting in on interviews and other debriefings she was involved with. "They know her testimony would bury them," Mal said.

Hamilton nodded. "She knows it too. But Jesus Christ, give her a minute. She's not even healed up yet."

Physically, he meant. Mentally and emotionally, Miss Gomez would never be the same. God, it made Mal sick to think of a woman being treated that way. The *Venenos* were freaking rabid animals, not men. And they needed to be exterminated, because that was the only way to stop it. Otherwise they would just keep doing the same damn fucked-up shit over and over.

Hamilton straightened and turned toward him slightly. "Hey, don't you know someone who works for the D.C. U.S. Attorney's office?"

Mal's fingers froze around the beer bottle and he looked away from those steel gray eyes. Hamilton's timing on the subject was damn spooky. "Used to."

"So you're not in touch anymore?"

"No. Not for a few years now." Not by his choice. But it was what it was, so he'd respected her wishes and stayed away from her. He still thought about her all the time, though.

"Do they still work there?"

"Yes." She was an Assistant U.S. Attorney now. On track to follow in her hallowed father's footsteps and become the U.S. Attorney.

Suddenly the beer tasted sickeningly bitter in his mouth. Mal set the bottle down in front of him.

Hamilton turned back to face the bar. "Might need to have you introduce us so I can get a meeting. They need to back off with Victoria. She's a fighter, and she's motivated. When she's ready, she'll take the stand and nail those assholes to the wall for what they did to her and the others. But if they keep pushing her like this…" He shook his head, jaw set.

"Sure," Mal answered, even as dread coiled like a snake in the pit of his stomach. Even after all this time, reaching out to Rowan would be like ripping the bandages off the half-healed wound in his heart. She probably didn't even think about him anymore. He wished he could say the same about her.

Some things, a man just didn't get over. Like finally working up the courage to risk his heart on a woman who was way out of his league, only to have her slam the door in his face.

Chapter Seven

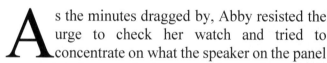

As the minutes dragged by, Abby resisted the urge to check her watch and tried to concentrate on what the speaker on the panel was saying. It was only day one of the conference but her focus was shot to hell already, and had been for the past two hours.

Time was crawling along, torturing her with its slow passage when all she wanted was to get out of here and meet Kai. He was picking her up here at the Grand Wailea Hotel as soon as she finished up. She couldn't *wait*.

The speaker was droning on about the latest research on prescription opioids here in Hawaii contributing to the opioid crisis, as compared to the mainland. Information she was well versed in because of her position within the company, so she'd heard it all a hundred times before.

Anytime now, guys. Wrap it up.

The past nine days had been a total blur, and in her precious downtime all she could think about was Kai. Would trying a relationship with him be a huge mistake? That kiss sure as hell hadn't felt like a mistake. No, it had felt like everything she'd been missing.

Every time she thought about it, her body lit up all over again. No man had ever affected her like that with a single kiss. He was also a good man, with a good heart. Dependable. Fun. Dedicated. Nothing like the men she'd been with before.

After what she'd been through, Abby wouldn't tolerate cheating, or any kind of abuse. Not ever again. As far as she could tell she didn't have to worry about those things with Kai, but because of her history she would be wary in the beginning. But he was loyal to his teammates, and he'd hung in there with Shelley for way longer than he should have.

She yanked her attention back to the presentation as the conference organizer stepped up to the microphone at the center of the stage.

"If anyone would like to make a donation in Doctor Bradshaw's honor, the family would prefer that in lieu of flowers. I have a list of charities the family has specified here if you are so inclined at the end of the panel discussion."

It was a sober reminder, and made her feel even worse for letting her mind wander. Dr. Bradshaw was a pain management specialist, and was supposed to have led the panel discussion. But he'd been murdered a few days ago, his body found next to his car at his medical clinic after someone had shot him repeatedly at point blank range.

It had been all over the papers and news here, the conference giving the awful story even more visibility. He'd been a church and family man, well-liked and respected, with lots of volunteer work within the community. Everyone seemed shocked at his murder. So far the police had no suspects, and no motive for the killing. Rumors she'd heard today at lunch suggested Bradshaw's colleagues blamed a junkie looking for opioids.

Incredibly sad and ironic, considering this panel was about the impact of opiate addiction, the root causes and the epidemic it had become around the world. Here in Hawaii, most of the synthetic "designer" drugs came from Asia, while most of the cocaine and heroin was supplied by the lethal *Veneno* cartel.

Abby hated those bastards with a passion. They were ruthless monsters, had no qualms about who they targeted or killed, even kidnapping the daughter of Kai's teammate and selling women into sexual slavery.

The hotel and conference staff had added extra security, just in case the attack wasn't random. All the heavy hitters from the pharmaceutical world were here, and a good chunk of the world's leading pain specialists.

As soon as the panel wrapped up, she texted Kai and made a donation to one of the charities Dr. Bradshaw had volunteered at. She hurried up to her room to change and freshen up, then made her way down to the lobby to wait for Kai, fighting the nervous flutters in her stomach. They liked and trusted one another. But was that enough, to warrant risking their friendship on this? There were still so many things she didn't know about him.

Based on the way he'd kissed her, and her reaction to it, things were going to move fast if she went ahead with this. She was afraid of losing him if this didn't work out, and told herself she was stupid to consider it given he was only a few weeks out of his relationship with Shelley.

Yet even all that wasn't enough to kill the hope and excitement inside her. Her mind was made up. She would see how things went, talk to him early on and make sure he was on board with maintaining their friendship if this didn't pan out. That was key for her before she was willing to agree to anything else.

A warm, tropical breeze bathed her when she stepped outside into the night, rustling the fronds of the palm trees overhead. The smell here was incredible, and she'd noticed it when she'd stepped off the plane at the airport. Green. Lush.

Tiki torches flickered around the entrance, and the scent of gardenias filled the balmy air. Lord, it really was paradise here. She couldn't wait to see more of it with Kai.

Moments later, a cherry red convertible Mustang pulled up. Her heart skipped when she saw Kai at the wheel. He broke into a wide grin when he saw her, and heat pooled low in her belly.

Smiling, she hitched the strap of her purse up higher onto her shoulder and hurried to the car. He climbed out and came around to meet her, six-foot-four of powerful, sexy man that made her heart trip all over itself.

"*Aloha*," she laughed as she got close to him.

"*Aloha*, shortcake," he murmured, and pulled her into a big bear hug.

Abby barely stifled a groan as her entire body went haywire. Oh, his voice. A deep, velvet rumble. All that strength and warmth wrapped around her like a protective blanket…it turned her to mush. And he smelled amazing, something soapy and spicy and all man.

Every last one of her pragmatic thoughts about their friendship being paramount to anything else went poof at the feel of his arms around her. "Good to see you."

"Good to see you too." He eased up on the hug and leaned his head back to look down at her, the warm light from the tiki torches reflecting off his bronze skin. One hand stroked over her hair, the side of her face as he stared into her eyes. "You look gorgeous."

Her cheeks heated but she didn't even have time to utter a thank you before he bent his head and claimed her lips with his. Abby leaned into him, her palms flattened against his broad chest. The kiss was slow and firm, screaming of possession and ending with a slight nip to her lower lip.

A slow smile curved his mouth as he pulled away, watching her. "So, you hungry?"

Famished. And not necessarily for food. She just wasn't sure how fast she was willing to move with this, even if her skin was suddenly hypersensitive and her nipples were hard. "Yes."

"Good. My grandma's been cooking up a feast all day."

She blinked at him. "Your grandma?"

He nodded. "I already committed to dinner with her tonight, and promised I'd bring you along. I want you to meet her. That okay?"

Well... Meeting his family seemed like a lot of pressure considering they weren't even in a relationship yet. She'd envisioned spending time just the two of them tonight, so she could get a feel of what was happening and talk about what they both wanted.

On the other hand, it felt good to know he was comfortable introducing her to the woman who'd raised him. And maybe it was a blessing that they wouldn't be alone, so their chemistry couldn't get in the way and cloud her judgment.

"Sure." She couldn't help but smile as he took her hand and led her to the Mustang. He opened her door for her, waited for her to settle into the plush leather bucket seat before closing the door and rounding the hood.

Once he was inside he did up his seatbelt, paused in the act of reaching for the keys in the ignition, and instead lifted a hand to cradle the side of her face, bringing her gaze to his. He must have had the seat pushed all the way back to accommodate his long legs, but he still looked crammed into the car. "I'm really glad you're here," he murmured.

Oh, man. There was no way she could stay just friends with him. "Me too."

Kai grinned, kissed her softly, then started the car and pulled out of the hotel parking lot. "How's the conference going so far?" he asked as he turned onto a wide street lined with lush monkeypod trees, their huge, leafy canopies spreading out overhead like giant green umbrellas.

"Pretty good." She drew in a deep breath of the fresh, tropical-scented air and told him about Dr. Bradshaw and the extra security.

"Yeah, it's been all over the news. You okay?"

"Yes, fine. What about you, how was your week with the team?"

"Helluva lot of fun, actually. We worked long days, but we had fun too."

"That's good." She paused. "What is it you do, exactly? I've been dying to ask you. Can you tell me?"

"Wish I could. I want to, and I trust you, but for security reasons I can't. Yet."

"Yet?" As in, he would once they'd been together for a certain amount of time?

"Yeah."

She decided to let that drop because she wasn't ready to look too far ahead and just wanted to take things one day at a time with him. He drove her up the west coast of the island, through Kehei and then north across Maui's "neck" toward the airport. But before reaching it, Kai turned south, heading inland toward the heart of the island.

"This is the upcountry," he told her. "My *tutu* moved up here to Pukalani after I joined the Marines. It's quieter up here. She loves it."

"Oh, where did you grow up?"

"Wailuku. West of where the airport is."

Out here there were no towns, only farms and ranches and houses dotted along the foothills of the ancient mountains. The road was a twisting black ribbon as they climbed into the hills in the darkness, lit only by the Mustang's headlights.

Kai pointed out sugarcane and pineapple plantations along the way, told her ancient Hawaiian legends about how the island of Maui was formed, when Maui pulled it from the depths of the ocean with his magical fishhook.

"Here we are," he said, turning down a long driveway. It was too dark out to see much, but the land sloped gently away from the tidy little yellow house set in the middle of the lot.

A tiny, thin woman with deep bronze skin and a head of thick white hair appeared at the door, her wrinkled face lighting up when she saw them. "*Aloha.*"

"*Aloha, Tutu,*" Kai said, stepping forward to embrace her. Abby loved that he was so openly affectionate with his grandmother. He turned toward her. "This is Abby."

His grandmother inclined her head with a big smile. "Abby. *E komo mai.*" She gestured for Abby to come in.

"*Aloha,* Mrs. Maka. *Mahalo* for inviting me," she answered, using the full extent of her Hawaiian vocabulary in those two short sentences.

The woman's sharp brown eyes darted to Kai. "You didn't tell me she's as pretty as a fairy princess," she said with a heavy accent.

"Well, I didn't want to spoil the surprise."

Abby blushed and didn't know what to say, relieved when Kai led her inside to the entryway.

"Take off your shoes," he whispered, sliding off his flip-flops.

Abby did the same, lining them up neatly at the door. His grandmother was already in the kitchen, and whatever she was cooking smelled so good that Abby's stomach growled. She followed Kai into the cozy, tidy space, taking in all the bright colors and tropical plants lined up in vivid clay pots on the windowsills. "Can I help with anything?" she asked.

"No," his grandma answered, smiling at Abby over her shoulder. "Kai told me how much you love food. I like a girl who likes food."

"Well then you and I are going to get along great."

The old woman grinned. "He also said what a fabulous cook you are, but tonight, we want you to just relax. We want you to feel at home, so we cooked you our favorite Hawaiian dishes to sample."

"We?" she said, looking at Kai. "You made this together?" It was sweet that he'd told his grandmother that she was a good cook. If he'd been talking to her about Abby, that had to mean something, right?

"Yes, ma'am. I wanted your first home-cooked Hawaiian dinner to be memorable."

Warmth filled her chest. None of the men she'd been with had ever appreciated or understood her love of food. She wasn't sure whether Kai had done this in a deliberate attempt at seduction, but that's exactly what it was. And it was working.

"Well I can't wait to taste everything." She was fascinated by the various foods laid out on platters, thrilled at the prospect of eating local cuisine prepared by Kai and his grandma.

The older woman flapped a hand at Kai without looking up from what she was doing at the counter.

"Go pour her a glass of plantation tea and take her out onto the lanai."

Kai winked at Abby and moved to the fridge to pour her a glass from a chilled pitcher. "It's iced tea with pineapple juice," he said, handing it to her.

"Freshly squeezed pineapple juice," grandma interjected, stirring something over by the stove. "None of this juice from a carton nonsense. Fresh Maui pineapple and home-brewed tea."

Abby resisted the urge to put a hand over her heart. She was all about making things from scratch and ditching the processed crap. "I think I already love her," she murmured to Kai.

He grinned back. "Knew you would. Come on." Setting a hand on her lower back, he guided her through the small living space that adjoined the kitchen, and out through a large set of sliding glass doors onto the lanai.

"Ohhh," she breathed when they stepped outside onto the wooden deck. "This is incredible."

"Yeah. *Tutu* has a real gift."

It was like a little wonderland back here. The wood deck led to a small brick patio, and everything was enclosed by a wall of green, lit up by strands of fairy lights. And the *smell*. She'd never get enough of it.

Palm trees anchored the corners, their curved fronds rustling gently in the warm breeze, carrying the sweet scent of flowers and bringing the soft music of wind chimes to life. A variety plants in various shades of green, red, orange and pink surrounded the space, giving it the feel of total seclusion. Little statues and figurines peeked out from their hiding places where they'd been tucked in amongst the plants and pots.

"It's so private and peaceful," she said, closing her eyes and taking a deep breath to better enjoy the lush scents.

"Here's the best spot," he said, lacing his fingers through hers and tugging her to a swinging bench set in the far-left corner, tucked beneath a wrought iron arbor dripping with some kind of multi-colored flowering vine. Bougainvillea, Abby thought it was called.

She sat next to him, savoring the private moment and the chance to lean into his hard frame, the glass of ice-cold tea in her hand. Draping an arm over the back of the swing, he played with the back of her hair gently, setting the suddenly oversensitive nerve endings in her nape on fire. "Look up," he murmured.

Feeling a little drugged by his nearness and the gentle caress of his fingertips, Abby tipped her head back. There in the midnight blue sky, a half-moon glowed through the palm fronds, bathing everything with a pale silvery light. "This is unbelievable," she whispered. Romantic. Magical. A thousand times more poignant because she was sharing it with Kai.

"You should have seen her old place, where I grew up. It was close to the ocean, so at night we would sit out back in the garden and look out over the water. It was really something." He glanced down at her. "How's your tea?"

She took a sip, sighed at the refreshing, not overly sweet taste. "It's my new favorite drink."

His low chuckle made her insides flutter. "I thought you'd like it."

What wasn't to like? This…date, if that's what it was, wasn't what she'd expected, but it was better. And something she never would have had the chance to experience if they'd gone for dinner back in town somewhere.

Abby studied him, letting her gaze travel over every line of his proud, chiseled face. She needed to know where they stood before this went any farther, what he wanted. Because she didn't want to risk her heart all on her own, and there was no way she could keep her heart out of the equation if they continued down this path.

She'd just opened her mouth to ask him where they stood when his grandmother called out from the house. "Time to eat. Bring Abby in here so we can show her what we made."

She and Kai shared a private smile. This time she reached for his hand, her heart skipping a beat at the way he squeezed hers in silent acknowledgment. Anticipation and arousal built inside her, every brush of his arm against her, every time she breathed in his scent adding to the heat between them.

In the kitchen, his grandma stood holding out a large plate to Abby, a proud smile on her kind face. "We'll do a big cookout with a kalua pig another time, but for now…enjoy."

There was so much food Abby might have been astounded if she wasn't used to the size of Kai's appetite. He explained what every dish was, and she tried some of everything. Lomi-lomi salmon, ahi poke, steamed mahi mahi fish wrapped in banana leaves. Laulau, little bundles of pulled pork wrapped and steamed inside taro leaves. Spam musubi—a kind of sushi made out of *actual* Spam, from a can and everything—fried rice, assorted Hawaiian fruits, and…poi.

"Always wanted to try this," Abby said, spooning some of the purple paste onto her plate.

"Eat it with a bite of something, not on its own. Otherwise it's like wallpaper paste," Kai said.

She laughed and continued filling her plate. He had a mound of food already piled on his. "What's your favorite?" she asked grandma.

"The *mahi mahi*," she answered. "I got it from the market this morning. They catch it fresh every day. You'll never taste anything better."

Abby believed it. "And what about you?" she asked Kai.

"*Kalua* pork," he answered without missing a beat. "You'll probably have it at the windup luau at the resort at the end of the conference, but if not, I'll make sure you get some before you leave the island."

Sounded like a plan to her.

All three of them sat at the table outside on the deck overlooking the magical oasis grandma had created. Abby didn't love the poi, but everything else was incredible. "Oh, I'm so full, but I can't stop eating."

Grandma smiled, delighted. "I'm glad you like our food."

"I love it." She eyed Kai, who was halfway through his second plate. "And here I was made to believe you could only cook steak and salad."

He shrugged, one side of his mouth tipping upward. "Can't give away all my secrets at once, can I?" The way he looked at her, the unmistakable male hunger for something other than food in his eyes, had her whole body buzzing with arousal.

Abby grabbed her tea and swallowed a few mouthfuls to cool herself off. It would be way too easy to give into the need he created in her. She had to keep her head on straight, have that talk with him before they were past the point of no return.

After dinner Abby insisted on helping clean up, asking grandma countless questions about the recipes and cooking methods. Once everything was put away, grandma told her stories about Kai and even pulled out old photo albums for them to look through.

"This is Kai and…Hani," grandma said, faltering slightly on the mention of the second name as she stopped at a picture of the two bare-chested boys with fishing rods over their shoulders. "Kai was around twelve or so here, and Hani ten or eleven. They were on their way down to the beach to catch something for dinner."

Abby glanced at Kai, next to her on the couch. His expression was unreadable, a slight tension in his square jaw that hinted at inner turmoil.

"They were like brothers and best friends all in one," the old woman continued, a wistfulness in her voice that tugged at Abby. "He promised to come by and see you while you're here," she said to Kai.

The hand on Abby's shoulder tightened slightly. "*Tutu*…"

She shrugged, her expression and posture becoming defensive. "I asked him to. You're *ohana*, Kai. And *ohana* is the most important thing."

Kai didn't respond, and Abby didn't dare ask any

questions, instead pointing to the next picture to change the subject. "How old was Kai here?" He was in his high school football uniform, already head and shoulders taller than most of his teammates, the proud expression on his face and confident posture hinting at the strength that would make him into the man he was today.

"Fifteen," grandma said, her face softening into a fond smile. "Look how handsome he was, even back then."

A little under an hour later, Abby bit back another yawn and blinked to clear her blurred vision. She was so damn tired, but didn't want the night to end.

"I think the time change is catching up with Abby," Kai said, the hand cupping her shoulder rubbing gently. "I'd better get her back to her hotel. Conference starts early in the morning."

Abby didn't argue. At the door she slipped on her shoes, thanked her hostess for a wonderful evening, and reached out a hand.

Kai's grandma looked down at it, snorted and held out her arms instead. Abby's heart melted. She stepped into the embrace, the feel of those thin but loving arms around her making her throat tighten. She was such a sweet lady. "Thank you for having me."

"No, thank *you*," grandma said, squeezing her tight. "I hope you'll come back again before you leave." Then, in a whisper, "You're good for my boy."

Abby hoped so. But were they good for each other? She'd gotten that wrong before, with disastrous results.

It stayed on her mind the entire drive back to Wailea. She and Kai got along well, but so had she and Roger, at least in the beginning. Did she and Kai have enough in common to have something that would last? She wanted to believe they did.

They were quiet at first, but then the questions in her mind became so loud she couldn't contain them any longer. "Can we talk about us?" she asked him.

He glanced over at her as he steered down the mountain road, the silvery light of the moon frosting his inky hair. "Sure."

"Okay, so where do we stand right now?"

The hint of a smile played around the edge of his mouth as he focused back on the road. "You want an actual label for it?"

No. Yes. "I want to know what's going on here, so I'm sure we're on the same page." *Because I don't want to make a fool out of myself and get my heart broken again.* And he was the one man who could definitely make a fool out of her.

"What do you want?" he countered.

Grrr. She frowned at him. "*Oh,* no. You first."

"Pretty sure I already made that plain around the corner from the elevator the night you came to my place."

The mention of the kiss triggered a total sensory recall of it. Screw subtlety. "You made it plain you want in my pants, yeah. Is that all you want?" It better not be.

He shot her a disbelieving look and raised a coal-black eyebrow. "No. I want you."

Those words, in that deep, sexy voice, sent a shiver through her. "What does that mean? For the duration of this trip? Longer? And how do we know it would even work between us? Is it worth risking what we've already got, when we might find out we're not compatible?"

"Isn't it worth giving it a chance, and finding out for sure?"

She considered that for a moment. "Only if you swear to me we'll still be friends if it doesn't work out." Even though no one could promise that, she needed to know he valued their friendship as much as she did, or no dice.

He inclined his head. "I swear."

Easier said than done, once people had been intimate and feelings had been hurt when one person broke it off down the road. "So what—"

She broke off when he raised her hand to his lips, pressed a slow, damp kiss to the backs of her knuckles, sending a rush of goosebumps up her arm. "Look. I know you're still hesitant about this, and I'm trying not to push. How about we just take it one day at a time, enjoy each other's company while we're here, and see where things go?"

Because I'm not wired that way? She needed to know the details in advance. "And if they go well, we'd be exclusive?"

He gave her a heated look, his intense gaze dropping to her lips. "We're exclusive starting now. I would never share you."

Another wave of heat cascaded over her at the possessive tone in his voice. The idea of being Kai's alone, the recipient of all that intense masculine focus and heat... Her insides squeezed, that all too familiar throb reigniting between her thighs. "Okay," she agreed, trying and failing to stem the excitement coursing through her. "One day at a time, and we'll see where things go."

"Okay." He kissed her hand again, the hint of dampness as he trailed his tongue across her knuckle insanely arousing.

The drive back was gorgeous, the warm night air whipping around them in the open convertible. Abby glanced at him, drinking in the sight of his profile, the power of his arms and shoulders. He turned her on big time, but he also made her feel safe.

Safe in a way she hadn't with anyone else. He would take care of her, protect her if need be. And it meant so much to her that he'd planned that wonderful, unforgettable meal for her. Her stomach was full, she was warm, and in good hands.

By the time they reached the Grand Wailea, it was nearly midnight and she was almost asleep. She sat up in her seat, fighting another yawn. "Sorry. I guess my internal clock hasn't adjusted yet."

"It's okay." He got out and hurried around to open her door for her, then took her hand and helped her out.

Abby gazed up at him in the flickering light of the tiki torches, indecision tugging at her. Should she ask him to come upstairs, rather than him driving back to his grandmother's for the night?

Her thoughts scattered when he wrapped one thick arm around her waist and pulled her close, her breasts pressed to the solid wall of his chest. His other hand came up to cradle the side of her face as he leaned down and placed his mouth on hers.

Shocking heat bolted through her, taking her off

guard. She'd sworn to take this one day at a time, but her body hated that plan. It wanted Kai, relief from the ache he created inside it, and it wanted that *now*.

She clung to his shoulders, slid her hands up into his short, thick hair and met each velvet stroke of his tongue, each caress of his lips. The way he held her, hungry and possessive but still gentle, turned her inside out. Within a minute she teetered right there on the edge of control, on the point of caving and asking him to come up to her room.

But Kai surprised her by ending the kiss and releasing her. "I know it's late, and you've got a long day ahead of you tomorrow, plus your internal clock's all screwed up right now. You need a good night's sleep."

At first she wasn't certain she'd heard him right. She barely caught herself before she could blurt out the words that would seal their fate and change everything irrevocably.

Stay with me tonight.

The tiny amount of self-control she still possessed held firm. She put on a smile for him, nodded. "Yeah. See you tomorrow?"

His dark eyes heated to molten pools in the torchlight. "Shortcake, that's a promise." And with that he climbed back into the Mustang and drove away.

Abby stared after him, her body aching with unfulfilled need. The deflated, overwhelming sense of disappointment as his taillights faded away in the distance sealed the deal for her.

She wanted Kai. She trusted him. What was the point in denying herself any longer? She'd been alone for long enough and had her head on straight, was going into this with clear eyes.

So, no. Her mind was made up. New Abby was woman enough to take what she wanted.

Next time she had the chance, she was climbing that sexy mountain of muscle like a goddamn tree.

Chapter Eight

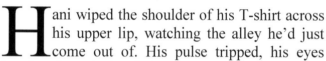

Hani wiped the shoulder of his T-shirt across his upper lip, watching the alley he'd just come out of. His pulse tripped, his eyes burning from lack of sleep. Even the uppers he'd taken to help combat the fatigue weren't working anymore.

Juan was here on the island. He'd heard it from some of his contacts on the street. The meeting—or summons—would happen soon.

He was strung out, twitchy as hell. Someone must have talked. It was the only reason why someone like Juan would want to come and check up on him personally.

Fear curdled in his gut. How much did his new handler know about him and what he'd been up to? How much did the cartel know about him and the crew he ran? Were they watching him right now?

The *Venenos* had eyes and ears everywhere on

this island. Throughout the islands, and back on the mainland too.

A shadowy figure appeared out of the twilit alley where Hani had just delivered some product to one of his best dealers. A man, wearing a hoodie, the hood pulled up to conceal his face.

Hani tensed behind the wheel of his truck, ready to peel out of there, but relaxed slightly when the man stepped into a dying ray of sunset filtering through the trees next to the rundown building in Happy Valley. Another guy from the crew Hani ran.

The man approached the truck, stopped and waited while Hani undid the window a few inches. "Howzit, *brah*?" Hani asked, speaking in Pidgin.

"Ho, *brah*. Dere's a *haole wahini* askin' 'bout you. Not from 'roun here."

Hani frowned. A non-local white woman was asking about him? "Asking what?"

"Wants to know who runs da black tar."

Lots of people sold black tar heroin here on the island. "How d'you know she means me?"

"Been showin' a picture of 'notha *haole* girl. Wants to know who sold her da black tar. Then she ask who sold *dem* da black tar."

"Fo' real?" Ballsy of her, walking into a place like Happy Valley and asking those kinds of questions. Questions that could get you killed here.

A nod.

That was a helluva lot of detective work for a *haole* woman to be asking on these streets. Maybe she was a reporter looking for a story. "People talkin' to her?" He had a hard time believing they would. The addicts and street people here wanted to stay anonymous. They didn't talk to cops, reporters or outsiders.

The man shrugged. "Dunno. Just heard 'bout it. She offering money.. Thought you'd wanna know."

Hani didn't like it, especially the money part. People here were desperate. Was she connected to this Juan guy or the cartel somehow? They were sneaky, ruthless. He wouldn't put it past them to use a woman to try to get the intel they wanted. "Thanks, *brah*." He needed to find out who this *haole* woman was and put a stop to her meddling.

"K'den." He walked away and melted back into the shadows.

Hani's phone rang. He glanced at the display, dread squeezing his throat when he saw the number. Juan. "Yeah," he answered, steeling himself.

"I'm in town and been doing some research. Heard some white lady's looking to find out who's selling my product in your area."

Hani clenched his jaw. Juan had probably paid the woman off to do it. "I heard. I'll take care of it."

"Also heard your cousin's in town."

He went rigid in his seat. He was well aware that Kai was in town. His *tutu* had called to tell him yesterday. "And?"

"You watch your tone, *cabrón*," Juan snapped. "I told you what would happen if your cousin showed up here. Now he has. So this is a test. Are you loyal to us, or the fucking DEA?"

Hani knew the answer to that. But he didn't dare say it. "I'll handle it."

"You'd better. I've got eyes on you at all times, *muchacho*. You take him out, you get the bounty. If not…" He let the pause build, making the threat plain. "Bullets are cheap. Would cost me less to put a couple in you and get a new distributor, plus it minimizes the risk. Know what I'm saying?"

Yeah, Hani did. "I said I'd handle it."

"We'll meet after it's done. You've got seventy-two hours, starting now." The line went dead.

Hani curled his fingers tighter around the phone and took a deep breath even though it felt like a concrete slab was lying on his chest. Three days to have someone kill Kai?

There was no way. Absolutely no way he could do it, or be involved. Which left only two options.

Hani could warn him. Except doing that would alert Kai to what he's been up to, and then his cousin would have no choice but to alert the authorities, including the DEA. Hani knew him. That boy scout part of Kai's personality couldn't be overridden, not even for family.

So really, Hani only had one choice. He had to get Kai to leave. Scaring him away wasn't an option. Nothing scared Kai. Hani had to figure out a way to shove him off the island. Push him away for good, for both their sakes.

His chest felt full of lead as he raised his phone and dialed Kai's cell number. His *tutu* had given it to him the other day.

"Maka," his cousin answered.

The sound of that familiar, deep voice hit Hani like a punch to the gut. He swallowed hard, fought the rush of emotions and memories away. "Hey, cuz. It's me."

A pause. "Hani?" Wariness was clear in his voice.

"Yeah. *Tutu* said you're home for a visit."

"Got in yesterday."

"How you been?"

"I'm good," he answered cautiously. "You?"

My life is a jacked-up, steaming pile of shit. Thanks for asking. And I'm about as close to rock bottom as a person can get. But I don't want either of us to die, so I have to do what I can to stop this. "Doin' good. You busy tonight? I was thinkin' we could meet up somewhere."

The silence that followed weighed heavy on Hani, pressing the anvil of guilt harder into his chest. It was the first time either of them had offered an olive branch to the other since their falling out years ago. When Kai told him they wouldn't have any kind of relationship until Hani cleaned up his life and turned legit.

God, how he wished he'd listened to his cousin.

"I'd like that," Kai said after a long pause, taking Hani by surprise. "But I've already got plans."

Stupid, to feel a rush of disappointment. Yet he did. "No worries. We can—"

"I've got a friend staying at the Grand Wailea. I'm going there for dinner at eight-thirty."

Hani hesitated, then forced himself to keep going. "I can meet you there. Just to say hey, catch up a little." He'd have to be careful on his way over there, make sure no one was following him.

"I don't know."

Desperation quickened his heart rate. "It's been a long time, Kai. Too long."

His cousin sighed. "Yeah. Yeah, it has." Another pause. "All right, meet me in the lobby then."

Hani released the breath he'd been holding. Kai probably thought having a third person there would act as a kind of icebreaker, but whoever it was represented the equivalent of a human monkey wrench in Hani's plan. And yet…

Goddamn it, he missed Kai. Missed him like hell, and had all this time. Hani had to do the hard thing soon and shove Kai away hard enough to make him leave the island. But before that happened, he was selfish enough to want some time with him. Not a lot, or it would make his plan impossible. So he'd take what he could get.

"Okay," he said. "Meet you there." He checked his watch. It was seven-thirty now. He had just enough time to run home and change if he was going to make it down to Wailea in time.

"All right. See you."

"See you." Hani lowered the phone to his lap, the sting of tears burning the back of his throat. He cleared it and swallowed, forced all that shit away as he started his truck and drove to his place.

He was so deep in his thoughts about Kai and what he would have to do, that only partway there did he remember about the *haole* woman who'd been asking about him, and Juan's warning that he was being watched. Hani kept checking his mirrors but it was too late now to discern whether or not anyone was following him, because this part of Kahului was busy and there was a line of cars behind him. He swore under his breath, dots of perspiration breaking out over his upper lip.

Vowing to be more careful from now on, he stayed vigilant as he parked behind his luxury townhouse and headed inside. Showered, shaved and changed into a dress shirt and khaki pants, he got back in his truck and headed for the west side of the island.

A few cars stayed behind him on the highway there, but the one directly behind him wasn't tailgating as if afraid of losing him, and none of the others were passing to try and get closer. His gut told him he was still in the clear, though there were plenty of other ways the cartel could track him.

He relaxed, the nerves buzzing in his stomach now mostly to do with the upcoming reunion with Kai. Shame crawled through him, threatened to smother him. He'd made bad choices in his life and it was way too late to fix any of them now. He was in too deep. There was no escape. He was nothing but a pawn of the *Veneno* cartel, and an expendable one at that.

Maybe Kai can get me out.

As soon as the desperate thought flashed into his head, he dismissed it. He'd done shitty things and trafficked dope for a living because until now it had been easy money. Kai was already in enough danger. Maybe their *tutu* as well. For once in his life, Hani had to put someone else's wellbeing before his and think of the only two people he really cared about in this world.

The streets of Wailea were quiet, filled only with the wealthy tourists who paid obscene amounts of money to stay at this luxurious part of the island. He only ever came here on business, whether for meetings or to deliver shipments of product to his dealers who sold to the people who stayed there. And the Grand Wailea was the area's crown jewel.

He drove up to the luxurious main entrance and handed the keys to the valet, glancing behind him as he stepped out into the sultry night air. A few cars behind him were familiar. Again, none of them concerned him. He would go meet Kai, play it cool, pull him aside for a minute and say something awful to make a clean break, then something else to try and make him leave the island tomorrow.

As he turned toward the open entryway into the hotel lobby, he spotted a familiar figure heading his way. A few inches taller than him, built like a freaking linebacker.

The rush of emotion he'd been trying to hold back burst free, thickening his throat, and his whole plan crumbled around him. Unable to help himself, he broke into a smile and walked faster, drawn to his cousin like a junkie to his next fix.

Kai stopped, his expression closed. Distant. But as Hani came nearer his cousin's face changed, split into a reluctant grin that made Hani's heart catch. "Hey," Kai said.

Overcome by a sudden wave of emotion, Hani walked right up to him, wrapped his arms around those massive shoulders in a back-slapping hug. His chest ached, ready to split open. "Good to see you, *hoahānau*," he said, his voice rough.

Kai hugged him back. "You too, man." He half-turned away from Hani and reached out a hand to someone standing behind him. "And this, this is Abby."

Hani's smile slipped, freezing in place as he stared at the newcomer. She was about five-five, with short, platinum blond hair and bright blue eyes, wearing a purple dress that made her pale skin glow. She was pretty, and not Kai's usual type at all, since he always went for leggy brunette model-types...

Yet the unmistakable pride on his cousin's face as he looked at her with that smile made Hani's stomach sink. He'd seen that look once before, when Kai had brought a girl home during his time in the Marine Corps. He knew what it meant, because he knew Kai better than anyone. Even their *tutu*.

"Hi, Hani," she said, offering her hand politely, everything about her radiating poise and confidence. This one wasn't shy. She knew who and what she was, and she looked him straight in the eye when she spoke to him. "Nice to meet you."

He shook her hand, numb inside. "Yeah. Same." Fuck. Kai was in love with her. Or if not, well on his way there. They both had a long history of shitty relationships. From what *Tutu* had told him about Kai's most recent relationship with some girl named Shelley, Kai hadn't been happy in a long time. But it was obvious he was happy now, with Abby.

More guilt piled onto the growing mountain he carried on his shoulders. He hadn't even considered that Kai would be meeting a woman, let alone one he was involved with. Hani didn't want her or his cousin getting hurt because of him. What the hell was he going to do now? He couldn't say the things he needed to in front of her, it would cause too much of a scene.

Kai slid an arm around Abby's shoulders and pulled her in tight to his body, the gesture possessive and protective all at once. "Let's head down to the restaurant and get our table. Then we can catch up." He turned away with Abby.

"How the heck do you pronounce it, anyway?" she asked.

"What, *Humuhumunukunukuapua'a*?" Kai laughed at her dumbstruck expression. "It's the Hawaiian name for the reef triggerfish. Our state fish."

The answering smile she gave Kai made Hani's insides writhe. Dammit. That was the fanciest restaurant in the whole place.

What now? He shouldn't have come. Shouldn't be here at all, it was too risky. And how the hell was he supposed to pull off his plan now, in that setting with all kinds of people around as witnesses? Stupid. God, why was he always so stupid? "I can't stay for dinner," he blurted out.

Kai stopped and looked back at him in surprise, frowning. "Why not?"

"Something last second came up on my way here. But I'll have a quick drink with you first, before I go."

Those deep brown eyes held his for a long moment, the warmth in them cooling. Then Kai nodded. "All right."

Hani exhaled a long, quiet breath as his cousin turned away and kept walking. He couldn't tell Kai off here. So tonight was a reprieve of sorts, but it didn't change the inevitable. Tomorrow he would have to tell Kai what he'd come here to say, no matter how much it would gut him to do it, and hope the hell it was enough to work. Hell, he had to try.

Better for his cousin to hate him forever than Kai

or his girlfriend winding up dead from a *Veneno* bullet.

****

Inside her rental car parked out of sight of everyone coming and going from the fancy hotel, Diane stared at the picture on her phone that one of the people she'd bribed had texted her. It was definitely the same man she'd followed here.

Hani Maka. The name of the man who trafficked the black tar heroin that had killed Bailey.

He'd just gone inside a few minutes ago. She hadn't been stupid enough to follow him in there. Too many witnesses and who knew how many security cameras. But she had managed to snap a few pictures on her phone when he'd met up with a couple.

She'd been here yesterday, doing some recon. The hotel was hosting a big pharma conference. From her research she'd learned that one company in particular was a big manufacturer of fentanyl. The poison the cartel thugs mixed into their heroin and cocaine.

That shit had killed Bailey. Diane was trying to identify a target here at the conference. She'd narrowed it down to someone from NextGen Pharmaceuticals. The CEO of the company was here. He had to know what his poison was doing to the world, but he and his shareholders didn't give a shit as long as the profits continued to roll in.

Diane focused on Hani's picture once more. She hated how good-looking he was. She'd wanted him to be ugly. As ugly as the evil inside him that drove him to make a living distributing poison that killed people's children.

Had Bailey known him? Would he even remember her if Diane confronted him?

Didn't matter. Tamping down the hot rage, she scrolled to the next photo and enlarged it. Hani had met another big Hawaiian guy, who was with a woman.

Diane focused on the woman. She was dressed in business attire, a teal blouse and black pencil skirt, and she had something around her neck. A lanyard.

Squinting at it through the glasses she used while driving, a shock of cold ran through her when she read the credentials. Abby McKinley. NextGen Pharmaceuticals. And she was meeting with Hani.

Why the hell would a NextGen employee be meeting with a known drug trafficker? Unless…

She swallowed as a combination of anger and revulsion twisted her stomach. Unless the cartel was working with NextGen to supply the toxic drugs to make addicts and keep demand for their poison high.

Shaken, she started her vehicle and began the drive back to Kaanapali where she was staying. Halfway there, the anger and revulsion had turned into determination. She turned right at the highway and drove across the island, heading to Happy Valley. Once there she found a parking spot near a vacant house and got out to start her canvassing.

Wearing the same wig and outfit from earlier, she tucked her pistol into the loose waistband of her jeans—she was losing weight like crazy, still having no appetite—and went in search of the addict she'd last talked to. The street people here knew things other residents didn't.

She found him a block from their previous meeting, in the midst of shooting up. He clenched and unclenched his fist as he lowered the needle and removed the elastic band serving as a tourniquet, looked up at her with bleary eyes and scowled.

"Why you here, *haole*?" he ground out, his expression hostile and suspicious. "I told you not to come 'roun here again."

Diane was well aware that the word was meant as a deliberate slur. It was laughable. She was so beyond the realm of words hurting her, he had no idea.

She crouched next to him, heart pounding, and held up her phone—along with a hundred dollar bill. "I just saw Hani talking with this man. He looks like he might be a local. Do you know him?"

The man stared at the money for a moment, then squinted hard at the picture and broke into a chuckle.

Diane frowned and lowered the phone. "What's funny?"

"Oh, man. Ain't seen him 'round here for years."

"You know him? This guy?" she tapped the big Hawaiian in the photo. Or at least, he looked Hawaiian.

"Yeah, *haole*, I know him. *Moke* from 'roun here. Grew up in the neighborhood. Name's Kai. They're cousins. Heard from someone that he's with the DEA now."

Diane gasped, her muscles grabbing tight. "DEA?"

"Yeah. That's what people say."

Holy shit. This was so much more corrupt and

twisted than she had ever imagined. This DEA agent was working with the cartel and the pharmaceutical industry? "They're cousins," she repeated, wanting to make sure she hadn't misunderstood somehow.

"That's what I said," he bit out, and snatched the money from her fingers.

Diane shoved to her feet and hurried back to her rental car, her mind whirling. The police weren't on to her yet. No one was looking for her, and no one ever would, because she had no criminal history of any sort. She still had time, but likely not much, so she had to act fast.

She had to be careful now. Watch over her shoulder every step along the way. Exhaustion haunted her, ready to take her down the moment her adrenaline levels dropped. She needed to go to a motel and crash, eat something before she planned her next move.

But in the morning, she would figure out a way to kill her new targets. She was going to kill all three of them before they could take any more innocent lives.

Chapter Nine

"Your first night there together, and he takes you to visit his *grandma*?"

Abby laughed at the outrage in Cindy's voice on the other end of the phone. "She raised him. It was a big deal for him to take me to meet her. The two of them had spent the entire day cooking dinner for me. It was amazing."

"And?"

"And what?"

Cindy made a frustrated sound. "I could strangle you for torturing me like this. You know exactly what."

"We're not in the friend zone anymore, but we haven't rushed things either." That was good. It was also playing hell on her self-control. He made her want to dive head first into the deep end and figure the rest out later.

A pause. "I'm really disappointed in you right

now."

Abby bit back a laugh at the disgust in her friend's voice. "No, it's a good thing. I've had time to think, and we talked about us. We've agreed to take things one day at a time and see where things go." Although it was driving her nuts, waiting to take the next step with him now that she'd decided to go for it.

"You're insane. You know that? One, for thinking you can fool me into thinking you're not ga-ga over him, and two, for not jumping on board that train and riding it as far as it'll take you. Riding it *hard*, Abs."

She laughed again. "I love you, Cin. You always look out for my best interest."

"I do, just like you do for me. And in light of that…just a friendly reminder that he's on the rebound."

"I know. But I've decided to give us a shot anyhow."

"I'm proud of you, babe. Really. I know how hard it is to put yourself out there after what you went through with Roger. I can imagine how much tougher it is when it's a guy you already care about, and he comes with an added risk."

"Well, I'm a big girl and I'm going into this with eyes wide open."

"Good for you. So. What did you guys do last night?"

"He met me here for dinner." At the most romantic restaurant she'd ever been to in her life. Named something she couldn't pronounce, set on a series of koi ponds, with the rush of a waterfall in the background and lush tropical gardens surrounding it. "We only had an hour together before I had to go to a work mixer." She hadn't invited him because things were still new between them and she hadn't wanted to introduce him to her boss yet. "And I met his cousin briefly too. That was weird, though."

"Why?"

"He seemed really happy to see Kai when he first walked into the lobby, but when he noticed me, he kind of froze up. He stayed for one drink with us and made some lame excuse about why he couldn't stay. He was only with us for about twenty minutes, and the whole time there was this awkward tension between them. I thought it was because of me, but Kai said afterward that it wasn't."

"Then what was the problem?"

"They had a falling out years ago. Hani got into a bad lifestyle and Kai refused to condone it. This is the first time they've seen each other since then, and they've got this unspoken don't ask, don't tell thing happening." Kai had been different after Hani left. Quieter, a little distracted, but she'd had to leave for the mixer before they could really talk about it. She could tell the way his cousin had blown off the visit had upset him.

"So nothing happened last night after the cousin left?"

"We didn't have time," Abby said with a chuckle. "He left when I had to go to the mixer." She'd wanted to meet up with him after the mixer, but then thought better of it. Her self-control was already weak where he was concerned.

"And what about tonight?"

"He's got plans with a bunch of old friends. He hasn't seen them in a couple years, so I'm doing my own thing."

Cindy made a frustrated sound. "How many days do you guys have left, then?"

"Three here. But it's not like we're up against a deadline or anything. We live in the same city."

"When he's in town."

"Yeah. I like that we're both busy, though. I couldn't stand it if he was clingy."

"Well just make sure you keep me updated if anything…changes."

Abby shook her head in amusement. "I will."

"Oh, hey, any news about that doctor who was killed last week?"

"Nothing new that I know of. Read in the paper here this morning that they still have no leads. Security's been beefed up here at the conference, so don't worry."

"Okay. Good. I gotta run. Enjoy your evening in paradise."

"I will. Love you."

"Love you too. Bye."

Abby slipped her phone back into her purse and took out her camera as she wandered the grounds. The sun was high in the sky, making it too hot to sit outside unless she was in the shade. She'd planned to go sit by the pool and read a book for a while, but instead she decided to wander around the property a little bit.

Beyond the long, rectangular pool lined with dolphin statues, a gorgeous white chapel sat in the middle of the lush green lawn. Birds called around her, darting from tree to tree as the breeze sighed through the leaves and palm fronds. She snapped a few pictures of it, making a mental note to come back at sunset or twilight to get different shots.

Her phone rang in her purse. She dug it out, excitement leaping in her veins when she saw Kai's number. "Hi, I was just thinking about you."

"Well that's nice to hear. You done for the day there?"

"Wrapped up my last session about forty minutes ago. I'm playing tourist, taking all kinds of pictures of the grounds now."

"You up for an excursion?"

"I might be, except I thought you had plans."

"I do, but I miss you too damn much, so I want you to come too."

Aww, that was sweet. Tiny butterfly wings began to flutter low in her belly. If she said yes, it was almost certain she would wind up in bed with him tonight.

"How do you feel about camping?" he asked before she could respond.

Camping? "I'm...on the fence about it. Why?"

"Buddy of mine owns a place on the beach just south of Lahaina, and he's gonna let us camp there for the night. You told me you've never snorkeled, which is criminal, so we'll do that before having dinner at my buddy's place, then camp overnight on the beach. You've never slept in a tent on a Hawaiian beach before, and we need to mark that off your bucket list before you go too."

Her insides fluttered, a mix of nerves and anticipation. Sleeping in a tent on the beach with Kai sounded enticing, and pretty damn romantic. But only because it was with him. "I have to be back here for a nine a.m. start."

"No problem. I'll make sure you're back in time to shower and get ready."

She bit her lower lip, a smile tugging at it. "Okay, then."

"Good," he said, sounding pleased. "I'll pick you up. How soon can you be ready?"

"I just need to pack. What should I wear?"

"Whatever you want. But bring your bikini. You brought a bikini, right?"

Apprehension hit her, the time-honored response to the idea of being in a bathing suit in public still as strong as ever. The thought of Kai, an insanely gorgeous man in prime condition who was used to dating model-worthy women seeing her in her bathing suit, filled her with dread. "Maybe."

"If not, we'll buy you one on the way up. Go grab whatever you need. I'll be there in half an hour."

No way she was passing this up, bathing suit phobia or not. She wasn't fourteen anymore. She was a grown damn woman, and she knew what she wanted. Him. "All right. See you soon."

"Looking forward to it, shortcake."

Abby couldn't wipe the smile from her face as she hurried back to her room, changed into a sundress and packed an overnight bag. She threw in sleep shorts and a tank top, but if things went well, she wouldn't be wearing them long. If at all.

Refusing to let herself overthink it, she headed to the lobby, her heart stuttering when she saw Kai there waiting for her. He pushed his shades up onto the top of his head and pulled her into a hug, burying his face in the curve of her neck, his lips brushing against her skin. "Missed you."

Please, it's only been fifteen hours since you last saw me.

She bit the flippant response back before it could burst out, and melted a little. This was Kai. It wasn't fair to verbally push him away just because she was afraid of getting hurt. She didn't have to keep her guard up with him. Didn't have to use that edge she'd created in the wake of her relationship with Roger to protect herself and keep him at a distance. If they were going to take a shot at this, she had to give him her authentic self.

"Missed you too," she murmured, meaning it.

He kissed her cheek, her jaw, his lips lingering at the edge of her mouth for a moment before claiming it in a slow, tender caress. Her heart was beating faster when he eased away and caught her hand in his. "You look gorgeous," he said, his voice a deep rumble as his gaze slid over the length of her body and back up.

Heat built inside her, making her skin extra sensitive. "Thank you. You do too." But he always did.

Grinning, he raised her hand to his mouth, kissed it, and started for the entrance, the promise of what was coming hanging in the air between them. "You're gonna love this, I promise."

She knew she would. It was what would happen afterward that worried her. She refused to let that spoil everything else, though. For once she was going to live in the moment and take a risk.

They arrived at Kai's friend's house at a little before three. A cute, Hawaiian-style bungalow sat in the middle of the property, surrounded by a lush green lawn, some overgrown plants and tall palms behind the house. The moment he parked and shut off the engine, the crash of the waves reached her. When she got out, the briny scent of it filled her nose, mixing with the perfume of tropical plants.

He took her hand, gave her an intimate smile that had her toes curling in her flip-flops. "Come on, I'll introduce you to everyone."

She followed him around back, where five guys were all standing around a large stone-ringed pit. All friends from his childhood. He introduced her to them, kept his hand on her waist the entire time she shook hands. They all gave her curious looks but were friendly enough as they greeted her.

"And, as promised," Kai told her, pointing at the pit, "Kalua pork for dinner, baked in a traditional *imu*. Another Maui bucket list item, I believe."

"Oh, wow, you guys have a whole pig roasting in there?" She took a step closer. The pig was placed over a fire in the pit lined with hot rocks and banana leaves. They covered it with wet burlap, more banana leaves, more hot rocks, then sand and dirt and cooked it until it shredded apart. Just digging and prepping the pit was a ton of work.

"Well, most of one," one of his friends answered. "You like to cook?"

"I love to cook. But I've never done anything like this." She gestured to the *imu* dug into the ground. "Wish I'd been there to watch you prep it."

Kai wrapped an arm around her shoulders. "I would've brought you here to see it, but we had to get it cooking by seven this morning."

Abby gazed up at him. "You did this for me, didn't you?" Because she was pretty sure that going through the laborious process of making kalua pork wasn't something he and his friends normally did on an average Thursday.

"Maybe," he murmured. "Some women like flowers or gifts. You love food, and I do too. So I'm gonna keep giving you what you love." He searched her eyes for a moment before pressing a tender kiss to her forehead that made her chest ache.

Oh, man, he was claiming little pieces of her heart with every one of these gestures, and she had no hope of ever getting them back again. More than that, she didn't *want* to. "You get me," she whispered, her throat a little tight. No one had ever understood her like that. Or cared to find out what truly made her happy.

Kai kissed her temple then laced his long fingers through hers and squeezed. "Let me show you our campsite."

Abby walked with him down the lawn and over the line of brush and tree debris that scattered across the edge of the sand. Before her, the ocean spread out in a sparkling expanse, at least a dozen different shades of turquoise glowing in the sunlight, with gentle waves lapping against the shore. "Oh, it's so beautiful."

"It belonged to his grandparents. They passed it down to him in their will. And there's our room for the night," he said, pointing to the left. She followed his arm to the tent already pitched and waiting on the sand beneath the shade of a giant banyan tree whose canopy arched over the beach. They'd be able to hear the sound of the waves all night, and still have total privacy.

Excitement stirred in her belly. "It's perfect."

His smile warmed her from the inside out. "You up for some snorkeling?"

She wasn't in a rush to put on her suit. "Shouldn't we stay and help get the rest of the dinner ready?"

"Nah, the boys've got it covered. I already did the grunt work." He tugged on her hand, coaxing. "Come on. Let's get you into your bikini."

More and more nervous with each step, she went with him to the tent, then slipped inside to change while he waited outside and got the snorkeling stuff ready. She pulled on the bright teal bottoms with the ruffled little skirt that hid the most hated part of her body, then struggled with the ties on the top, dreading and looking forward to this at the same time.

Wishing she had a mirror to check everything, she mentally berated herself, but still felt a hundred times better once she had her cover up on. Floppy-brimmed sunhat in place, she paused at the tent flap, took a deep breath to gather her courage, and pulled up on the zipper.

Kai was right there at the entrance waiting for her—in nothing but a pair of swim trunks. Abby forgot to breathe as she stared at him, her fingers still grasping the zipper tab. She'd imagined what he'd look like without a shirt for so long, but this…this was beyond the realm of anything she'd fantasized about. He was all hard, cut muscle, those gorgeous, thick black tribal tattoos swirling over his sculpted left pec, shoulder, and down his upper arm in intricate patterns.

She was so caught up in staring at him that she forgot to be self-conscious of him seeing her until he said, "You planning to snorkel in the cover up?"

Her gaze jerked to his, that old, familiar anxiety tingling in her gut once again. "Um, no." She fought the urge to fidget, her muscles suddenly tight as cables. "I thought maybe we'd wait until..." Until it was dark enough that he wouldn't be able to see every imperfection on her body highlighted by the bright, unforgiving sun.

He shook his head at her, eyes brimming with amusement. "You got sunscreen on?"

"Oh." Turning, she dug out the can from her bag.

Kai took it from her with a heavy sigh that was full of disappointment. "You mainlanders." He tossed it back in her bag, caught her hand before she could protest and pulled her out of the tent into the shade. "That stuff's toxic as hell to our coral and marine life, and gives our sea turtles cancer. You don't want to give our sacred *honu* cancer, do you?"

"No, of course not, but—"

"I brought some other stuff, just in case. Gotta make sure we protect that pretty fair skin from this sun, or it'll burn you to a crisp in no time." Bending, he spread out a towel on the sand and straightened, the sheer authority of him as he stood in front of her making her stomach do a little flip. God, that was sexy. "Take off the cover up and lie face down."

Abby squirmed inside. Having him see her thighs and butt up close and personal right off the bat?

He raised a dark eyebrow. "You're not getting shy with me, are you, shortcake?"

Yep. But she wasn't going to let her insecurity ruin this. That was Old Abby BS. Old Abby would have stayed in her cover up in the shade the entire time. New Abby was confident, knew who she was and what she wanted. Didn't give a shit what other people thought about her body.

New Abby also wanted Kai. So he could just deal with a bit of cellulite, stretch marks and a few jiggly spots.

Drawing her New Abby armor around her, she pulled off the cover up and went straight to the towel, lying flat on her stomach, thankful that at least in this position she didn't have to look at his face.

Her entire body buzzed with awareness as he knelt beside her in the sand. A cap popped open, and she jumped slightly when his large hands touched between her shoulder blades.

"Cold?" he murmured.

"A little," she said, fighting the urge to tense as his hands began to smooth the sunblock over her skin.

"It'll warm up fast."

She was already hot and on her way to overheating, and all he'd done was touch her back. She bit the inside of her cheek as he worked his way across her shoulders and down the length of her spine, his touch firm and slow and so damn erotic she was throbbing and wet by the time he reached the small of her back. He smoothed the lotion over her skin like she was the most precious thing in the universe to him, being careful to cover every inch of her.

Abby couldn't help but flinch when he shifted

lower and flipped up the skirt of her bikini bottoms. Her muscles went rigid, her heart hammering as her mind flashed back to that horrific field trip at the end of ninth grade when she'd come out of the changing room wearing her new red bathing suit to find the rest of the class watching her. She'd been so excited about the trip, about wearing her new suit.

She'd also been carrying an extra twenty pounds back then, resulting in a few rolls. Which was why she'd agonized over selecting a new swimsuit, one that would make her feel confident about how she looked, and maybe get her noticed by the boy she had a crush on.

Instead of a fun day at the pool with her friends that she'd been looking forward to for weeks, it turned out to be her nightmare. The boys in her class had been mean little shits, making snide comments that cut deeper than knives because the teacher hadn't come out of the changing room yet. Including the boy she'd had a crush on.

Quick, get a harpoon, there's a beached whale on deck!

Must be jelly 'cause jam don't shake like that!

Kai's hands stilled, squeezing the backs of her thighs. "Hey. Relax." He shook her legs gently.

With effort, Abby exhaled and forced her muscles to loosen, shoving those memories back into the box she'd put them in. Some part of her would always feel like that awkward, overweight and self-conscious teenager.

"That's better," Kai murmured, and resumed the motion of his hands.

Now that she'd consciously surrendered that most

vulnerable part of herself to him, it felt like a weight lifted from her. He wasn't making snide comments, didn't appear disgusted by what he saw, just kept going with those smooth, firm yet gentle strokes over her most hated body parts. And with every glide of his palms and fingers, something loosened inside her. Healed.

Closing her eyes against the sudden sting there, she swallowed back the lump clogging her throat and gave into his touch, grateful that he was unaware of her thoughts.

By the time he'd finished with her calves she was a human puddle laid out on the towel, utterly relaxed. Safe.

And aroused as all hell.

"Okay, turn over."

At his low command she slowly rolled onto her back, unashamed by the way her nipples pressed against the fabric of her top. There was no way to hide it anyway, and she wanted him to see what he'd done to her.

Kai's gaze stopped at her breasts, the desire kindling there giving her a heady rush of feminine power she hadn't felt in…maybe forever. "You're so beautiful," he said softly.

From any other man she would have dismissed those words and assumed he was either flat out lying or just trying to get in her pants. But not Kai. She believed him because that look on his face, like he was thinking about all the things he wanted to do to her, combined with his touch—those were real.

Closing her eyes, she let herself drift while he spread the sunscreen all over the front of her, making her tingle and throb. He finished by pushing her sunhat off and tossing it aside, kneeling over her to smooth the cool lotion over her forehead, cheeks and nose. Abby had never felt so cherished or wanted.

"Okay, all done." He withdrew his hands, causing her to open her eyes and look up at him. His face was directly above hers, giving her a prime view of those powerful shoulders, arms and chest, that gorgeous, chiseled face. "Ready for some fun in the water?"

Her entire body ached with need. What she wanted was to drag him into the tent and do bad, bad things to him. But that wasn't going to work when it was broad daylight and five of his friends were wandering around. And this continual build of arousal was too delicious to end now.

"Okay," she whispered back.

He stood and reached down a hand for her, the sensual promise in his eyes making her heart pound. "Come on, shortcake. Let me show you my idea of paradise."

Chapter Ten

A few days ago, Kai thought the most fun part of this trip was during that race with Freeman back on Oahu, but he'd been wrong. Dead wrong. Nothing could touch what he'd experienced with Abby this afternoon while they played in the water together.

"That was incredible," Abby gushed, tossing her snorkeling gear to the sand beside their tent. They'd been in the water for almost an hour, exploring the reef just offshore. The water was calm, the tide just beginning to come in, the sun dipping low on the horizon, about an hour away from setting.

Kai smiled. "Glad you had fun."

Rubbing the sunscreen into her creamy skin had made him hard as stone, but he'd also seen something from her that surprised him. She'd hesitated before coming out of the tent in her swimsuit, and she'd been almost shy with him at first, as though she'd been anxious about him seeing her body.

If she'd only known how desperate he was to see her, she wouldn't have worried in the first place. He'd loved what he'd seen, couldn't wait to see *all* of her. Thankfully she'd relaxed after he'd told her how beautiful she was. Once he'd helped her with her fins, mask and snorkel and gotten her into the water, she'd loved it. He'd pointed out all the different fish and a couple of sea turtles.

She gave him a coy look as she pushed her wet bangs out of her face. "You sure know how to show a girl a good time."

He'd just shared his love of the ocean with her, and romanced her with food he'd known she would love. But he wanted to show her so much more. Like how amazing chemistry translated to incredible sex, for example. That was at the top of his list right now. "Oh, shortcake, you ain't seen nothing yet."

Her cheeks turned pink but she didn't look away, a grin tugging at her lips. "You sound very sure of yourself."

"I'm pretty confident in my abilities." He'd show her exactly how much fun he could be soon enough. Heat gathered low in his belly, his growing erection pressing against the front of his swim shorts. "One more quick swim before we shower up for dinner?"

"Okay." She studied him, her gaze lingering on his chest, sliding lower, making the shorts even tighter before she met his eyes again. "I've never seen anyone as good as you in the water before. You're like a fish. Or a merman."

"Well, my name does mean 'sea'." Without giving her any warning, he bent at the waist and grabbed her, hoisting her over his shoulder.

She shrieked out a laugh and grabbed at his waist. "Kai! Put me down!"

"Nope." He whacked a hand across her left butt cheek and carried her back into the water, waiting until he was waist deep before gripping her hips and tossing her into the waves.

He caught a glimpse of shock on her face, her wide, pretty blue eyes just before she went under. She surfaced two seconds later with an expression of horror, her hands clutching her bikini top to her breasts, which had come undone at the back of her neck.

Chuckling, he took a wading step toward her. "Uh oh, wardrobe malfunction. Need a hand?"

She narrowed her eyes at him. "I'd splash you for that, but my hands are full right now."

They were full, all right. "I'll help. I'll hold the top in place while you tie it."

She snorted. "No, I'll hold and you tie. You think I'm that easy?"

God, he loved her sass, her confidence. "No, you're not easy at all, except for when it comes to being with you," he murmured, bending to kiss the tip of her nose as he pulled the ties into place at her nape and did them up.

Abby gazed up at him with those gorgeous, vivid blue eyes, looking like a little blonde water nymph. A sexy one. Then her hand flashed out, shoving a wave of water right into his face. He sputtered and coughed, wiped the water away to give her a mock glare.

"Serves you right," she said, and bravely stood her

ground.

Kai held her gaze, the latent heat and tension building between them. Quick as a striking shark, he scooped her out of the water, holding her across his chest, one arm beneath her thighs and the other around her back.

She squealed and locked her arms around his neck, clinging to him. "Don't throw me again!"

Chuckling, he cuddled her closer, loving the feel of her pressed to him, the way she buried her face in his neck. "Okay. But only because you feel so good up against me like this."

Abby relaxed a little, hummed in appreciation and nuzzled the side of his neck, the drag of her lips across his skin sending a wave of desire through him. "You feel good too. And I gotta say, it's a real novelty being swept off my feet. Last guy who tried it hurt his back and could barely move for a week," she added with a little laugh.

He squeezed her tighter to him, giving her another display of his strength as his muscles flexed against her. Yeah, he was a big guy, and he worked hard to stay in this condition. Knowing his body turned her on was a big ego boost. "Well then he must have been a wimp, because you don't weigh very much." He could hold her all day.

"Very gallant of you to say so." She opened her mouth on his neck, sucked gently, making the breath lock in his throat. "Mmm, you're all salty."

Suppressing a growl of longing, Kai slid the hand around her ribs up to cup the back of her head and bring her mouth to his. She settled into his hold and cradled the side of his face with one palm, her mouth soft and warm and inviting beneath his own. Every stroke of her tongue against his sent another rush of blood between his legs.

More than anything he wanted to pluck the bow at her nape undone, peel the cups of her bikini top down to reveal her breasts, finally see if they were the shade of pink he imagined before driving her wild with his mouth.

"Hey! If you two can bear to stop sucking face for a few minutes, it's time to eat," one of his buddies called out from shore. "Dinner's in fifteen, and we're not saving any pork for you if you're late."

Kai ended the kiss reluctantly and pressed his forehead to hers. He was hard and aching, ravenous to get Abby naked and under him. "Not gonna lie, kind of regretting bringing you here, because now we're gonna have to hang out with them until we can go to bed."

She kissed him softly, her lips curving. "I don't know. I'm kind of loving the whole anticipation thing."

He was too, in a way. And she was totally worth the wait.

He carried her out of the water, ignoring her protests, only setting her down once they'd reached the tent. She hurriedly slipped her cover up on, then grabbed her bag and walked hand-in-hand with him up to the house where she had first shower.

He was waiting for her in the hallway when the door opened, releasing a cloud of Abby-scented steam. She appeared a moment later wearing a turquoise sundress that clung to the curve of her breasts and hips, the hem flaring out in little ruffles around mid-thigh.

Kai caught her, lifted her off the floor and turned, pinning her to the wall for another scorching kiss, letting her feel what she did to him, how much he wanted her. Reining the hunger in, he released her slowly, taking savage satisfaction in her dilated pupils, her rapid breathing. "I want you so damn much," he said, his voice low, gruff.

Her fingers clenched around the tops of his shoulders and she moaned softly. "How long until bed time?"

"Hours," he groaned, and released her before he could decide to hell with it, carry her into the bathroom and take the edge off for them both.

It took an act of will not to take his own edge off in the shower. Clean and dressed in shorts and a T-shirt, he found Abby helping his buddies get the last of the sides set out on the long picnic table in the backyard. He could tell they all liked her from the way they teased her, and she gave it right back, earning even more respect from them. Yet another way she was different from Shelley. Shelley never would have fit in here, would have been clingy and demanding.

When they'd all filled their plates, Kai snagged her around the waist and pulled her into his lap in the lawn chair he'd taken. "I want your first bite of kalua pork to be from my fingers," he murmured, low enough that only she could hear him over the trill of birds in the nearby garden.

Her eyes flicked up to his, arousal and amusement gleaming there. "You don't need to keep seducing me with food. I'm already at a steady simmer."

"Well, can't hurt." Pure male satisfaction slid through him as he selected a bite of the succulent pork and brought it to her lips. Abby's cheeks turned an adorable shade of pink and she glanced around for a moment, but then dipped her head and parted her lips, accepting the morsel from his fingers.

"Mmmm," she moaned, closing her eyes as she chewed. "Oh, it almost melts in my mouth."

His cock swelled at the enjoyment on her face, made worse by the sweet pressure of her ass in his lap. He selected another bite and raised it to her mouth, watching with erotic fascination as her lips closed around it. Abby adored food the way some women adored jewelry or clothes, but there was something so erotic and primal about feeding her the thing she loved by his own hand.

"Am I interrupting?" a dry voice said from beside him.

Kai glanced up at their host, Jonah, who had a plate piled high with food in one hand, and a beer in the other, a wry expression on his face. "Nah, man. Sit down," he said, his entire body tightening when Abby's tongue flicked out to lick at his fingertips before she withdrew and slid off his lap to take the chair next to him.

Clearing his throat, Kai put his plate in his lap to hide the evidence of his arousal, his entire body strung taut as he tried to make casual conversation with his friend. No woman had ever turned him inside out the way Abby did. No woman had ever made him ache like she did.

It had taken him a long time to see that Shelley was broken, and that no amount of reassurance or effort from him would ever have changed it. Abby was almost her polar opposite. She wanted him, but didn't *need* him. Not in the fragile, *please take care of me and fill the black hole of need inside me* way the others had. She was strong and independent, could take care of herself.

It was a double-edged sword, because, well, he wanted her to need him in some ways.

More than anything, right now he wanted to wrap her up in his arms and breathe her in, lay her down and claim her with his body, watch her face as he took her to the edge of release and pushed her over it. He wanted to lie beside her in the dark and hold her while she drifted off to sleep, and wake up next to her in the morning.

Somehow, he managed to force his mind off getting Abby alone in their tent and enjoy time with his buddies. They built a fire and sat around the crackling flames while Jonah played his guitar for a while, the smell of it taking Kai right back to his childhood and the countless campouts he'd had with Hani. Abby was so quiet at one point he looked over to check that she was still awake, and saw her frowning in confusion at him.

"What's wrong?" he asked, reaching for her hand.

She curled her fingers around his, one side of her mouth tipping upward. "I've only had two beers, but I swear I only caught a few words of that whole conversation. It sounded like English, but not."

It took him a moment to realize what he'd done. "Pidgin," he said with a wince. "Sorry, I just slipped into it without realizing."

"Yeah, sorry," Jonah said. "Old habits die hard,

right big guy?" He smacked Kai on the chest.

"It's okay," she said with a wave, and leaned close, resting her head on his shoulder. "Just glad I'm not going crazy."

Kai wrapped his arm around her shoulders and kissed the top of her head, breathing in the clean scent of her shampoo mixed with the campfire, his soul sighing in contentment. She belonged with him. Did she feel it too?

A chorus of greetings lifted his gaze across the campfire, where the others were gathered around a newcomer. Kai's abs contracted when they parted and Hani's face appeared beyond the flickering flames. His cousin's eyes caught his, flicked from Kai to Abby.

Hani's big, toothy smile slipped. Froze for a moment before fading away, his expression turning almost hostile as he stared at first her, then Kai. Kai instantly bristled, his protective instincts surging to the surface. What was Hani's problem with Abby? She'd been nothing but polite and friendly to him, even during that awkward drink they'd shared last night.

Abby sat up, pulling away from him. Kai tightened his hold. "No. You stay right where you are."

She tugged his hand off her shoulder. "I should go. I'm pretty tired from all that sun and water and food. Think I'll get ready for bed and turn in." She gave him a sensual smile that dimmed his annoyance considerably before she walked toward the house.

Reluctantly Kai watched her go, resentment for his cousin growing inside him.

"What's with Hani?" Jonah asked quietly once Abby was in the house.

"I dunno." Yeah, he and Hani had their differences, and Kai was sure his cousin was still involved with bad shit here on the island. He'd made it a point to avoid the topic and not look into it out of respect for his cousin and *tutu*, but if Hani continued to be an asshole and treat Abby in a way that made her uncomfortable, then Kai was going to have words with him.

Hani stayed near the back of the house, talking with the others, pointedly avoiding him. When Abby came out the back door a few minutes later, everyone stopped talking.

She paused, her gaze darting to Hani. Kai pushed to his feet and stalked toward them, ready to put Hani in his place, but Abby smiled, said goodnight and breezed past them, classy to a fault.

Kai took her hand when she reached him. "You don't need to leave."

"It's okay, I'm ready for bed. And it seems like you guys need to talk." She put on another smile, lifted on tiptoe to kiss him softly. "I'll wait up for you."

Kai nodded, jaw tense as he stared at Hani. "I'll be there soon." He wanted to follow her right now and do everything he'd been fantasizing about all day—hell, for weeks—but he wasn't leaving like this. It was high time he and Hani set things straight between them, and the little asshole needed to be reminded of his manners.

The others backed away awkwardly as Kai strode toward Hani, who stood there with a defiant expression on his face. Everyone else retreated to the far side of the fire pit.

Kai stopped a foot away from him, uncaring that they had an audience. "You got a problem, cousin?" he asked in a hard voice.

Something flickered in Hani's dark eyes, but it was gone before Kai could figure out what it was. "Maybe I do."

Kai folded his arms across his chest. "Enlighten me."

Hani's jaw flexed. He looked away from Kai, his gaze pausing on the others all pretending not to be staring from across the fire pit, then coming back to his. "Not here."

"Why not?"

"I need to talk to you in private."

"Front yard private enough for you?"

"No." He glanced down the path, where Abby had just reached the edge of the sand on her way to their tent. "You leaving here tomorrow?"

"Yeah."

"What time?"

"Early."

"Fine. I'll talk to you then." Without another word, Hani turned and walked off, leaving Kai staring after him. Stewing.

Like hell. Like fucking *hell*.

Kai stormed after him, determined to have this out and get to the bottom of whatever the hell was going on here. "Hani," he barked.

Up ahead out front of the house, Hani drew up short, his back to Kai. "I said I'll talk to you tomorrow," he bit out, the sound of passing traffic coming from the highway at the end of the drive.

Fuck that. "Be a man, turn around and say what you gotta say," he taunted.

Slowly, Hani turned to face him. It was dark here, so dark Kai could barely make out the set expression on his cousin's face. "You want it here and now?"

Kai planted his feet, folded his arms across his chest. "Yeah. So start talking."

Hani stared at him a long moment. "Fine, you asked for it. You—"

A loud bang reverberated through the air.

Hani ducked and whirled around, his hand going to the back of his waistband to pull out the pistol he'd hidden beneath his shirt. Kai reacted instinctively at his cousin's response, tensing and glancing around.

But there was nothing. No movement. No threat that he could see.

He glanced back at his cousin.

Hani was still half-crouched in a defensive position, scanning the darkness around them as though he expected an ambush at any moment, the fear rolling off him so strong Kai could almost smell it.

A softer bang followed a moment later, coming from somewhere down the highway.

Not a gunshot. Just a car backfiring.

Hani slowly straightened and lowered his arm, his posture tense, pistol still in his grip.

"Jesus Christ, Hani," Kai muttered, heartsick at the irrefutable evidence in front of him. "What the fuck have you gotten yourself into now?"

Hani spun around to glare at him. "Nothing. Leave me the hell alone." He stalked to his truck.

Kai stood there while his cousin climbed inside the cab, started it and drove off down the long driveway, an oily sensation coating the pit of his stomach. What the hell was going on?

Something was off. Way off. Hani might be a punk sometimes, but he'd never disrespected Kai or been rude to a woman before. And Abby wasn't just some woman, she was Kai's lady. Then there was Hani's reaction just now, as though he'd been afraid someone was shooting at him.

Maybe Hani was even deeper into the drug scene than Kai realized. Maybe he'd made some dangerous enemies, like the ones who had killed that dealer last week and dumped his body into the ocean.

Agitated, he turned and walked back to his chair by the fire. Everyone was watching him, not saying a word. He picked up his beer, took a sip, striving for calm. "Anyone know what the hell's with him?"

Jonah shook his head. "Nah, *brah*. No idea."

Kai didn't want to bring his *tutu* into this, but he might have to if he couldn't find out what the hell was going on. If Hani was in over his head the way Kai suspected he was, then he was going to need help. Big time help, from someone with connections that could offer him protection. Kai would do that for him, but only if Hani came clean and wanted out. If he didn't…Kai couldn't do anything for him.

He finished his beer, using the time to calm his thoughts. He and Hani would have this out at some point before Kai left, maybe even tomorrow if Hani was serious about coming back in the morning. He refused to allow his cousin to ruin what had been an otherwise awesome day, and the night stretching out ahead with Abby. Something he'd looked forward to for a long time now.

"I'm turning in," he announced, getting to his feet. He was anxious to see her, put the tension with Hani behind him and finally ease the relentless ache she'd created from the moment he'd held her that day in his apartment after Shelley walked out. "Night."

His friends all wished him a good night, and it said a lot about the abrupt change of mood in the evening that none of them made a snide remark about him going to Abby. He wouldn't have cared if they had. He didn't care about much at that moment except Abby.

His lady was waiting for him in their tent. Kai intended to claim her, rock her world, and show her that she was his.

Chapter Eleven

Abby's heartbeat quickened when she heard the footsteps in the sand outside the tent, hushed beneath the lap of the waves mere yards away.

Kai.

The entire time with him today had been foreplay. Hot, decadent foreplay. Her body ached for him, even the light brush of the sheet against her naked skin sending a rush of arousal through her.

His big shadow appeared behind the tent flap. He crouched, and the soft rasp of the zipper came as the two halves parted. Kai ducked inside, paused when he saw her lying there watching him, the moonlight illuminating one side of his face.

"Hi," she whispered, pushing up on her elbows, the sheet and quilt revealing her bare shoulders.

"Hi." He yanked the zipper back down, enclosing them in their private cocoon, then straightened.

Abby sat up and drew the covers off her, the soft, filtered light coming through the tent roof revealing her body to him without illuminating all the imperfections. She felt seductive. Beautiful, even.

Kai seemed to freeze for a moment as he stared at her naked body. A low, guttural sound came out of him and he reached for the hem of his shirt, peeling it over his head and tossing it aside as he moved toward her. Nearly six-and-a-half-feet of powerful, hungry male about to pounce.

Abby reached for him as he straddled her legs, sliding her hands into his hair as he took hold of her face and fused their mouths together. She made a sound of need and opened to the hot caress of his tongue, her heart pounding its way out of her chest. He kissed her hard and deep, as though he was starving for her and it had been weeks since he'd last seen her instead of mere minutes. Arousal burst into a raging fire that was both thrilling and terrifying in its intensity. She'd never wanted anyone this much, was afraid of getting addicted to him.

He leaned forward, one hand on the back of her head as he lowered her to the foam mattress. She groaned as he kissed his way to her jaw and neck, stretching that big, hard body out on top of her.

"I was gonna go so slow," he rasped out against her skin, nipping the tender spot just beneath her ear. "Savor every last inch of you, but you've got me wound so tight I just wanna eat you up."

Abby gripped the back of his head to hold him closer and slid her other hand over his back, savoring the warm, smooth skin and the hard muscles rippling beneath it.

Those big, gorgeous hands cupped the sides of her breasts and pushed them together. She had only a second to gasp in a breath and catch the intense expression on his face before he lowered his head and took one hard, aching nipple between his lips.

Her mewl of pleasure filled the tent. She parted her legs for him, lost in sensation as the hard length of his erection settled against her mound, his mouth sucking her sensitive flesh so tenderly.

Pleasure sizzled through her, the hot throb between her thighs intensifying. Part of her couldn't believe this was actually happening. Kai was her friend, and she was still a little worried about what would happen after this, but it was too damn good to hesitate or regret her decision now.

She tugged on his hair, bringing his lips back to hers for another deep, hungry kiss, then he nipped gently at her lower lip and turned his attention to her other breast. Abby squirmed beneath him, eyes closed, one hand in his hair and the other clutching his shoulder. His tongue flicked over her nipple then slid over the curve of her breast.

He shifted his hips, lifting the pressure of his erection from her, that wicked mouth moving lower and lower, over her belly. He curled his hands around her hips, darted his tongue into her belly button. One hand smoothed over the top of her thigh, his fingers gliding over the top of her mound in a light, seductive touch that made her shudder.

She bit her lip and tried to remember to breathe, in an agony of suspense as she awaited his next move. This was so much more intense than she'd bargained for.

He growled low in his throat when his teasing fingers met her drenched folds. "Gotta taste you, shortcake. Hold on tight." He eased one of her legs over to give him room.

She dug her fingers in harder, taking his warning to heart. The heat of his breath against her most sensitive spot made her shiver. Then the smooth, warm stroke of his tongue followed, ripping a cry from her. Kai clamped his hands around her hip and thigh, holding her open as he licked and kissed and sucked.

Raw pleasure flowed through her, melting her bones at the same time as it drew all her muscles tight, her belly and thighs quivering. He focused on her pulsing clit for long moments, making her pant and moan, then thrust his tongue inside her.

Her hips came off the mattress, her body locking tight. God, oh, God, she was going to come if he—

He made another of those low, hungry sounds and withdrew to caress her clit. A slow, velvet glide that made the ache so sharp she whimpered, the breath halting in her throat. Oh, Jesus, she needed more. Craved him so much she could barely breathe.

"You close?" he murmured, licking softly. Expertly.

"Yes." It came out tight, almost frantic, her muscles clenching. This wasn't even remotely normal for her. He had complete control over her body.

He sat up. Abby bit back a cry of protest and sat up, reached out to help him as he stripped off his shorts and underwear. He turned back to her on his knees, ripping open a condom packet. She looked down the length of that gorgeous torso to where he gripped the base of his cock.

The shadows there were too dark for her to see much, but she wrapped her hand around him, reveled in his harsh groan as she closed her fingers around his girth. He was a big boy. All over. She couldn't wait to feel him inside her, relieving the emptiness, taking away that gnawing ache.

Kai closed his hand around hers and guided her over his hot, rigid flesh for two slow, sensual strokes, then pushed hers away and rolled the condom on. "Down," he said in a gruff voice, planting one hand on her sternum and pressing her backward.

The instant her back hit the mattress he took her thighs, opening them as he settled over her, belly to belly, his cock nestled between her folds. One hand holding the back of her head, his mouth came down on hers while he rocked forward, sliding the heated length of his erection over her clit. Abby moaned and grabbed his hip, the other curling around his nape to anchor herself.

He did it again, again, until she was writhing beneath him, desperate for penetration. "You want me in you?" he murmured against her lips.

"Yes," she gasped. "Hurry." She was dying for it. Because this was Kai.

Coming up on his forearms, still holding her head in one hand, he stared down into her face and shifted his hips. Heat and pressure registered between her legs for a moment, then the muscles beneath her grasping hand contracted and he pushed forward in a slow surge.

Abby's eyes slammed shut. She sucked in a breath

at the heavy, delicious stretch of him burying himself inside her. God, he was thick. And hard.

"Oh, fuck, you feel so good…" He withdrew a little and thrust forward again, her wetness making the motion effortless.

She squirmed beneath him, trying to get the contact she needed on her clit.

Instantly he seized her hip to still her. Bending down for a slow, deep kiss, he smothered her whimper of need.

Strong hands gripped her thighs, pushing them together. He settled his own outside hers, keeping her legs tight together, his cock still lodged deep inside her. Abby slid her arms around him and clung to his shoulders as he stretched out over top of her, instinctively wrapping her calves around his, wanting him closer. Deeper.

His mouth was at her ear now, the weight of his torso distributed along hers, pinning her to the mattress. Easing his hips back, he withdrew a little and stopped, his head resting above and to the side of hers, his warm breath stirring the top of her hair. "Tip your hips downward," he commanded in a tight whisper.

She did. And he rocked forward, sliding the base of his cock directly over her clit.

Oh, Jesus…

Her ragged gasp filled the tent. Clutching him for dear life, she began moving without conscious thought, hips rolling with his, trying to find exactly the right angle to give her the stimulation she needed to send her over the edge.

"Slower," he rasped out, his breaths coming faster

now, the muscles in his shoulders and back bunched tight as he worked her with small, stroking motions of his hips.

Abby moaned and shuddered, sweat slicking her skin. She was so wet, so swollen, and he was hitting every one of her hot spots with each slow, sensual glide against her. Within a minute they'd found the right motion and rhythm, but she couldn't hold it. It felt so good and she was too desperate to go slow now.

Kai groaned and held his tempo, the weight and strength of his body keeping her safely anchored while she was about to fly apart. "You gonna come for me, Abby?" he coaxed, his mouth pressed tight to her hair.

She had no choice. It was like being caught in a powerful rip current, the elemental force of it too strong to pull herself free.

Loud, uncontrollable moans rolled from her throat and she didn't care if anyone overheard her, all ability to think gone, the incredible building pleasure and frantic need for release driving her movements. She rubbed against him, each motion stimulating her clit and sliding the head of his cock against the secret spot inside her.

It was too much, yet not enough. She chased that elusive release with single-minded intent, and soon it was right there, a sweet, bright glow at the edge of her consciousness.

"That's right, baby, rub your clit on my cock…"

The deep rumble of his voice, one more sweet glide, and she shattered. Her wild cries echoed in her ears as her body came apart beneath him, clenching around the length of his cock.

Panting, weak, she went limp against the mattress and held him to her, every muscle in her body quivering. He'd shaken her to her core with that masterful display of tender, skilled dominance.

As she lay there, her body recovering, her mind flashed back to what Shelley had said to her. *You don't know what he's like. What it's like to be with him.*

Shit, Abby so got what she'd meant now. If this was any indication of what sex was like with Kai, and not just a one-off anomaly, then Abby could understand how he was capable of ruining a woman for anyone else.

And now I'm ruined too.

She swallowed, tried to stem the bubble of anxiety rising inside her chest. They'd agreed to take things one day at a time. But holy hell, what a difference a day could make. His attentiveness, his easy affection, the food he'd been spoiling her with, the mind-melting sex… God, how was she going to be able to let him go now? She hoped she wouldn't have to.

Kai groaned and came up on his forearms, pulling her focus back to him. He was still hard inside her, had to be hurting. She wanted to give him as much pleasure as he'd given her.

She turned her face toward him and kissed the edge of his jaw. He shifted to gently push her thighs open with his. His lips covered hers as he eased back and thrust forward, sliding deep once more. Meeting the caress of his tongue, Abby wrapped her arms around his broad back.

When he eased his hips back she put a hand on the

side of his face, stopping him. She gazed up at him in the soft light, drinking in the lines of that gorgeous face, the tension in it, the stark need in his dark eyes. Need for *her*.

Holding his gaze, she settled her feet flat on the sheet and rolled her hips, sinking him deep inside her. Kai sucked in a sharp breath, nostrils flaring. His eyes slid shut, his big body shuddering all over before he gained control and opened his eyes to stare down at her. "Do it again."

Wrapping her hand around his nape, she did, holding his gaze the entire time.

"Yeah, Abby, stroke me," he groaned, his head dropping forward, eyes squeezing shut.

Sensual power softened with an aching tenderness flowed through her. A breathless, tension-laced silence filled the tent. She watched his face intently as she stroked him with her body, tracking every tiny nuance of his expression. And so she knew the moment he'd reached his limit.

His face tightened. He plunged one hand into her hair, his other arm coming around her hips, crushing her to him as he took over and thrust deep and fast.

Abby held him tight, squeezed her thighs around his hips, the guttural sounds he was making sending a thrill through her. His fist tightened in her hair and he drove deep, a harsh groan vibrating against her ear as his big body shuddered in the throes of his orgasm.

He was hot and heavy atop her, his twitching muscles slowly relaxing. She stroked his hair, the breadth of his shoulders and down his back, tracing every ridge and hollow, savoring every moment of the closeness.

With a soft moan he kissed the side of her jaw, her lips, then lifted his upper body off her and withdrew gently. He turned away from her for a moment to deal with the condom, and stretched out on his side facing her. Lifting a hand, he stroked her bangs from her damp forehead, trailed a fingertip down the bridge of her nose to her mouth, where she kissed it.

A slow, intimate smile curved his lips. "Now how's that for chemistry?"

She grinned. "Pretty damn great." How the hell had she ever done without it before? She resented missing out on it before now, and yet grateful that she'd experienced it for the first time with Kai. He'd made everything about this day unforgettable.

Chuckling, he drew her into his arms and pressed a kiss to the crown of her head. "How do you feel about spooning?" he murmured.

"I'm a huge fan."

"Good, me too. Roll over." He turned her, pulled her back into the curve of his body, then drew the covers over them and wrapped those warm, solid arms around her.

Abby sighed and snuggled closer, her body replete, fighting the questions about them in her mind as the gentle rush of the waves filled her ears.

She shook the thoughts away, made up her mind to enjoy the here and now. Tomorrow would come soon enough. Whatever happened between them after tonight, she would just have to deal with it as it came.

Chapter Twelve

Kai opened his eyes in the faint light that signaled dawn was coming, and smiled sleepily. Gentle waves lapped softly at the sand yards from the tent, and birds sang in the nearby trees. Abby was snuggled into him, her back to his chest, the sweet pressure of her ass pressed against his groin. She was dead asleep, her breaths slow and even, the sweep of her lashes forming crescent shadows against her fair skin.

The feel of her, remembering what they'd done last night, had his cock starting to swell. He'd thought they'd be good together, but last night had been so insanely hot. He'd wondered what it would be like to combine that kind of chemistry with someone he shared a base of friendship and respect with. Now he knew.

He'd never be the same again.

She'd given herself to him so sweetly,

surrendering control to him. That took trust, and it humbled him that she placed hers in him.

He wasn't perfect. He was cocky and proud, loved to play practical jokes. There was a reason he liked to be the center of attention and the life of the party. And why he'd continually engaged in dysfunctional relationships with emotionally unavailable women. Thankfully Abby was the opposite of that.

He tightened his arm around her ribs, careful not to wake her as he wrestled with his inner demons.

When his mother had left him behind, he'd barely been out of diapers. Too young to understand anything about it except that she'd abandoned him.

It wasn't until the shit show of a breakup with Shelley that he'd finally confronted the emotional and psychological impact of it. Acknowledging that he'd always wondered if it was something he'd done that had made his mom leave. That maybe she'd been able to leave him so easily because he wasn't loveable.

He breathed in the sweet scent of Abby's shampoo, letting the uncomfortable thoughts tumble through his mind. Even though his *tutu* had stepped in and given him the love he'd craved so badly, it couldn't fill the hole his mother had left in his heart.

Wasn't easy for him to admit, but the plain truth of it was, all his life he'd been searching for love and acceptance. Craving it on a level so intense that he would do anything to get them. He'd found it in one form with the Marine Corps, and he had it with his FAST Bravo brothers. But he'd never found it in a woman. And a deeply buried part of him worried that he wasn't worthy of real, unconditional love.

Until Abby.

In every other romantic relationship he'd been in, he'd given and given and given in a futile attempt to prove himself worthy to his partner, all the while aware at least on a subconscious level that it would never be enough. He'd done that to himself over and over in an endless, toxic cycle, maybe as a form of self-punishment because some part of him thought he deserved it.

Until Abby had shone a light on the secret place deep down inside him that he'd been too terrified to look at. It had not only opened his eyes to what was really going on, it had made him see her and what he wanted in a whole new light.

To be loved for who he was, faults and all. To have a peaceful, devoted relationship with someone he trusted and respected.

He knew on a gut-deep level that the answer to all of that was sleeping in his arms right now. If he could just find a way to convince her that he was the one.

Kai nuzzled the top of her head, the silky, platinum strands catching in the stubble on his jaw. She stirred slightly, that sexy body shifting against him. He tightened his arm around her, skimmed his lips over the vulnerable skin on her nape, down the side of her neck.

Her swift inhalation and the sudden tension in her muscles told him she was wide awake. "Morning," he whispered, sucking at her skin softly.

She made a purring sound and angled her head to give him better access. "Morning already?" Her voice was pure, sleepy contentment.

"Mmm." They still had a couple hours before she

needed to head back to the resort. She was naked and warm and soft, and he wasn't going to waste a moment of their remaining time together.

He slipped the covers off them, commenced with slow sweeps of his hands over all her gorgeous curves and hollows, building her arousal. She tried to turn toward him but he stilled her with a solid grip on her hip, keeping her right where he wanted her.

Every caress of his fingertips over sensitive flesh earned him sighs and then soft, pleading gasps. When she was mewling and moving restlessly, he reached between her legs to cup her in his palm, adding pressure to her clit with the heel of his hand while he eased two fingers into her slick core.

"Ohh," she breathed, her body arching in a lovely bow.

Kai played with her, his mouth busy on her neck, his other hand squeezing one hard nipple. They were a soft, rosy pink, even prettier than he'd imagined. And so sensitive that every movement of his fingers made her gasp and moan.

God, he wanted inside her so bad. He was hard as granite, aching for her.

As he withdrew his fingers to slide them up and down the side of her swollen clit, she whimpered and clamped a hand around his wrist, her hips moving with his touch. Her breathing hitched, a soft, almost desperate whimper escaping.

Kai withdrew his hand, quickly sheathed himself with another condom from his wallet, and tucked back in behind her, easing one of her legs forward. Opening her for him.

Grasping the base of his cock, he moved into

position and slid the swollen head inside. He groaned and scraped his teeth along her nape at the feel of her tight, slick walls squeezing him. She surged back to meet him, trying to push him deeper, but he refused to be rushed, instead holding her still with an arm around her hips, the other snaking beneath her to caress her folds and clit.

A soft, liquid moan rolled out of her throat. Kai whispered to her, getting lost in sensation, taking her with slow, easy thrusts, angling his hips to ensure he hit her inner sweet spot.

Her panting breaths turned into gasps and moans, the muscles in her thighs and belly quivering as she neared the peak. She dug her fingers into his forearm and let out a sob as her release hit, her core squeezing him in rhythmic pulses that pushed him past the last of his control.

Wrapping both arms around her tight, he growled into her neck and surged deep, letting the pleasure take him. Her name chanted in his head. *Abby. Abby...*

When he could breathe again he withdrew gently, got rid of the condom and gathered her back into his arms again. A warm wave of fatigue washed over him, along with a sense of peace he hadn't felt before. Ever. He was so damn thankful that Abby had shown him what this was like. He'd do anything for her.

Anything except let her go.

Abby groaned, her body warm and soft in the cradle of his own. "I don't ever want to get up. Don't make me get up."

His deep chuckle ruffled the top of her hair.

"Don't tempt me, shortcake." He'd love nothing more than to keep her here all day and night, hidden away from the rest of the world. But unfortunately, reality awaited them both.

He woke her up twenty minutes before they had to leave, reluctantly peeled himself away from her, dressed and left the tent. The sun was barely up.

He grabbed a quick shower, had just snuck out the back door to head back to the tent, but stopped when he saw Hani there waiting for him, arms folded across his chest as he leaned against the picnic table.

Kai's hand froze on the doorknob as he met his cousin's hard, unwelcoming gaze.

"You're up early," Hani said, a hostile expression on his face.

Kai straightened, bracing himself for the coming battle. No point in avoiding this any longer. They'd have this out right here and now.

"WHAT DO YOU want, Hani?"

Hani steeled himself, forced himself to hold that dark, wary gaze even though his insides were writhing with guilt. It wasn't good enough that Kai was leaving the island in a few days. He needed to leave the island *now*. Hurting him this way was the only thing Hani could think of to have a shot at making that happen. "Need to talk to you."

"Get vertical when you talk to me."

The low command wasn't sharp, but it was hard as steel and held a deadly edge to it, the tone of a man accustomed to having his orders obeyed. Hani reacted instinctively, straightening and uncrossing his arms, shoving his hands into his pockets instead.

He'd worshipped Kai his entire existence, the strong, protective brother that life hadn't given him but circumstances had.

Kai had taught him how to swim and ride a bike, how to catch fish and stand up for himself. Later, he'd taught Hani how to steal cars and catch girls. Then he'd moved on to a bigger, better life, leaving their rough, crime-riddled neighborhood behind— and Hani with it.

Kai had chosen the harder road. The right road. While Hani had chosen the wrong one, unknowingly leading them both to this very moment.

Now he had to betray everything they meant to each other. Destroy it to save the man he'd idolized forever.

"Better. Now, talk." Kai cocked his head, waiting.

Hani hadn't been able to do this last night, he'd lost his nerve at the last moment, but he couldn't put it off any longer. He had the whole argument figured out now, had rehearsed it in his mind on the way over. Kai's life was in danger here. Hani's words might not be enough to make him leave the island, but they were all he could think of, so he had to try.

"Why'd you come back here, Kai? You wanted to show off your *haole* whore to everyone from the old neighborhood?"

Shock flared in his cousin's eyes at the slur, quickly replaced by rage. "What did you just say to me?"

"You heard me."

Kai took a menacing step forward, his jaw set. "You better hope I didn't hear right."

"You did."

His cousin stopped, inhaled deeply as though trying to calm himself, his stare never wavering. "What the hell is your problem, man? You don't even know Abby."

He couldn't stop now. He might not be able to extricate himself from the life he'd created, but he sure as hell wouldn't allow Kai's blood to wind up on his hands. "I don't need to know her. She's just another one of your drama queen sluts you like to parade around, pretending you're the man, like you're better than the rest of us. Well, you're not."

Kai flinched at the verbal punch, and it felt like someone had driven a dagger through Hani's chest.

He blurted out the rest before he lost the will to continue. "News flash, Kai. We don't need you here. We don't want you here. You up and leave us behind for a better life just like our mothers did to us." He gave Kai a scathing look, dying a little inside. His voice shook, and he prayed Kai thought it was out of anger.

"You're no better than them," he spat. "You like to talk about how we're *ohana*, but you don't even know what the fuck that means anymore, because you've been gone too long. You turned your back on me, *Tutu,* and our people years ago and I'll never forgive you for it. You ever stop to think about anybody but yourself? Like *Tutu*?"

"What about her?"

"The people back in the old town, the locals, they know you turned your back on everyone. You think she deserves the insults and the way they talk about her behind her back?"

Kai's jaw flexed. "What are you talking about?"

"Yeah, she takes their shit every time she goes into town, defends you at every turn. All without ever telling you how it really is for her."

A hint of uncertainty flickered in that imposing gaze. "I'll talk to her."

"You'll talk? What the hell good is that gonna do, huh? It's been like that for years, ever since you left. And the longer you stay here, the harder it is for *Tutu* to watch you leave again. So do us all a favor, take your woman back to the damn mainland you love so much and fucking stay there. You're not one of us anymore, so stop pretending."

Kai paled, and Hani's stomach twisted so hard he feared he would puke right then and there. "What the fuck, Hani?" he rasped out, the stricken note in his voice almost more than Hani could bear. "I didn't turn my back on anyone," he bit out, jabbing his index finger into his own chest for emphasis. "I might have left for the mainland because of my career, but *you're* the one who turned your back on all of us. You were too smart for everyone else, including me, wouldn't listen to a goddamn thing I said. No, instead you took the easy way out with the losers from the old neighborhood, and look where you've wound up. Right in the same place we started, staring at a dead end, and now you're running scared because of it. That was *your* choice, not mine. No one forced you into it."

Hani's mouth went dry. The words cut deep, because they were true, and the truth hurt. Almost as much as having to do this. "I don't need your approval, you egotistical asshole."

Kai's eyes cut sharply to Hani's right. Hani

swiveled his head to find Abby standing at the end of the path leading to the beach with a bag looped over her shoulder, looking between them uncertainly.

She took a step backward. "Sorry. I'll just go wait—"

"How long have you been with him?" Hani demanded of her.

She stopped, faced him, and he couldn't help but admire her poise. She was calm as she stood her ground and confronted him. Raised her chin to give him a cool, *you-don't-intimidate-me* stare.

"Not long, I'll bet. Well then, let me give you a little tip and save you some heartache."

"Shut up, Hani," Kai snarled.

Hani ignored him. Abby was Kai's other weak spot. So he would keep hitting that to get this done. He hoped it worked, because he didn't know what the hell else to do. "He seems like a great guy, until you get to know him."

"I think I know him pretty well," she answered evenly.

"Yeah? Do you even know what he does for a living?"

"Yes."

No she didn't. Not everything. Kai wouldn't be able to tell her, for security reasons. "Really? You know he's with the DEA?"

"Yes." Her expression was impassive, but her eyes were cool. She didn't like the way Hani was talking about him. Was prepared to defend him. Christ, Hani wished he'd been able to get to know this one. Hoped Kai knew what he had in her.

"So then you know he's part of FAST Bravo,

huh?"

At that, Kai drew in a shocked breath. Abby stared at Hani, uncertain, before her gaze shifted to Kai.

"Ah, you didn't know that. Well, I'm not surprised." Hani turned slowly to face his cousin, a derisive smile in place, using it as armor, and clucked his tongue. "How come you didn't tell her? Don't trust her? Or me, for that matter. *Tutu* either, since you didn't tell either of us. But Abby? That's not very forthcoming and honest of you, is it? Doesn't bode well for a new relationship between you two. Didn't you think she'd wonder what you got up to when you're gone all the time?"

Kai's nostrils flared, his eyes narrowing in warning. "Shut. Up."

He eyed Abby, let his gaze rake over her body in a way that was blatantly disrespectful. "Or maybe he was just looking for a good fuck while he was here. I hope you made last night worth his while."

"You son of a bitch," Kai snarled, and came at him.

Hani tensed, brought his hands up to try and deflect the punch he was sure was coming. Kai grabbed the front of his shirt instead and wrenched him forward until only his toes touched the ground.

Hani gripped the thick wrists holding him prisoner, his throat tightening at the fury and hurt in his cousin's eyes. "Get your goddamn hands off me."

"Who told you," Kai growled, the muscles in his shoulders standing out beneath his T-shirt, fists twisting the fabric of Hani's shirt. "Who told you about my job?"

"Doesn't matter. Point is, you lied to us all, didn't

even tell your own family what you really did for a living. Because even though we're *ohana*, you still don't trust us. *That's* the truth, and we're better off without you."

"It's got nothing to do with trust, you stupid *asshole*." Kai shoved him away.

Hani stumbled back and fell into the picnic table, catching the edge across the middle of his back. Pain radiated down his spine. He welcomed it.

Quickly righting himself, he shot Kai a look of pure hatred. "Or maybe you had an ulterior motive, huh? Playing it cool when you come home for a 'visit'," he said, using his fingers for air quotations, "when you're really here to keep tabs on me and report back to your bosses."

"Why, you got something to hide?" Kai grated out, his voice like gravel. "Is that why you're packing now? Why you got so spooked last night when that car backfired? Huh? Someone after you?"

Shame curled inside him. He stuffed it down, kept the sneer in place as he jerked his chin at Abby. "Fuck you, Kai. Take your *haole* bitch, get outta here and leave me and *Tutu* the fuck alone," he snapped, spinning on his heel before Kai could reply. He stormed off to his truck, his legs unsteady with every step.

Kai didn't try to stop him. Didn't call out or come after him.

By the time Hani reached his truck, he could barely see the driveway through the sheen of tears in his eyes.

Chapter Thirteen

The tension inside the car finally registered when Kai pulled up to a stoplight just outside of Kehei.

He'd put the top up on the convertible before leaving Jonah's place because it was so early and still cool out, but since then he'd been too lost in his own head to notice Abby's uneasiness. So deep inside his head he hadn't realized he'd driven for a solid fifteen minutes without a word to her, leaving her so uncomfortable that she'd had to resort to staring out her window rather than look at or try to speak to him.

Drawing a deep breath, he glanced over at her. Her hands were folded together primly in her lap rather than twined with one of his, and she was doing everything but crawl into the backseat to give him space.

After what they'd shared last night and again this morning, it made him feel like a gigantic asshole.

"Sorry for ignoring you, and for what you overheard with Hani." For his cousin being an asshole to them both.

Abby swiveled her head to look at him. "It's okay." She searched his eyes. "Are you all right?"

"Yeah, I'm fine."

She nodded, and although she didn't look convinced, she let it go. "Okay."

He wasn't fine, it was eating at him from the inside like acid. "Hani's...changed," he said finally as he drove, feeling the need to explain. "He never used to be like that." Kai didn't even know who the hell that rude punk had been earlier this morning, but that wasn't his cousin.

Those gorgeous blue eyes filled with empathy. "Can I do anything?"

The gentle offer increased the ache in his chest. "No. Just...sorry I haven't been good company on the way here." He reached out to take one of her hands, twined his fingers through hers.

She shrugged. "You're upset. I'd be the same way."

At least Abby wasn't mad at him for the silent treatment bit. Shelley would have been. She would have been angry that he'd shut her out for the past fifteen minutes, and made sure he'd known with hurt, sidelong looks and verbal jabs. Abby hadn't done any of that.

Trying to put his annoyance aside, Kai changed the subject. "You hungry?"

She gave him a grateful smile that reassured him there were no hard or hurt feelings. "Starved."

"There's a bakery I love a couple minutes up the

road. We can grab some coffee and pastries and still have you back at the resort in plenty of time to get ready."

"Sounds good."

The little roadside bakery made the best caramel-macadamia sticky buns in the universe, fresh every morning. Kai ordered two for himself and one for Abby, a black coffee for him, and a vanilla latte for her. He sipped at his coffee back in the Mustang while she nibbled her bun and sipped at her latte.

"Oh, wow, this is insanely good," she mumbled around a mouthful of caramel and sticky bun. He wanted to lick it off her lips so bad.

"Best ever."

She licked her fingers, cast him a curious look. "Can I ask you something?"

Automatically his shoulders tensed, bracing for her to say something uncomfortable. "Yeah."

"What's a FAST team?"

The question took him off guard. He'd assumed she'd been about to ask something about him and Hani. Under normal circumstances he would say he couldn't tell her, for security reasons, but these circumstances weren't normal, and after this morning he didn't want secrets like that between them any longer. He trusted her, wanted something real with her. "It means Foreign Advisory and Support Team."

She watched him steadily, swallowed another mouthful. "I've never heard of it."

He took the turn toward Wailea. "No, most people haven't." So how had Hani? That unsettled him almost as much as what Hani had said. He had to tell his commander about it. "There are five teams, all of us tier one units. I'm on FAST Bravo. Each team is responsible for a different geographic area, helping foreign governments and units conduct counter-narcotic and counter-terrorist missions. For us, it's all over the place, but we do an annual four-month-long tour in Afghanistan in addition to whatever missions we're given elsewhere."

Her eyebrows went up and she stopped chewing. "Huh." She ran her gaze over his shoulders and chest. "That makes a lot of sense, though, and the deployments explain a lot about why you're sometimes gone for so long. Because I can't picture you sitting behind a desk."

He snorted. "Yeah, no. I'd lose my mind."

"So you guys are all former military? Or maybe...more?"

He loved how quick she was, how she was able to read between the lines. "Yes. Well, most of us. Granger—the guy who was doing a terrible job at lip-syncing to AC/DC—isn't former military. He was former DEA undercover."

"You said counter-terrorist missions. So that means the same kinds of things as the SEALs and whoever do too, right?"

A grin tugged at his mouth. Yep, she was quick on the uptake. "That's right."

"So you work with those kinds of units, then. Or at least train with them." At his surprised expression, she added, "I saw a documentary talking about that kind of thing a couple months ago."

He shook his head, glanced over at her. "Why are you so damn smart?"

Abby cocked her head, gave him an adorable smile. "Just am."

He stopped at a red light. "Well, since you are, I'll only say that what I told you is all classified info. Normally we can't tell our significant others what we do unless we get engaged or married. And even then, there are certain things we can't talk about."

She drew her head back in pretend shock, eyes wide. "Whoa, slow down, big guy. We said one day at a time. So that kind of talk is moving way too fast for me."

A bark of laughter escaped, stunning him. How the hell had she made him laugh when he'd been so damn miserable fifteen minutes earlier? "I needed that, thank you."

"You're welcome." She leaned across the seat to kiss him, her lips lingering on his for a moment before she settled back against her seat. "And thank you for trusting me. I promise not to tell anyone that you're a badass DEA operative. But now that I know…" She shook her head ruefully, watching him with an appreciative gleam in her eyes. "Just when I thought you couldn't possibly be any hotter."

The compliment shouldn't have inflated his ego to ridiculous proportions, but it did. "Yeah? Hell, if I'd known that, I would have told you earlier," he joked.

"No, it means more this way." This time she reached for his hand, twined their fingers together. Kai wished they had more time together right now, but the resort was only a few minutes away.

"How did Hani know?" she asked. "I mean, he kind of flung it out there like he was proving a point and you seemed surprised."

"That's a damn good question. Not even my *tutu* knows what I do." And he dreaded the answer. Although he had a pretty good idea of what it was.

Abby tightened her fingers around his. "Are you... Is it dangerous for you to be here?"

"Nah, I'm fine," he said, brushing it off. But the niggling in his gut said otherwise. It was too much of a coincidence that his personal info had been leaked to the cartel several weeks ago, and now his cousin who made his money in a less than respectable way knew Kai was a FAST member.

Which meant Hani was connected or at least in contact with someone within the *Veneno* cartel. As sickening as that thought was on its own, it also placed Kai in one hell of a moral predicament. Either he had to compromise his professional morals by turning a blind eye to protect his cousin, or he was forced to betray Hani by reporting his cousin and having him investigated. Possibly even arrested.

Although the decision had pretty much been taken out of his hands already. And that weighed heavy as hell on his heart.

Abby kept looking at him with that worried expression. He let go of her hand to slide his around her nape and squeeze gently. "It's okay, I promise."

She didn't seem convinced, but nodded and changed the subject as he pulled up in front of the hotel's main entrance. "So what are you going to do today?"

"I've gotta talk to my grandmother about Hani. And then I'm gonna have to talk to him as well, see where we go from there." He was looking forward to that as much as he would having a tooth pulled without any anesthetic. Commander Taggart was absolutely going to want to get to the bottom of this. Depending on what Kai found out, he would likely have to bring Hani in, for his cousin's protection as much as because Kai was obligated to do it.

She winced in sympathy. "I'm really sorry this is happening."

"Me too." He sighed. "Sorry I'm not the best company right now. I'm not sure how long this will take, so I don't know if I'll be able to see you tonight."

A look of irritation flickered across her face. "Kai. Stop," she said in a firm voice. "I understand. There's no need to apologize. I get it. You just take care of this, that's priority one, and I'm working all day anyway. I'll be here when you're done. But call me if I can help at all, okay? I'm here for you."

Her support and understanding floored him, especially with something this ugly in the early stages of their relationship. *So this is what a healthy, supportive one feels like.* It was a novel experience, for sure. "I appreciate that, thank you."

She leaned forward, took his face in her hands to give him a gentle smile that warmed him from the inside out. "You're welcome. Good luck," she said, brushing her lips over his in a teasing kiss that made him ache for more. "I'll be thinking about you."

He'd be thinking about her too, about their time in the tent last night and this morning. Wishing he was with her, rather than dealing with this bullshit.

With a soft growl, Kai pulled her closer, sliding his hand into the back of her hair as he deepened the kiss. She tasted like caramel and melted for him like sugar, warm and sweet on his tongue. When he broke the connection her eyes were dilated, her cheeks flushed, lips shiny. Damn, he didn't want to go. "I'll call you later."

"Okay." She leaned in for one last kiss, gave him a half-smile and climbed out of the car with her bag.

Once Abby was safely inside the hotel, Kai drove away and called Hamilton, who answered immediately. "Maka. How's life in paradise while the rest of us are trapped back here on the mainland in paperwork and admin hell?"

"Hey, Cap. Honestly? It could be better."

"Why, what's up?" His team leader's tone was sharp.

Kai expelled a hard breath. He couldn't ignore this predicament with Hani. It had to be dealt with. "I've got an unfolding situation here I might need a hand with."

****

Diane kept to the shadows as she followed the trafficker's progress through the most dangerous and impoverished area of Happy Valley. She was down to her last disguise, with a short black wig to complete her new look. Last night she'd managed to get some sleep, but it had been fitful. Bad dreams, guilt, grief, and the look on Dr. Bradshaw's face when she'd shot him down in cold blood.

She was a murderess.

Her mind rebelled at the idea, refused to believe she'd done it. Killing Bradshaw hadn't eased her grief at all. Maybe because there were still others she had to eliminate. Only once she was done would she be able to move forward.

For another thirty minutes she followed Hani, the now familiar weight of her pistol at the small of her back giving her a tiny measure of comfort. Twice she felt eyes on her tonight. Both times she found no one watching her. But someone was. Either the police or someone into the drug scene, she wasn't sure.

Her heart kicked against her ribs, fear mixing with the anxiety. *Hurry. Hurry, or they'll catch you.*

So far there hadn't been a good opportunity to shoot Hani. He'd been in and out of three different houses in the area, always moving fast, and always with people around. Too many witnesses for her to risk attacking here.

She stayed out of sight around the corner of a dilapidated shed on someone's property as Hani emerged from a run-down house next door and headed to his black pickup. Moving fast, Diane raced around to the alley behind the property, got in her rental and followed him, careful to keep a good distance.

Once she almost lost sight of him when she got stuck at a red light. Luckily, she spotted him again and kept going. Within a mile she realized he was heading home. She knew his address, had been by his luxury townhouse bought by dirty money already so she would know her way around, know where the easiest exits from the complex were.

When she struck, she had to make it fast.

Curling her hands around the steering wheel as he turned into the gated complex, she parked on the side of the road, facing back toward the highway for a quick getaway. She reached up an unsteady hand and curled her fingers around the locket she wore, rage and grief suffusing her.

This piece of shit lowlife lived in one of the most expensive and exclusive places in Kahului, paid for by the suffering of so many vulnerable people who'd become hooked on the poison he pedaled. While her daughter's ashes lay scattered in the ocean.

Her shoes crunched lightly on the gravel as she approached the gate, slipping through just as it began to swing shut. Hani's truck was in his driveway. He was still sitting in it. She could shoot him as he got out, then flee.

A prickle at the back of her neck stopped her cold. She froze, whipped her head around to search behind her, sure that someone was following her. Nothing but shadows met her gaze, but a moment later, headlight beams cut through the darkness and headed straight toward her.

She scrambled over to the sidewalk, stood there in the shadows cast by the roofline with her heart in her throat as a cherry red Mustang roared up and parked to the side of the gates. Had the driver seen her?

The driver's side door popped open.

Cursing, she darted across the small strip of lawn that separated the first two townhomes and ran for Hani's unit, determined to do this. She would wait for the right time, hopefully get him as he exited his truck, or maybe as he unlocked his front door.

This is for you, baby, she told Bailey silently, pushing past the fear threatening to drown her. *One down and a few more to go. I'll keep going until they stop me.*

She couldn't let anyone stop her. Not until everyone on her list was dead.

Chapter Fourteen

—◇◇◇◇◇—

After turning off his truck, Hani expelled a breath and pulled his phone out of his pocket, still buzzing. No surprise, it was Kai again. His cousin had called five times throughout the day, left three texts and one voicemail.

Hani, we need to talk. Call me.

Much as Hani wanted to—much as he would love for this whole thing to blow over and go away, it wasn't going to happen. The fight this morning had done its job; he'd seen the pain in his cousin's eyes. But had it been enough? If not, he had one last idea in mind.

Invent a reason that would convince Kai to take *Tutu* with him when he left, as a precaution. Juan's seventy-two-hour deadline was mere hours away. Time was running out fast, and Hani's life was in jeopardy just as much as Kai's now. The sooner Kai left, the better it would be for all of them.

Phone in hand, he exited the truck, breathing in the scent of grilled steak from somewhere down the street. He started to shut the door, stopped when a large, shadowy figure appeared down the sidewalk from his place. His whole body tensed, ready to either grab his weapon or jump back in the truck and take off. Then the streetlight overhead revealed his cousin.

Shit. Hani braced himself, thinking fast. "What are you doing here?" he called out. Dammit, Kai couldn't be here. Someone from the cartel was likely watching.

Kai kept coming, stalking toward him like a human heat-seeking missile, his expression hard. "Said I needed to talk to you."

Hani slammed the truck door shut and shook his head. "I got nothing more to say to you." Desperate, his mind raced as he tried to come up with a direct threat against *Tutu*. If anything would make Kai leave and take her with him, it was to protect her.

"Well I've got a thing or two to say to you," Kai fired back.

"Whatever." Turning his back on Kai, he started for his front door, knowing his cousin would follow.

He didn't even make it to his front steps. Didn't even hear Kai coming.

Out of nowhere a strong hand gripped his shoulder and jerked him around. Hani grabbed hold of the thick wrist clutching a fistful of his jacket and tried to wrench free but got nowhere.

With a hard glare directed at Kai, Hani planted both hands against his cousin's chest and shoved. Hard.

Kai let go. They stood there facing off, both breathing faster. The hard set to Kai's face and the anger in his eyes made Hani feel like shit. "Why are you still here, anyway?" Hani demanded, tugging on the hem of his jacket. Hadn't anything he'd said earlier made an impact?

"Because it's a free goddamn country, Hani, and I'm not done with you yet."

Hani shook his head, his heart beating like a frantic bird against the inside of his ribs. Fuck. "I already said everything I have to say this morning. Just go, Kai, and leave me the hell *alone*."

Kai glowered down at him. Hani was only a couple inches shorter than him, but Kai had a presence about him that made him seem at least a foot taller. Yet another way Hani had never measured up to his idol. "I came here, on my own, so we could talk like adults about this."

He let out an exasperated breath. "About what?" he asked tiredly.

Kai shook his head in frustration, his jaw tightening. "You seriously wanna leave things like this? Huh? It's killing *Tutu*." He glowered at Hani. "And how the hell did you find out the insider info on me?"

Hani flinched inside. "You think *this* is killing *Tutu*?" He let out a short, brittle laugh, thinking fast. What kind of threat could he name against her without giving his involvement with the *Venenos* away? At that moment, he couldn't think of anything. "It kills her more to keep watching you leave over and over, asshole. You want to stop breaking her heart? Go pack her up and take her back to the mainland with you. The sooner the better."

"Hani, for Christ's sake—"

He spun away, his heart in pieces. The thought of going through life without even his *tutu* there for him was like a knife to the chest, but if it kept her and Kai safe, that was all that mattered.

"*Hani.*"

He'd only taken two steps toward the door when movement caught his attention from the shadows to the left of his place.

A woman. Her unblinking gaze fixed on him in a way that made the hair on his nape stand on end. She was lifting her arm, had something in her hand.

Gun.

"This is for my daughter," she rasped out before he could move or say anything, and raised the weapon.

Hani sucked in a breath and reached back for the weapon in his waistband as he spun back toward Kai. "Get down!" he yelled, hand closing over the grip of his pistol.

Kai took a step toward him instead of away, face set in a hard expression. Heroic bastard was going to try to shield him.

No! Hani launched at him just as the shots rang out from behind.

It felt like a sledgehammer slammed into his back. Once, twice. Three times.

Deep, burning agony ripped through him, stealing his breath. He hit the cool concrete facedown. The woman was still shooting.

Strong hands grabbed the back of his jacket and dragged him behind the bed of his truck. Hani gasped and bucked. *Can't breathe.* Four more shots pinged off the back of it. Then silence.

Kai pulled Hani's weapon from his hand. Hani lay there sprawled out on his belly, struggling to breathe. But there was no air. Only pain. A white, fiery anguish while he battled to suck oxygen into his burning lungs. He panicked. Thrashed.

Strong hands turned him over. Propped him up. Held his face.

"Hani. Hani, look at me."

He struggled to focus his eyes. He tasted blood in his mouth, smelled the metallic edge to it as it bubbled out of his nose. A horrible wheezing sound happened every time he inhaled, choking on his own blood.

Kai's face was inches from his, those dark eyes so like his own, desperate. "Hani. Hold on. I've got help on the way." With one hand he held a cell phone to his ear.

Hani fought to stay alert, his breathing a tiny bit easier now that he was upright. The shooter. Where was she?

Kai had pulled off his shirt and was pressing it to the exit wounds on Hani's chest. The pressure hurt. He looked down at himself, at the river of blood pouring out of his body, already pooling around his lap.

I'm dying.

A bolt of terror ripped through him. He grabbed for one of Kai's wrists, clung desperately. He was too young to die. And he didn't want to go like this. "C-can't…breathe," he choked.

"You're doing fine, man. I'm right here, I'm not

leaving." Kai scanned the area where the woman had just been.

Hani pictured her face. He'd seen her around lately, couldn't remember where. Was she the woman who'd been asking about him?

Kai was speaking to someone on the phone, relaying Hani's situation and address. Still here. Trying to save him even after what Hani had said and done. Trying to save him even though the shooter was still out there somewhere. Might be coming back for another attack.

The bounty.

Oh, Jesus, no. He shook his head, the slight motion sapping his rapidly dwindling energy reserves. "G-go," he begged Kai.

Kai set the phone down and applied more pressure on the shirt against Hani's chest. "Not going anywhere. Just stay with me. Nice, slow breaths." His voice was steady. Calm, giving Hani a moment's hope that he had a chance. "Ambulance will be here in a few minutes."

The tiny flame of hope inside him snuffed out, leaving an icy darkness in its wake. He would be dead by then. And Kai…the woman might kill Kai too.

Hani had to save his cousin before it was too late.

KAI'S HEART SLAMMED out of control as he knelt in front of Hani, applying pressure to the wounds in his cousin's chest, and keeping an eye out for the armed female. She'd disappeared between Hani's townhome and the one next door, and Kai had been too busy trying to save his cousin to track her.

The wounds were bad. Hani was losing so much damn blood, and the pressure Kai applied wasn't helping. But he'd be goddamned if he was just going to sit here and watch his cousin bleed out in front of him.

"Hani," he said sharply when those deep brown eyes began to glaze over. "Hani, I need you to stay awake, okay? Just look at me and keep breathing nice and slow." He shoved down the panic at the sight of the blood frothing from his cousin's nose, mouth and chest, covering the black tribal tattoos that were almost identical to his own. They'd gotten them together when Kai graduated from high school.

Brothers, Hani had said proudly afterward. *Forever.*

Hani's fingers were still around Kai's wrist, but the grip was weakening with every minute. "Kai," he rasped, then coughed, flailed as he choked on his own blood, the panic on his face ripping Kai's insides to shreds.

He locked one hand around Hani's nape, leaned closer until their faces were mere inches apart. "I'm right here, man. Not going anywhere. You're gonna be fine." God dammit, where was the fucking ambulance? If it didn't get here soon, it would be too late.

Hani shuddered and opened his eyes. Tears spilled free, tracking down his cheeks, mixing with the blood in pink rivulets that dripped onto his bloody chest. "N-no," he wheezed, agony etched into his face.

Kai's chest compressed. "Yes, you are. Don't you dare give up on me."

Hani's eyes cleared a little at the authoritative tone, then clouded again. "You...not...s-safe," he gasped.

"The shooter's gone. It's all right, I'm keeping an eye out." Though most of his concentration was on Hani.

He shook his head again, this time with more force, irritation creeping into his expression. "G-*go*."

"*No*." The word was flat. Final. "Who was she, Hani? The woman who shot you." She'd said it was for her daughter. What the hell did she mean?

"Dunno..." He clamped his fingers down on Kai's wrist, squeezed with a strength that had to cost him. "Danger. B-bounty...on you." He wheezed in a horrible, gurgling breath, shuddered, his body seeming to sag. "*Venenos*."

More ice spread through Kai's gut, Hani's words confirming his worst fear. Hani was definitely connected with the cartel. And the bounty had been reissued here. "I'm not leaving you, Hani." Fuck them and their fucking bounty. "Save your strength. You can tell me later."

The grip on his wrist was weakening now, Hani's breathing slower. More labored. "S-sorry said...all that." His eyelids began to droop. He fought to open them, stared at Kai. "P-protect...you..."

A rush of tears burned Kai's eyes, his throat tightening. It all made sense now. Horrific, terrible sense. "I know." He squeezed Hani's nape, tried to somehow force some of his strength into his cousin's failing body. "I *know*, man."

Hani's eyes glazed over, his face going lax. "Don't...hate," he mumbled. "Love...you..."

Jesus, no, please... "Love you too, man. Now hold on. Hani, please, hold on for me," he begged, his voice ragged. "The sirens are coming. Hear them? Ambulance is almost here."

Hani's gaze shifted to his once more, clung for a second. "T-take...*Tutu*. Keep...safe." Then his eyes went hazy, the lids sliding closed.

Fuck this. *No.* "Hani." Kai gave him a little shake. No response.

"Hani! Goddamn it, you open your eyes and *look* at me."

Nothing. Then Hani crumpled, his body sagging as though someone had unplugged an invisible power supply.

All but choking on the lump in his throat, Kai slid the hand at Hani's nape to the carotid pulse point beneath the angle of his jaw. Only a slight flicker met his fingertips as the sound of the approaching sirens grew louder in the distance. Then it disappeared altogether.

No!

The denial was loud as a shout in Kai's head, his entire body rebelling at the evidence in front of him. He grabbed Hani's shoulders, lowered his upper body to the ground and immediately started chest compressions, determined to keep his cousin's heart beating.

He worked hard and fast, the muscles in his arms and shoulders burning, sweat beading on his face and chest. He didn't stop to check for a pulse. Couldn't, all his focus on the compressions.

The ambulance crew finally arrived. Kai was panting, bent over Hani and still hard at work as he relayed information to the paramedics. One checked for a pulse. Shook his head.

Kai refused to stop, kept going while they got the defibrillator ready. Panting, he eased back only when they had the paddles ready. He held his breath, his entire chest aching as the charge built in the machine.

They shocked him.

Hani's torso arched and fell. His eyes were still closed, his lips open now, blood continuing to pool around him. Kai's knees and hands were soaked with it.

They shocked him again.

A tiny blip appeared on the display screen.

Kai stared at the machine, heart in his throat, a burst of hope swelling inside his ribcage. *Come on, come on, please…*

Another shock. Hani arched again, then sagged.

This time there was no answering blip.

They kept working on him. Five minutes. Ten. Fifteen.

Finally, the paramedic eased back onto his heels, looked up at Kai. Icy numbness spread through Kai's chest at the look in those pale blue eyes. "He's gone," the man said quietly.

Kai sucked in a ragged breath, then a horrible, wounded sound ripped from his chest. He was shaking all over, his muscles quivering like plucked elastic bands.

"I'm sorry."

He didn't answer the man, just stared down at his cousin's still face. Hani had been trying to force him away for Kai's own safety. Had been trying to protect him. And now he was dead, shot by some woman who may or may not be affiliated to the *Venenos*.

The paramedic watched him in silence for a few moments. "Is there someone we can call for you?"

Jaw tight, Kai shook his head. With one last look at his cousin, he forced himself to his feet, swaying a second before he staggered off to the curb and dropped onto it like a sack of cement.

Part of him was numb. But inside him, a deep, burning rage intensified, twining with a rapidly swelling wave of grief. When it hit him, it would take him so far under he wasn't sure he'd be able to find the surface again.

His stomach twisted as he shifted to pull his phone out of his pocket. He needed to call his *tutu* and tell her about Hani. But not yet. He couldn't bear it. There was only one person he wanted to talk to right now.

He dialed her number with a shaking finger, held the phone to his ear while it rang. And when she picked up, something inside him cracked wide open.

He squeezed his eyes shut, dropped his head and sucked back a sob, managed to croak out her name before his voice broke. "*Abby*."

Chapter Fifteen

———◇◇◇◇◇———

At the pain in Kai's voice, Abby jackknifed upright on the chaise out on the lanai. "What's wrong?" she blurted, dropping her e-reader and putting her hand to her chest, right over her racing heart.

He made a choked sound and she shot off the chaise, shoving the sliding glass door to her suite open and stepping inside.

"Kai?" she said urgently after a pause, fear curling inside her. "Are you all right?"

"No," he rasped out.

Oh my God. "Are you hurt?"

"No. Just…"

"What?" My God, what had happened? She rushed to the bathroom, dumped her robe on the floor and started pulling on a pair of jeans, her phone tucked between her ear and shoulder.

"Hani," he managed after a moment. "He's dead."

She froze, hands on the button of her jeans. "*What?*" she gasped.

"A woman shot him. I was standing there talking to him, and she came out of nowhere, opened fire on us."

Jesus. "Where are you?"

"His place. The ambulance and cops just got here."

So he was sitting there while Hani's body lay just a short distance away. *Oh, Kai...* "Sweetheart, I'm so sorry." She ached for him. "What can I do to help?"

"Nothing. I just... I wanted to call you."

"Do you want me to meet you there?"

"No. I don't want you to see any of this."

His refusal stung, but she shoved it aside. This wasn't even a little bit about her right now. "Okay. Can I call anyone for you?"

"No. Thanks," he added. "I've gotta talk to the cops and go to the hospital to get everything taken care of. Then I have to go tell my *tutu* that—" His voice broke, and so did her heart. Tears rushed to her eyes, his pain echoing clearly across the line.

"I'm here if you need anything, okay? Call me if you want me to meet you at the hospital." she said softly.

"Okay." A pause, and he dragged in a shaky breath. "I gotta go."

"'Kay. Talk to you later?"

"Yeah. Bye."

"Bye." She hung up, a lead weight in the center of her chest. She wished she were there so she could wrap her arms around him and somehow ease the pain. God, he shouldn't be alone right now. He'd gone there to make peace with Hani, and instead had seen him gunned down in cold blood.

****

Kai's heart sunk into the pit of his stomach as he climbed the two front steps to his *tutu's* house hours later. At the door, he stopped, unable to twist the knob.

He'd never imagined having to do anything like this. Once he walked inside, everything would change. And he didn't think he could bear to see his beloved *tutu's* reaction to what he had to tell her.

Hani. You need to do this for Hani. The words burned inside him, strengthening his resolve.

Gathering his courage, he took a few deep breaths, steadied himself and walked in. The quiet sound of the TV came from the living room. He slipped off his shoes and walked down the hall, his legs and chest like lead.

His *tutu* smiled at him from the couch when he walked in. "Hi." The smile quickly faded when he just stood there, face grim. "What's wrong?" she asked, frowning in concern. "Did something happen with Abby?"

God, it hurt that she was so concerned about his happiness. "No." He swallowed and crossed to the couch, sinking down beside her and taking her hand. It was so small folded in his own. Fragile and wrinkled, age spots on the back. He made himself hold her gaze, unable to shield her from the pain he was about to inflict, or ease the fear in her eyes.

"Something terrible's happened," he said in a

rough voice. "And there's no easy way to say it."

She stared back at him in alarm, her fingers curling in his. "What is it?"

It took every bit of strength he had to say the words. "Hani's gone."

She jerked, shock and confusion filling her eyes. "Gone?"

Kai nodded, aching inside. "He died a few hours ago, *Tutu.* I'm sorry." He could barely get the last bit out his throat was so tight.

She jerked her hand from his, shook her head in denial. "What? No. I just talked to him when he was on his way home…"

He set his jaw. He'd debated how much to tell her on the way up here from the hospital, had planned to spare her all the details he could. "He's gone, *Tutu.* I was there."

A grief-stricken, terror-filled wail shot out of her. She jumped to her feet, stood there staring down at him in disbelief, shaking all over. "No! No, not Hani. Not my sweet Hani…"

When Kai stared back at her helplessly, the tears started. Great, gut-wrenching sobs that tore from her chest and ripped his heart open with their agony.

Cursing inwardly, Kai got up and went to her, pulled her to him. "I'm sorry." *Sorry I couldn't save him. Sorry that I didn't realize how much trouble he was in. Sorry I couldn't stop it.*

She slammed a frail hand against his chest, grabbed his shirt with both fists and shook him, staring up into his face, her cheeks streaked with tears. "How? How did this happen?"

Fuck. She was going to find out eventually, but

he'd hoped it wouldn't be tonight. He couldn't lie to her though. "He was shot."

Her horrified cry made more tears burn the backs of his eyes. "No!"

Kai slid a hand to the back of her head and tucked it into his chest. "I'm sorry," he whispered, feeling helpless for the second time that night. "So sorry."

"Hani," she wailed, the shrillness of it sending a cold shiver corkscrewing up his spine. "My poor Hani, oh, God, *why*!"

"It was fast," he added quickly, not giving a shit that it was a lie. He was willing to say anything that might lessen the pain for her. "He didn't suffer. And I was with him right until the end. He said to tell you he loved you." He choked on the last words, overcome by a tidal wave of grief. Burying his face in her soft, white hair, he held on tight and fought to breathe.

His *tutu* clung to him and sobbed out her unimaginable loss, her hot tears soaking the front of his shirt.

****

Not knowing what the hell to do with herself, Abby paced around her room. It had already been a long day before Kai's awful phone call. Up to that point she'd so been looking forward to hearing from him once he finished up with Hani, hoping everything went well and they'd smoothed things over. Never had she imagined something like this would happen.

It was understandable that Kai didn't want her

there right now. They were still new. Neither one of them was sure what the boundaries or rules were yet. He was still in shock and had so much to deal with. Talking with the police. Giving a statement at the local station. Handling everything that came with Hani being placed in the morgue. Then telling his poor grandma what had happened.

For now, much as it upset her, there was nothing she could do to help.

So she called Cindy. Her friend didn't pick up, so Abby left a message. She kept her phone with her as she paced around the room.

Sitting out on the lanai now held no appeal whatsoever. She tried reading, but her eyes kept skipping over the same lines again and again, her focus shot. Finally, she turned on the TV and lay there channel surfing for a while, but nothing held her interest for long.

She forced herself to watch a movie. When it finished she checked her phone. More than two hours had passed since Kai's call. Was he still talking to the police? At the hospital? At his grandmother's?

Wanting to be supportive but not invasive, she sent him a quick text. *Thinking of you. Wrapping you up in a big hug in my mind.*

His reply came back a few minutes later. *Thanks. At my grandma's. Just told her. She took it hard. Call you later. Miss you.*

She blew out a breath and typed back *Miss you too*, then added an XO. His grandmother had raised both him and Hani. This would be like losing one of her own children. Abby hated to think about the level of grief they were both experiencing. It distressed her not to be there for him or helping in some way.

If this had happened back when Kai lived across the hall from her, Abby would have made him a bunch of dishes to freeze and taken them over. He and his grandma shouldn't have to worry about trivial things like cooking, cleaning and laundry right now. She could do all of that for them, show them she cared and try to help in her own way.

Kai said he missed her. And he was hurting. "I can't just sit here and do nothing," she muttered in frustration, and decided to call her boss.

Normally she wouldn't simply show up on Kai's doorstep without being invited at a time like this, but these were extenuating circumstances. If it turned out to be awkward, she would just drop off the food and leave, wait until he was ready to see her. But her gut said he wanted to see her and was either trying to be the alpha male who didn't need anyone during a crisis, or was afraid to lean on her too much early on in their relationship.

"Abby. What's up?" her boss asked.

"The session starts at ten tomorrow, yes?"

"Right."

"If I miss the opening meet and greet, would that be okay with you?"

"I guess so, but I'd sure like you there. Why, something wrong?"

She sighed. "Something's come up. The guy I'm—" Dating? Involved with? "seeing called a while ago. His cousin was just gunned down in front of him. I'd like to go to his place tonight, see if I can help with anything."

"Oh, damn, I'm sorry. Yeah, for sure you can miss

the meet and greet."

"Thanks. I might still make it. I'll be back in lots of time for the panel presentation, though."

"All right, sounds good. You'll call me if anything changes?"

"Yes. But don't worry, I'll be there for the panel no matter what." After she got off the phone she went straight to the closet and packed an overnight bag, then went down to the lobby and hailed a taxi. She stopped at a grocery store to pick up some ingredients, and gave the driver half-assed directions to Kai's grandmother's place upcountry.

She worried she'd gotten them lost, relying on landmarks she'd only seen once in the dark, then she spotted the red Mustang parked at the other end of the driveway. "Here, this one," she told the driver, who pulled in. A few dim lights glowed from inside the house.

Jitters started up in her belly when she unloaded her bags from the trunk and started for the front door. The driver waited where he was, engine running. Abby wasn't sure what kind of reception she was going to get, so she might need a return trip back to the resort.

Shifting the bags into a more comfortable position, she drew a deep breath and knocked on the front door. Heavy footsteps approached. The door swung open. Kai's face showed his surprise at seeing her there. With a hesitant smile she opened her mouth to say hi, but then he pulled the bags from her, dumped them on the front porch, and dragged her into his arms.

Abby hugged him back in silence, her heart

squeezing at the fierce way he held her, his face buried into the curve of her neck. He inhaled deeply, a tiny shudder rippling through him as he held her. She kissed the top of his head, stroked a hand over his back. She hurt for him. Hated what he'd seen, and that he was in so much pain.

At last he straightened, his arms still around her. "How did you find your way here?" he asked softly, looking at the taxi.

"I got lucky and remembered the turns." She released him, gestured to the bags. "I brought you guys some food. I can stay and make something for you, or I can just leave it here if you want privacy."

His gaze swung back to hers. Held. "You took a taxi to the other side of the island in the middle of the night to come to me, and you think I'd want you to leave?"

"Well, I don't want to impose, and I showed up uninvited and unannounced."

Kai waved to the driver, signaling for him to leave, and snagged Abby's hand. "You're staying."

The anxiety in her chest eased. "Okay."

Before she could bend down to get the food, he'd snatched up the groceries and her overnight bag. Abby followed him inside the entryway. The house was still and quiet. Eerily so. "Is your grandmother still up?" she whispered.

"No. She finally cried herself out about half an hour ago. I had to carry her to her bed."

"Oh, the poor thing." The image was heartbreaking. "And what about you?" He looked okay, but he was damn good at the brave face thing.

"I don't think it's really hit me yet," he answered,

unloading the groceries onto the counter.

Abby didn't offer to help or try to take over, sensing that he needed something to do right now. "Yeah."

He crumpled the plastic bags together in a ball and tossed them onto the counter beside the fridge, then faced her, expelling a deep breath. "I'm glad you came."

"Me too." He looked tired. And there was still blood around his fingernails.

She swallowed, tried not to stare at them. "Have you eaten?"

"No. I'm not hungry."

That in itself spoke volumes about how upset he was. She'd never known him to pass up a meal.

"And I still need a shower."

"Why don't you go take one, and I'll make you something? Maybe you'll feel like eating later. I brought the stuff for your favorite, my lasagna."

"You don't have to do that."

"I want to." She wanted to take care of him, in any way he'd let her. "Let me do this for you. I'll be quiet. And this way there'll be plenty of leftovers for your grandma for the next few days. I don't want her worrying about cooking or anything like that right now."

Kai studied her for a long moment, as though he couldn't believe she'd do such a thing for him. "Okay," he finally said. "Thanks."

"It's nothing." She wished she could do more. Things had changed for her over the past twenty-four hours. She and Kai had forged a new kind of bond, and it was more powerful than anything she'd felt before. She would do anything for him.

"Back in a bit."

She nodded, her gaze following him as he moved out of the kitchen and disappeared down the short hallway into what she assumed was a bathroom. A few moments later she heard the rush of water through the old pipes.

Being as quiet as possible, she got to work on the lasagna, finding the equipment she needed in various drawers and cupboards. She'd made this dish so often she knew the recipe by heart, and she'd bought enough for a double batch. By the time she was done prepping all the ingredients and assembling the lasagna, the water shut off in the bathroom. Wiping her hands on a kitchen towel, she popped the large casserole dish into the preheated oven.

In forty minutes, Kai's favorite comfort dish would be ready. Maybe he'd even feel like eating some. Until then, she would be here for him and listen to whatever he wanted to tell her.

****

Diane's hands were no longer shaking as she drove the final few miles to her motel in Kaanapali. A different motel from last night, because she was too paranoid to stay more than one night in each place.

The adrenaline rush that had fueled her on the long drive here was gone, leaving her mentally and physically exhausted. She couldn't believe she'd had the guts to shoot Hani. So many times, she'd almost chickened out. Then, standing in the shadows between the townhouses while he talked with that dirty DEA agent, something had snapped. She'd shot Hani several times, had fired at the agent too, but hadn't been brave enough to risk staying longer to chase him around the back of the truck and try again.

She had no idea how she'd gotten away. People must have seen her. They had definitely heard the shots. The agent would have called the cops.

Being on edge for so long was eating away at her. She'd stopped partway here to throw her disposable raincoat and wig in a Dumpster outside a restaurant in Lahaina. Hani must be dead now, considering how many times she'd hit him center mass at close range. He couldn't ID her. But that agent could.

Dragging her purse from the passenger seat, her half-empty pistol safely tucked away inside, she exited her vehicle. She'd parked right at the base of the stairs leading to her second-floor room, allowing her to get to it as quickly as possible.

Two steps from the base of the staircase, she froze when a man appeared out of the shadows to confront her. She started to reach for her pistol, heart in her throat, but the man held up a hand in warning.

"Don't," was all he said. He had an accent.

Diane stood there frozen, ready to bolt if he took another step toward her.

He didn't. Merely stood there staring at her, the dim glare of the nearby streetlamp gleaming on his dark hair and black leather jacket. "I saw what you did."

What? Her insides curdled. She started to take a step backward, but he stopped her with a single word.

"*Stop.*" It was so cold, so full of menace, that she

automatically stilled. The man cocked his head, revealing a dark goatee and mustache. His black eyes glittered at her, the icy calculation there chilling her. Was he a cop? Something worse?

She darted a frantic glance around. Was he alone? Was anyone watching them?

"Why'd you kill him?"

Her gaze snapped back to him, the muscles in her jaw trembling. "I don't know what you're talking about," she grated out.

Without looking away he held up his phone and touched the screen. A video clip started playing, showing a view from across and down the street from Hani's unit.

Diane blanched when it showed her coming out from between the detached townhomes and opening fire on Hani. She held her breath, flinched as the bullets struck him, taking him to the pavement. She hated seeing it. Her belly clenched with guilt and fear.

The man lowered his phone, that dead-eyed stare making her skin crawl and her heart hammer. "Why'd you do it?" he repeated.

She couldn't answer. Couldn't even swallow she was so scared.

"I could turn you in."

An image of prison popped into her head. Her in an orange jumpsuit, her ankles and wrists shackled in cuffs and chains. A big, uniformed guard escorting her into her cell. The finality of the metallic clang when the door locked. An image of her future.

He raised a taunting eyebrow. "You gonna tell me?"

"He killed my daughter with his drugs," she forced out, her voice shaking.

His expression never changed. "So you wanted revenge."

"Yes," she hissed, the anger growing now, burning away the terror that had frozen her.

He raked his chilly gaze over her, a smirk twisting his mouth. "I wouldn't have thought someone like you would have the guts. I'm impressed."

I don't care what you think. She raised her chin, glared back at him. She'd gone into this knowing she would pay eventually. At least she'd killed two of the people responsible for Bailey's death. It wasn't enough, but it was something.

The smirk turned into a grin. "I like your attitude. So I'll give you a choice, since it benefits us both."

She eyed him warily, darted another glance around to make sure no one else was watching. "You a cop?"

He gave a cold laugh. "No."

"A dealer?"

"I'm a businessman."

Yeah, she could guess what business he was in. Her lips curled in disgust.

"You want revenge?" When she stared at him in defiance, he continued. "The guy with Hani was his cousin. He's a DEA agent."

She drew in a deep breath, squeezed her hands into fists. "And?"

"Guess you haven't heard, but there's a bounty on his head."

Bounty? Diane nearly laughed. What did she care about money? Her life was over, and soon enough she'd be going to jail for the rest of her days.

"You take him out, and I'll give you ten percent of the money."

"I'm not interested."

"No?" He cocked his head. "Then what if I told you I could get you off this island without being detected? They'd never find you." He watched her like she was a pinned insect. "No jail time. Just a fresh start in Mexico, and a shitload of money to live on."

Diane blinked as she considered it. Bailey had loved Mexico. They'd vacationed there twice together at different resorts. Such a happy time in their lives, lots of great laughs and memories. She could have that instead of constant pain every time she drew a breath of Maui air? But she didn't for one second think she could trust him. "And why would you do that?"

"Because then we both get what we want."

She eyed him. "If you saw it, why didn't you do it yourself and get the bounty? You were right there."

"Because I have people like you to do it for me."

Asshole. There was every chance this man was connected to the very cartel that manufactured and supplied the drugs that had killed her daughter. If so, she should kill him right here and now. And yet he'd just offered her a way out. Her *only* way out that she could see. An option she hadn't believed existed.

"You're either in or you're out," he said flatly. "If you're in, I'll hold up my end of the bargain once the job is done. If you're out, I'll make an anonymous tip and you'll be in jail before midnight. Your choice."

It wasn't much of a choice. Except by going along

with his offer, she might still be able to kill the last two people on her list. She might even get away with it.

"I've got eyes all over this island. Over all the islands," he told her, a smug gleam in his eyes. "I've got some on you right now, and will until this is finished, one way or the other. My way is the only way out for you."

Diane drew in an unsteady breath, stood up taller. "Fine. I'll do it." She wanted the agent dead anyway, and she'd agree to anything if it bought her more time to kill the others too.

He nodded once. "That's good to hear, *señora.* That's very good. For you." He turned away and started walking. "I'll be in touch with instructions soon."

What? "How?" He didn't even have her number, and there was no way in hell she was staying the night here, low cash supply or not.

"Don't you worry about that," he said over his shoulder just as a silver Lexus pulled up. He climbed into the back passenger seat. The dome light was disabled, but enough light from the streetlamp showed two big men in the front seats for a moment before the car drove off.

Shaken, Diane hurried straight back to her rental car and drove off in the opposite direction the Lexus had gone. No place was safe anymore.

The clock was ticking even faster now. She had no idea where the hell to go from here, only a gut-deep certainty that she'd just sold her already damned soul to the devil.

Chapter Sixteen

Kai stood in the shower until the water turned cold, letting it pound over his head and shoulders, against his back. It ran clear now, not the faint pink that it had at first when he'd washed the residual blood from his hands and forearms. He scrubbed at his nail beds one last time to make sure they were clean, his stomach rolling at the thought of Hani's blood being trapped on his skin for a moment longer.

Abby showing up had lifted the weight he'd been carrying on his shoulders. He was amazed that she'd done that for him, had somehow found her way here without the address. She'd bought groceries, was in the kitchen right now making his favorite meal. God, he was crazy about her. She was so good to him, for him. No wonder he was falling for her.

It had been building for a while now. He'd already cared about her way more than as a mere friend before he'd kissed her the first time. Tonight, she'd been the first person he'd wanted to call after what had happened. That said so much about his trust in her. And when she'd shown up on his doorstep with her arms full of food because she cared and wanted to be here for him, his already battered heart had split wide open.

He shut off the water, dried himself. It was impossible to grasp that his cousin was gone. Would take a while for that to sink in. Even longer for him to be able to forget the look on Hani's face tonight, the things he'd said with his dying breaths.

Abby was on the couch in the living room when he came out dressed in clean jeans and a fresh shirt. She gave him an uncertain smile, her legs tucked beneath her, bare feet poking out, her toes polished with bright pink. "Lasagna will be ready in just over half an hour."

"Smells amazing." He still wasn't hungry. Right now, all he wanted was to be close to her.

Lowering himself next to her on the sofa, he curled an arm around her shoulders and pulled her to his chest. Abby wrapped herself around him, laid her head over his heart.

And Kai pulled in the first full breath he'd taken in the past four hours. Along with Hani's murder, the bounty was still heavy on his mind. He'd spoken to his commander about it, and the local cops were having someone come out to watch his *tutu's* house soon, just in case there was a threat against her. Otherwise Kai wouldn't be here, and wouldn't have let Abby stay either.

"Thank you for being here." He had to hide the

intensity of his feelings so as not to scare her off. She already didn't trust that he was in a good headspace after breaking up with Shelley. She might not believe him if he told her the truth right now.

This relationship was different for him. Abby was solid all the way through her character. Someone he could trust and lean on, independent and confident enough to be able to tolerate his hectic work and travel schedule, the stress of his job. He'd never been with a woman who was all of those things. Had never imagined anyone like Abby would want him.

"You doing okay?" she asked softly, rubbing a hand over his chest.

"Better with you here." He kissed the top of her head, breathed in the scent of her shampoo. This was exactly what he'd needed and never would have asked for. They'd only been together a few days and already Abby intuitively knew him better than anyone else he'd ever been in a relationship with.

She was quiet, snuggled up against him, offering comfort and support without saying a word. Giving him the time and space to talk about it if he wanted, not pushing him. Damn, she was such a sweetheart. He slid a hand up and down her back, basking in the peace she gave him.

"I can't believe he's gone," he finally said after a while. "And to lose him like that…" He shook his head, pulled in a deep breath. "I saw the woman when I pulled up, but I didn't think anything of it. Then, when I was talking to Hani by his truck, she came out of nowhere. 'This is for my daughter', she said, and started firing." Kai had gone over it a thousand times in his head. What had she meant?

Had Hani been involved with the daughter and broken her heart? Gotten her pregnant and bailed? It was all Kai could think of, other than maybe the daughter had taken it so hard she'd killed herself over it.

Abby made a sympathetic sound and hugged him tighter.

Kai gathered his thoughts for a moment. "I went there thinking I was going to take him down a peg or twenty, put him in his place and set him straight for the way he'd acted and the things he said yesterday. Instead I watched him die. And while he was laying there, bleeding out in front of me, you know what he said?"

She tipped her face up to look at him. "What?" she whispered.

"That he'd done it to protect me." He ran his fingers through her short hair, his insides twisting as he recalled it. "He didn't know who the shooter was, but he'd been trying to push me away to protect me. Because apparently the *Veneno* cartel still has a bounty on my head and they know I'm here on the island."

Abby sucked in a breath, fear lighting the depths of her pretty blue eyes.

"He thought if he shoved me away hard enough, that I would leave the island. Turn my back on him and just walk away." He clenched his jaw. "Knowing he thought I'd do that hurts almost as much as losing him."

"Ah, Kai." Laying her cheek back on his chest, she exhaled hard. "Did you tell the police? About the bounty?"

"Yes. Talked to my CO and team leader about it too. The cops have Hani's phone right now, but the DEA and FBI are involved in the investigation as well. They're trying to figure out who Hani's *Veneno* contact is. I'm betting the woman is involved with them too." Kai considered it his personal mission to take them down. Once he found out who was responsible for Hani's murder, whoever had done this would pay. He'd sworn it to Hani before Kai had left his cousin's body in the morgue earlier.

"Think they've got people out looking for you right now?" she asked worriedly.

"Maybe. The cops are sending someone out to watch the house tonight, and get me a new rental. The Mustang stands out way too much."

"And so do you." She hugged him tighter, made a sound of distress. "I couldn't stand it if anything happened to you."

He hadn't wanted to frighten her, but he loved that she cared about him so much. Setting a finger beneath her chin, he tipped her face up and met her eyes. "Nothing's gonna happen to me. There's too much heat on the cartel now with everything that's happened. And I'm only here for another couple days. As soon as I get all the legal stuff taken care of, I'll stay for Hani's funeral, then fly home."

"Want me to stay with you until after the service?"

Her question was quiet, but sincere. And it helped fill the hole inside him that Hani's death had created. "It means a lot that you'd do that."

She frowned in concern. "I care about you. I hate to see you hurting and I want to be here for you. I can change my return flight and push it back a couple of days, no problem."

The woman was holding his beating heart in her hands right now, and she didn't even realize it. Kai brought her head back to his chest once more, kissed her temple. "Thank you. Let's see what happens, okay?" He didn't want to screw up her work schedule.

"Okay."

They sat like that for a while, just holding onto each other in the quiet stillness of the house while the air became perfumed with the scent of baking lasagna. Then Abby's phone chimed softly on the coffee table. She sat up to silence it. "As soon as I take it out of the oven it'll need about ten minutes to rest on the counter before it's ready." She stood.

"Want a hand with anything?"

"No, you just sit here and relax. I found your favorite beer at the store, too. Want one?"

"God, I'd love one."

He dropped his head back onto the back of the sofa and watched the gentle sway of her hips as she walked into the kitchen. He was still reeling from what had happened, a little numb at times, and Abby was the only thing that made it bearable. She came back a minute later with an icy cold bottle of his favorite beer.

"Thanks." He took a swig, let out a groan as it slid down his parched throat.

"Think you can eat in a few minutes?" she asked quietly, rubbing his shoulder.

He loved how affectionate she was, how comfortable she was with touching him. He craved it from her. "Because it's your lasagna, yes." He'd try some, see how it settled.

"Good." She glanced toward the darkened hallway that led to the bedrooms. "What can we do for her?"

"Just let her sleep. She was exhausted. And she's pretty private, doesn't want anyone to see her grieving. Not even me."

Abby made a sad face. "It's just so horrible and wrong."

Kai nodded. "Hani made a lot of bad choices in his life, but he still had a good heart underneath all the bad shit he did." As proved by his dying words. "He didn't deserve to die like that."

"No." She gave him a squeeze and got up, returning a few minutes later with two plates filled with piping hot lasagna. She sat beside him, raised her glass of water in a toast. "To Hani. May he rest in peace."

Touched, Kai tapped his beer to her glass. "*E ho'omaha me ka maluhia, hoahānau,*" he murmured, and took a sip. *Rest in peace, cousin.*

A sudden lump formed in his throat as it hit home that Hani would never get to know Abby. He would have loved her, given the chance. And though she and Kai had only just gotten together, he already felt like Abby was The One. She was under his skin and burrowing deeper each passing day, and with every little thing she did to help and show how much she cared, she stole another piece of his heart.

They ate in silence together. He was surprisingly hungry, even had a second helping before finishing his beer and heading to the kitchen with their plates. Abby had already hand-washed the other dishes, leaving them drying in the rack beside the sink. While she wrapped up the leftover lasagna and put it in the fridge, he loaded their plates into the dishwasher and turned it on so his *tutu* would have one less thing to worry about tomorrow.

Then he took Abby's hand and led her out to the lanai, where they sat cuddled up on the bench in the corner while the breeze blew around them, filling the air with the delicate music of the wind chimes. For a moment, Kai could almost believe it was Hani's spirit passing by.

At length he told Abby about the Hawaiian belief that deceased loved ones continue to fulfill the obligations of *ohana* from the next realm. He talked about what Hani had been like as a child and as a teenager, the things they used to do together. "We used to love pulling pranks on *Tutu*. April Fool's Day was almost as good as Christmas around here. Changing the sugar for her coffee out for salt. Covering the toilet seat with plastic wrap. Stuff like that."

"So basically, you were both holy terrors."

He smiled fondly. "Yeah. We got into our share of trouble. And it was me who always got us out of it." *Except for tonight.* His smile vanished, a sick feeling swirling in his gut. Shit, this was hard.

Abby stroked his arm. "What else did you guys like to do together?"

"Swimming, surfing. Fishing. Man, Hani loved to fish more than anybody I ever knew. And he was lucky at it, too." He listed off a half-dozen other of his favorite memories, including the day they'd gotten inked together. Talking about Hani helped dull the pain a little, but then he reached a point where he just felt hollow inside.

"It's late. You must be tired," she murmured, rubbing his arm.

"Yeah. Let's go to bed." He needed to hold her against him in the darkness. Didn't think he could bear it otherwise.

She tilted her head back to meet his eyes. "You sure you want me to stay?"

How could she ever doubt that? "God, yes." He needed her on a level he couldn't put into words. If he had her beside him in the darkness tonight, he could get through the night.

Inside they got ready for bed. He was stretched out in the guest bed wearing only his boxers when she stepped into the room wearing a thigh-length pink sleep shirt and a shy smile that turned him inside out.

"Are you sure this is okay?" she whispered, casting an uncertain glance at the wall to her left. "I don't want to offend her."

"Yeah, I'm sure." It wasn't ideal that his *tutu's* room was right next to theirs, but hell if he was going to worry about it right now. He held out an arm in invitation. "C'mere."

She crawled in beside him, and the moment the length of her body slid against his, he let out a deep sigh, wrapping his arms around her back. She was soft and warm, giving him the solace of her embrace. And it helped. A lot.

As they lay there her breath created a warm little circle on his chest, her quiet exhalations stirring nerve endings in his skin. Cradled against her abdomen, his cock hardened.

Abby skimmed her lips over his breastbone, her hands wandering over his back, his ribs. Kai nuzzled the top of her head, stroking his hands down the length of her body, relearning her shape. Impatient to feel all of it without a thin cotton barrier in the way.

She kissed his chest, a slow, erotic press of her lips right over his heart before trailing more of them toward his left nipple. He dragged in a breath and slid a hand into her hair as her tongue teased the hard little point, groaned deep in his throat when she closed her lips around it and sucked. She took her time, teasing first one then the other, slowly working her way up to his neck while her hand trailed down his ribs to his hip, grasped his pulsing erection through the thin fabric of his boxers.

Kai dragged her mouth to his, growling in relief and hunger at the feel of her hand around him. She stroked him, squeezed as her tongue caressed his, lighting his entire body on fire.

The sleep shirt had to go.

He peeled it up and over her head, dumping it aside before locking one arm around her hips, the other around the back of her head. Abby pushed at his shoulder, still kissing him, and he obeyed her silent command, rolling to his back. She sat up on her knees, giving him a gorgeous view of her creamy skin glowing in the faint light coming in from the lanai. Her round breasts were sheer perfection, nipples hard and flushed a deep pink.

Before he could touch them, she gripped the waistband of his boxers and tugged them down over his hips. He helped her get them off, closed his eyes in bliss as her soft hand curled around his naked length, her teeth nipping at his jaw gently. He shuddered at her touch, the sensual way she stroked him.

She sucked at his earlobe, her voice a husky, sexy rasp that sent a shiver of anticipation down his spine. "I want to taste you," she whispered. "Been thinking about it for so long."

His whole body throbbed at the thought of her sweet lips closing around his cock. He shuddered as she worked him with her hand and began a downward path with her mouth. She took her time here too, seeming to savor every ridge and hollow of his muscles, making sexy little sounds of approval in her throat that drove him nuts. By the time she reached his hipbone, he was holding his breath, sweat popping out on his skin.

The warm, velvet stroke of her tongue at the crease of his thigh made him bite back a curse. He set his jaw, pushed back the covers with one hand so he could watch what she was doing to him.

Her pale blond hair seemed to glow in the unearthly light seeping in around the blinds. And then she looked up the length of his body at him, the vivid blue of her eyes like that of a match strike, the unmistakable heat and tenderness there stealing what was left of his breath.

Her lashes lowered and she licked her lips as she held him there in her fist, the engorged head shiny with his arousal. Her tongue peeked out to lap at it. Kai let out a throttled groan and squeezed her hair gently, silently begging. He needed her mouth on him so bad it was all he could do to lie still.

Slowly, oh so slowly, Abby kissed the crown of his cock. Kai inhaled sharply, a shudder rolling through him. And finally, when his muscles were as taut as cables and he couldn't stand the burn anymore, she parted her lips and sucked the head into her mouth.

His eyes slammed shut as pure pleasure radiated up his spine, his mouth opening on a soundless groan of ecstasy. His fingers contracted in her hair, holding her close, conveying his need.

She didn't tease him now, sucking with firm pressure that made his eyes roll to the back of his head, the flick of her tongue against the underside of the head pushing him right to the edge. He enjoyed it for as long as he dared, his orgasm barreling toward him with startling speed and intensity.

"Abby, oh, God, stop," he finally gasped out in a ragged whisper.

She paused, her mouth still engulfing him, and peered up at him questioningly. The sight damn near undid him.

Gathering up the tattered remnants of his control, Kai reached down to grasp the base of his cock and gently ease her off him. He groaned again, sucking in air, his swollen length throbbing with every heartbeat.

Before she could ask him what he was doing, he sat up, grabbed her and flipped her onto her stomach, quickly stretching out over top of her so that he was plastered to the full length of her back. Abby gasped and squirmed beneath him while he nibbled at her neck, sliding one hand beneath her to play with her breast and the other to find the hot, slick place between her thighs.

She was hot against his fingertips, and silky soft, the slick evidence of her arousal coating his caressing fingers. Sucking him off made her hot, and holy hell, there was no bigger turn-on in the world than that.

"Kai," she whispered, the breathless edge to her voice filling him with satisfaction.

"Want to be inside you when I come, shortcake. But I need you to come first," he murmured back, reaching one hand out for his jeans, lying strewn across the chair beside the bed. He fished out a condom, rolled it on, and stretched out full length against her back, the tip of his cock nestled in her folds, wrapping both arms around her so his hands could resume their former positions. "You ready?" he whispered against her shoulder.

A tiny quiver ran through her, and she nodded. "Yes."

Kai eased forward, burying his length inside her with a single, slow thrust that dragged a rumbling growl from his throat. She made a soft mewling sound and struggled beneath him, widening her thighs slightly to allow his fingers better contact with her clit.

His heart hammered at his ribs, his breathing ragged as sensation streaked through him. So tight and warm, her core squeezing him. "Abby, God," he rasped out, and started moving, unable to stay still a moment longer.

Her breathing changed, her body tensing beneath him. His muscles coiled along with hers, pulled taut as the pleasure intensified and kept building, driven along by the feel of her slick walls clenching around him and her soft little whimpers of arousal and need. He fought back the need to come and focused on what his hands were doing, playing with her hard nipple, caressing her swollen clit.

"Gonna come," she groaned in a whisper, shuddering. Her head came off the bed, spine arching as she neared the peak.

Yeah, shortcake, come for me. Kai squeezed his eyes shut and pressed his face into the curve of her shoulder, his hips rocking, every glide forward stroking his cock over her G-spot until she came. She bucked beneath him and buried her face in the mattress, her cries of release muffled against the covers.

Stilling his hands, Kai wrapped his arms all the way around her and held on tight as he plunged into her, driving deep one last time. He bit back the shout that tried to rip free of his throat as he found his own release. He shuddered, locked deep inside her, her core still rippling around him.

Mind wiped clean by the pleasure, exhaustion hit him like a brick wall. He relaxed against her as he caught his breath, careful to keep some of his weight off her so he didn't crush her into the mattress. She was such a tiny little thing compared to him. Tiny but fierce in her own way, and also caring and loyal.

With a groan he withdrew and rolled off her, pausing to kiss the back of her shoulder blade before he dealt with the condom. Lying down next to her, he pulled her into his arms, her back nestled against his front, and drew the covers over them. His entire body was relaxed, even though the pain of Hani's loss was still heavy on his mind.

"Do you think we were quiet enough?" she whispered in the silence.

The question surprised him so much he huffed out a laugh, amazed that he could laugh at all after such a horrific day. "Yeah, I think so."

"Because I don't know how I'd ever face your grandma again if we weren't."

Grinning, he kissed the back of her neck. "Nah, she likes you. And if she did hear, she'd just be glad that you're here with me right now."

"I'm glad I'm here for you too."

He kissed the back of her head and snuggled her closer, grateful for her presence and comfort. *I'm falling in love with you, shortcake.*

He didn't dare say it. Abby had been through the ringer where men were concerned. If he told her his true feelings now, it might freak her out, or she might dismiss them out of hand. More time. He'd give her more time, wait until things settled down and they found their footing once they got back home.

He just hoped he wasn't falling in love alone.

One minute he was breathing in the scent of Abby's perfume. The next, he was blinking against the bright morning sunshine streaming through the edges of the plantation-style shutters covering the guest bedroom windows.

Abby was curled into him, half-sprawled across his chest, her breathing slow and even in her sleep. As soon as that registered, images of Hani's last moments flashed through his head. The pain of it stopped his breath, a giant fist twisting his heart in a cruel grip.

Before he could move, his cell rang on the bedside

table. He grabbed it as Abby shifted off him and onto her side, watching him with sleepy blue eyes, tugging the covers over her bare breasts.

Kai glanced at the screen. It was still early, not even six. "Maka here," he murmured.

"Detective Carruthers," the man announced, his voice crisp, alert. "We've just got results back from the ballistics folks."

The words made him even more alert. *That was fast.* "Find anything?"

"Yeah. Ballistic fingerprints on the bullets taken from your cousin match the ones from a murder a few days ago. A doctor Bradshaw."

"I know about him." His murder had been all over the local news and papers. Now the same gun that had killed him had also killed Hani?

"Seems like our murderess has been busy."

Shit. Did the *Venenos* have female enforcers now? It was the only explanation Kai could think of. "So she's working on a hit list?"

Abby sat up, an alarmed expression on her face. Kai reached for her hand, gave it a squeeze and didn't let go, awaiting the detective's response.

"Looks that way. We've released her description and the composite sketch you helped us with to the media. It's a small island. Someone will know her. And then we'll find her and bring her in."

"Good. Thanks for the update." As soon as Kai got off the phone with the detective, he called Taggart, back home in Virginia. "Hey, it's me. Got an update about the situation here."

"I'm glad you called," his commander said. "We've got a bit of a situation here ourselves."

Chapter Seventeen

———◇◇◇◇———

Rowan Stewart paused a moment to tug on the bottom of her suit blazer and smooth her hands down the front of her matching pencil skirt before knocking on the closed office door. Malcolm might be here. His text early this morning had come as a complete shock.

Something important has come up at work. Can you make an early meeting at HQ this morning?

It was the first time she'd heard from him in almost a year, since the day she'd put an end to their budding relationship.

Doing that had been one of the hardest things she'd ever done, and seeing him again wouldn't be much easier, no matter what he might think to the contrary. She'd hated hurting him, but there'd been no other option. Better to end things early on than later, when it would have been even more painful. Hopefully by now he could admit that they were just too different to make a relationship possible.

A tall, well-muscled man with a strawberry-blond buzz cut and an intense aquamarine gaze opened the door. "Ms. Stewart?" He radiated an authority she instantly recognized as former military.

"Yes."

His expression warmed slightly. "I'm Commander Jared Taggart," he said, offering his hand. "Thanks for coming on such short notice."

She shook with him. His hand was huge, his grip firm, but not overbearing. Handshakes, eye contact and body language told her so much about a person. This man was tough, but not a bully. She was more than familiar with the latter. "My pleasure. Nice to meet you."

"You as well. Come on in."

She stepped inside, her heart jolting when her gaze landed on Malcolm, seated in a chair opposite his commander's desk. He was every bit as fit as he'd been the last time she'd seen him, wearing cargo pants and a black T-shirt that molded to his muscular torso.

He was pure, latent power curled up deceptively in that chair, like a resting panther. A few days' worth of black scruff covered his jaw, cheeks and upper lip, accentuating his luscious mouth. His skin was a beautiful deep brown, his eyes a few shades darker, like melted dark chocolate. They pinned her in place for a moment, unreadable, the penetrating intensity of them making her stomach flutter.

No fluttering. You're an Assistant U.S. Attorney, for Christ's sake, and you're here in an official capacity. Get it together. "Malcolm," she said politely, giving him a nod that was a little stiff because her neck muscles were so tense.

"Rowan." His deep, dark voice slid over her like rich, molten chocolate over ice cream. Not good for her, but tempting as hell. Exactly like the man.

Trying her best to pretend he had no effect on her, she took the chair next to his and faced Taggart as he seated himself behind his desk. "So the woman in question is here somewhere?" she asked.

"She's in the boardroom right now with her attorney and some other agents. She's refused to talk anymore to us about her situation without someone from your office being present."

"And what does she want from me?"

"To find out what deal the government can offer her." He leaned forward, resting his thick forearms on the surface of the desk, the muscles in his shoulders and chest bunching with the movement. "She showed up this morning with her lawyer right as the building opened and marched in here demanding to see me. Says she's got intel we need about the *Veneno* cartel. This is off the record, but one of my guys is in Maui and we just learned last night that the cartel has reissued a bounty on his head. They're looking for him there, already gunned down his cousin, and took shots at my agent. If this woman knows anything about the current situation or insider information about the cartel, I need to know it fast. You get what I'm saying?"

"Yes. Can I see her now?"

Taggart shared a look with Malcolm for a moment, then nodded. "Right this way."

She followed him down the hall and up an

elevator to the top floor, where the conference room was located. With every step she was conscious of Malcolm behind her, a silent, magnetic presence that was impossible to ignore. Was he still angry with her for breaking things off? Surely now he could see she'd done them both a favor by ending things when she had.

At the conference room, two middle-aged male agents stood flanking the door. "She won't talk," one of them said to Taggart. "Hopefully you can get something out of her."

"We'll take it from here." Taggart pushed open the door for her.

A slender woman somewhere in her mid or late-twenties sat at one end of the long table, dressed in jeans and an expensive-looking top, her long, chocolate-brown curls drawn back from her face in a sophisticated knot. Her makeup was classy and flawless, and Rowan noted the trademark red soles on her stilettos. Louboutins.

Whoever this woman was, she was polished and had money. Her middle-aged male attorney sat beside her, dressed in a business suit.

Rowan walked up to them with a professional smile in place. "I'm Rowan Stewart, with the U.S. Attorney's office."

They shook her hand, the woman's gaze darting suspiciously to Taggart and Freeman, who stood behind Rowan. "Hi." She didn't offer her name.

Rowan sat two chairs down from her while Taggart and Freeman sat on the opposite side of the table. "How can I help you, Miss…"

"My client needs protection," the lawyer said.

She focused on him. "Protection from what?"

The lawyer nodded at the woman, who then answered. "From people within the *Veneno* cartel. You give me and my mother protection, and I'll tell you everything I know." Her English was flawless, but spoken with a marked Spanish accent.

"Your mother?"

The woman nodded, swung her gaze to Taggart. "Can you do that?"

"Are you talking WITSEC?"

"I don't…I'm not sure." She glanced at her lawyer uncertainly.

"That's handled by the U.S. Marshal Service, not us. And whether or not they'd be willing to take you into the program will depend on who you are and whether you have anything useful to give us. So *who* are you?"

She set her jaw, her blue-gray eyes flashing with annoyance. "I'm Oceane Nieto."

Stunned silence met her words.

Surprised, Rowan glanced at Taggart and Malcolm for some guidance. The name meant something to them, because they were both staring at Oceane intently now.

"As in, Manny Nieto?" Taggart said.

Rowan didn't know that name either, but clearly something big was going on here.

Oceane's chin came up, quiet defiance written on her face. "He's my father."

Taggart sat back, never breaking eye contact with her. "Why are you here?"

"I told you, I need—"

"Why would you need protection if Manny's your

father?"

She lowered her gaze, swallowed. "Because it's not safe for us at home now. It's not safe for us anywhere."

Taggart stared at her. "Is that right."

A flash of anger crossed her face. "Would I have fled to the States, risked coming here to your headquarters otherwise? Given who my father is?"

Taggart crossed his arms over his chest, his expression hard. "Keep talking."

Oceane flicked a glance at Rowan before facing him again. "He can't protect us now."

"Why not?"

"I don't know. I…" She cleared her throat, drew a deep breath. "I was unaware of the full extent of my father's true business until a week ago."

Taggart's expression said he didn't believe a single word of that. "Uh huh."

"I *didn't*," she insisted. "My parents made sure to keep me removed from all of that my whole life. I lived with my mother near Veracruz, rarely even saw my father. As far as I knew he was a businessman involved with a few shady dealings, but never anything on this scale. Never with that kind of violent criminal association." She shifted in her seat, swallowed. "Then last week, everything changed. My mother came to me in the middle of the night, terrified. Your agency arrested someone within the…organization a few weeks ago, a lieutenant named—"

"Ruiz," Taggart said.

"Yes. It created a power vacuum, and my family was sucked into it. I didn't know what was happening until it was too late. Our personal security barely got us out of our house alive. A rival member attacked. There were…" She swallowed, drew in a breath. "People were killed. My mother finally told me everything while we were on the run, and we decided to escape here."

"So your father doesn't know where you are?"

"He will by now. We flew to Dallas and then connected here to Virginia late last night." She looked at Rowan. "I found a lawyer and came here to ask for your help."

"As Commander Taggart said, that will depend on a number of things," Rowan told her.

"Wait," Malcolm said, bringing everyone's eyes to him. He stared at Oceane, his expression full of suspicion. "How old are you?"

"Twenty-four."

"You're twenty-four, and yet you claim to know nothing about his involvement with the cartel your whole life?"

Oceane huffed out an irritated breath, her cheeks flushing. "I realize how that must sound to you, but it's the truth. I'd heard stories when I was younger. Then rumors, back when I was at college. But I never believed them. Never believed my father was capable of those things. Not the man I knew. My father is…he's a complicated man, and so was our relationship. I never lived with him. I didn't see him much or spend a lot of time with him over the years because he was always traveling."

"You mean living with his wife and moving around from place to place to avoid any assassination attempts," Taggart put in.

She dropped her gaze again. "Most likely." She seemed to gather her strength a moment, then raised her chin and squared her shoulders, meeting Taggart's gaze head on, and Rowan had to give her points, because his stare was intimidating as hell. "In light of everything that's happened, I can't go home, and I can no longer afford to be ignorant. My mother and I have no involvement with my father's business. We want to start a new life away from all of that. So I'm willing to give you whatever information I have in exchange for protection."

Rowan glanced at Taggart in astonishment. That was a hell of an offer, tossed right in their laps. Oceane seemed really damn naïve for someone in her mid-twenties. Did she realize what she was doing? Her so-called lawyer had been useless so far.

Taggart studied Oceane in silence for a long moment, then sat up straight. "You got any ID on you, Miss Nieto? Passport? Driver's license?"

She flushed, shook her head. "Not legal ones," she admitted.

"Figured not," he murmured, his tone dripping sarcasm. "This meeting is over until I can verify who you are."

Oceane's brave front faltered. A sheen of tears filled her eyes, but she blinked them back and answered. "Go ahead and check."

"Oh, I will," he said, getting to his feet and pulling out his phone. "I'm going outside to make a call," he said to Malcolm. "Keep her in that chair and don't let her out of your sight until I get back."

****

For over thirty minutes Malcolm stayed silent in his seat, listening carefully as Rowan talked with Ms. Nieto and her lawyer.

This was crazy.

He wasn't sure how much of her story he could swallow. Her body language and reactions rang true enough. But Manny Nieto's daughter fleeing a life of luxury in Mexico and running straight to DEA headquarters for protection? And willing to give them insider info against her father in exchange for it?

Excuse him if he was skeptical.

As for Rowan, she was cool and sophisticated as ever in that tailored skirt suit that hugged every line of her trim curves, her silky black hair pulled up into an elegant twist. It was hard as hell to sit here across from her and ignore his awareness of her. He thought he'd shut all his feelings off for her a long time ago, but apparently not. The sight of her still made him ache deep inside, yet she'd barely reacted at all when she'd walked into Taggart's office and seen him sitting there.

It drove him crazy to think she'd just moved on and gotten over him so fast when he couldn't do the same with her. Did she ever think about him now? Did she ever regret walking away? Wish she'd given them more of a chance?

The conference room door opened. They all looked over as Taggart strode back into the room.

The team commander took the seat beside Mal and faced Rowan. "So what have I missed?"

Rowan set her pen down and faced him with the

cool professionalism that had been drilled into her since she was a little girl. "I've advised Ms. Nieto about the legal ramifications regarding her situation," she said in her southern belle Georgia accent. "She would like protection in exchange for information, but is still undecided about whether WITSEC is a good choice for her and her mother." She looked at Ms. Nieto for clarification.

"I don't want to be separated from my mother," the woman said. "We're really close and she needs me more than ever. I've left her in a secure location with our private security members who we know are loyal to us. I don't trust anyone else."

Well then WITSEC wasn't going to be an option, was it? Malcolm felt obligated to educate her a little. "Given who you are, and what you're proposing, WITSEC is the only way you would both be protected."

Those blue-gray eyes flashed to his. "I can't be separated from my mother."

"If you want to be safe, then you'll have to be." Sorry, but there it was.

Taggart folded his arms. "But all that aside," he said to the woman, "you're willing to give us intel on your father and his inner circle, in exchange for asylum and protection for you and your mother. Have I got that right?"

She swallowed hard. "Y-yes." She whispered it and lowered her gaze, almost as if she was ashamed. Or possibly scared. Mal didn't blame her if it was the latter. The *Venenos* had a reputation for carrying out hideous killings on those who crossed them.

"Why?" Taggart pressed.

She lifted her gaze from the table to meet his. "Because I love my mother, and I want her to be safe. And because if all the things I've heard about my father are true, then…" She drew a deep breath. "Then I want to stop him from doing any more."

Mal barely kept from raising his eyebrows in surprise. That was noble of her, but a hell of a risk to take considering what she was offering.

"You think your father will just let the two of you go?" Taggart asked.

At that, she paled. "He might have done or ordered terrible things, but he would never harm us." She sounded certain of that. "His rivals would, though. They'd use us to get to him in an instant."

Taggart looked unconvinced. "You don't think he'd come after you even if you were helping us target him?"

She didn't respond to that. Taggart opened his mouth to say something else, but his phone rang. He checked the screen and stood. "She's here."

"Who?" Mal asked.

"Insider source." He crossed the room. The door opened just before he got there.

Hamilton walked in, held the door and looked over his shoulder at someone. A woman with jaw-length dark brown hair stepped inside the room and stopped, her wary gaze surveying the room.

It took Mal a few moments to realize who it was.

The change in her was startling, but then, the last time he'd seen her she'd been huddled beneath a blanket in the back of an ambulance when they'd raided Ruiz's hideout near Biloxi. She wore a scarf wrapped around her neck, even though it was humid and in the low eighties outside. Probably to hide the scarring where the slave collar they'd locked around her throat had dug into her skin.

Her anxious gaze flicked to Hamilton and stopped. The moment it did, her vigilant posture relaxed, and she walked over to stand at his side.

"This is Victoria Gomez," Hamilton announced as he took her elbow, standing like a sentinel beside her. His gaze zeroed in on Ms. Nieto at the far end of the table.

Victoria stared at the other woman with an almost hostile intensity, her body eerily still.

"Do you recognize her?" Hamilton asked her in low voice.

Victoria nodded, never looking away from her. "Oceane. Manny Nieto's illegitimate daughter."

Mal's gaze shot to Ms. Nieto in the tense pause that followed the verbal bombshell. Her cheeks flushed, and she seemed to bristle at the illegitimate tag. "My parents never married," she allowed, eyes narrowed. "But I *am* his daughter. His only child." She said it with an almost defiant pride, as if it should carry some sort of weight with everyone in the room.

Obviously, she had no fucking clue who she was talking to. Mal mentally shook his head at her.

Victoria's laugh was bitter. "Aren't you a lucky girl."

Ms. Nieto's bravado faded. She shifted her gaze to Hamilton for a moment, then back to Victoria. "Do I…know you?"

Victoria's dark gaze was icy. "No. But I know all about you. And I've seen pictures of you."

Mal watched Ms. Nieto carefully as she frowned

and glanced at Taggart. She seemed truly bewildered.

"Ms. Gomez was taken hostage by Ruiz's men and held captive for several weeks. While there she had the misfortune of becoming well acquainted with them and your father's men, against her will."

At those damning words, shock and horror filled her face. Mal was pretty damn good at reading people. Her reaction was either real, or she was the best damn actor he'd seen.

Her gaze swung back to Victoria, stricken, her face pale. "I'm sorry. Truly."

Victoria stared at her for another long moment, then looked away, dismissing her. "What else can I help you with?" she asked Taggart, her voice surprisingly strong. The woman might appear fragile and have wounded doe eyes, but there was a backbone of steel inside her. One that the *Venenos* would regret ever fucking with.

"Ruiz's capture caused a predictable power struggle within the cartel," Taggart answered. "Our sources are saying that Nieto's taken his place as lieutenant. *El Escorpion's* apparently given his blessing. We're trying to find out who Nieto's main players are. His most trusted insiders. One of them's reinstated a bounty on one of our team members, over in Maui. The threat is serious. Somebody killed our agent's cousin last night in front of him. We can't be certain he wasn't the intended target. Any names come to mind?"

Victoria thought about it for a second, then started listing off names. She'd been prisoner to those animals for several weeks, chained to the floor in a rotting shed out back of the property while they used and tortured her.

Mal didn't know the details of what they'd done to her during that time, but he could guess well enough, and judging from the physical damage she'd sustained, none of it was pretty. Her captors had intended to sell her into a human trafficking ring in southeast Asia, never thinking she would escape.

Except she had. And now every single thing they'd talked about so carelessly in front of their "slave" would come back to haunt them.

Sometimes—but not often enough—karma was a fucking awesome thing to behold.

He wrote each name down as she listed them, compiling a list to begin checking the moment he got out of this meeting. He was anxious to move on this, find out anything that might help out Maka. And the sooner he left the room, the sooner he wouldn't have to look at Rowan and be reminded of all he couldn't have.

"But I'll bet the guy you're looking for is Juan Montoya," Victoria finished, her voice ringing with hatred. "He runs most of Nieto's crew."

Ms. Nieto gasped.

Mal jerked his gaze to her.

She was even paler now, eyes full of horror. "That's…that's my father's best friend," she said in a shaky voice. "He's my godfather."

"Well he's also one of our top ten most wanted North American cartel members," Taggart muttered, before turning to Mal. "Bring that list to my office. We need to call Maka right away and bring him up to speed on all this."

Chapter Eighteen

———◇◇◇◇———

"So Nieto's for sure the new boss," Kai said into his cell phone, leaning back in the seat of his new rental. A freaking minivan, of all things.

"Looks that way," Hamilton answered. "You got the picture of Montoya I sent you?"

Juan Montoya, Nieto's supposed head enforcer. Reported to be here somewhere on the island, and likely the one who had put the word out about the bounty on Kai. "Yeah. I don't recognize him. Cops said they think he was in contact with Hani. They're still tracing the number from Hani's phone." The number they were looking for came from an encrypted phone. Who knew how long it would take them to crack it.

The police had learned a lot of things from Hani's phone so far. It still stunned Kai that his cousin had been trafficking *Veneno* heroin throughout the islands. He felt sick at heart that someone he'd been so close to had been in business with a cartel that Kai and his team had been risking their lives to battle at home and overseas for the past several years.

"Where are you right now?" Hamilton asked.

Kai scanned the parking lot, extra vigilant in light of all the shit that had gone down. He'd been careful on his way over, making sure no one was following him.

It was only five o'clock, but with everything he'd been juggling today it felt much later. Now he had the mother of all headaches pounding in his skull and his eyes burned from lack of sleep. His entire day had been eaten up with seeing to his *tutu*, making arrangements, and talking with the cops and investigators. Since the ballistics linked Hani's murder with the doctor's, the heat was on the female suspect.

"At the Grand Wailea. I'm meeting Abby once she's wrapped up the conference." Hard to believe it was only hours ago that he'd woken up next to her. A detective had brought the minivan to Kai, then driven Abby back to the resort in an unmarked car. They had extra security watching the conference, just in case.

"Cops haven't tracked down the female shooter yet?"

"No. Still no name, no known motive." Other than it had something to do with her daughter. How everything else fit with Hani and the *Venenos*, Kai wasn't sure. "I'm about to talk to the security guys in the hotel. Cops have briefed them about the female. I'll let them know about Montoya and their possible connection."

Stood to reason that the woman was working with or connected to Montoya somehow. There was a target on Kai's back. The female had seen him the other night. Had fired at him too. She might have seen him with Abby at some point.

Kai would make damn sure he did everything possible to protect his lady.

"Yeah, wouldn't hurt to tell them, be on the safe side. How's your grandma doing?"

He smothered a yawn and shifted his phone to his other ear. "I guess okay, all things considered. Some of her friends from the old town are with her right now."

That was the only reason he'd been willing to leave her. It hurt him to see her so devastated. For all his faults, she'd loved Hani with everything in her. Now her heart was

broken. And Kai hadn't told her about the threat against him, or how Hani had been trying to protect him. She was in enough pain, and damned if he would add more to her burden. At least she had cops stationed at her house to guard her.

"Any idea when the service is gonna be?" Hamilton asked.

"Wednesday afternoon at four."

"Taggart and I are thinking of coming out. Things are quiet here for the moment. If you wanted some backup, we could even fly out this afternoon."

This was why he loved his teammates. They cared. No matter how they bitched at each other occasionally or got on each other's nerves during deployments, they always worked it out. In times of crisis, they were there for one another. They weren't just a team—they were a family. "I appreciate the offer, man, but I'm good for now."

"Figured you'd say that. Just wanted you to know we're here for you."

"I know it."

"Okay, brother. Later."

"Later." Kai ended the call, took two ibuprofen tablets with a swig of water, and strode toward the Grand Wailea entrance.

The change of scenery was good for him, because he couldn't bear the thought of going back to his *tutu's* place right now. He needed to be with Abby. The mere knowledge that he would see her soon eased him inside, even if it was here, in the same place where Hani had met him only a few days ago. Kai was looking forward to unwinding with her, spending the entire night together before they had to face reality again in the morning.

I'm here, he texted her as he hit the lobby.

He went straight to the concierge desk and asked to see the head of security, while keeping an eye out for anyone watching him. Given his size, it was impossible for him not to stand out. Manny Nieto was a powerful man in his own right, might even have people from this very hotel on his payroll. The DEA was still compiling information about him, both from his daughter and other sources.

Not surprisingly, his daughter painted entirely different pictures of him from everyone else. Sources within the cartel characterized Nieto as an efficient and ruthless man, willing to consolidate power at any cost. Anyone who crossed him died in short order, and often, so did their families.

According to what Hamilton had told him this morning, those murders were mostly carried out on orders from Juan Montoya by his circle of trusted, elite enforcers. Word was they were all former Mexican special ops members.

His phone chimed with Abby's response. *Meet me by the pool in half an hour. I've rented us a private beachside cabana for dinner.*

Kai's mouth quirked up. Nice. His lady was going all out to make the evening special for them, no doubt in an effort to take his mind off everything else. She was such a sweetheart.

Okay, he replied, already looking forward to it. He wanted to shut out the rest of the world and focus only on her.

The head of security arrived. Kai showed him his agency ID and the man escorted him down to the security room. Five guards sat at various stations monitoring video feeds, from cameras mounted around the resort.

As efficiently as possible though without giving away anything classified, Kai brought them up to speed with what was going on, and showed them pictures of both the female suspect and Montoya. He sent the shots to the head of security's phone. "If you see either of them, alert me and the MPD right away. I'll report any new intel to my superiors."

The head guy nodded, held out Kai's phone to show the others the photos. "You staying here at the resort?" he asked Kai.

"Just for tonight. I'm having dinner with a friend in a little bit. If anything comes up, you can text or call me. I'll have my cell on me." He checked his watch on his way out the door. Abby should be wrapping up her final session of the conference right about now. He couldn't wait to see her.

He was halfway down the hall when a door opened behind him and the head of security called out. "Agent Maka?"

Kai stopped and turned around. "What's up?"

"Can you come back and look at this?"

A tingle of concern slid through him. "Sure." He strode back to the room, stepped inside and shut the door. Two guards stepped aside from the monitor they were looking at, making room for him.

"Play that back again," the security head ordered.

Arms folded across his chest, Kai stared at the screen while the video footage played.

"Watch right here," the man said to him.

The camera showed a young family walking in carrying their luggage. Thirty-ish man, woman, and two little kids.

Behind them by a few paces, another woman came into view. She wore a wide-brimmed sunhat and a Hawaiian-style dress. Kai zeroed in on her, his pulse beating faster. Her build was right, and she was approximately the right height to be the woman from last night.

She stopped a few yards behind the family and glanced around the lobby, the gesture almost nervous. For a moment she stared at something out of the camera's range, then glanced over her shoulder, revealing her face for an instant.

Kai's insides clamped tight. "Play that part back and freeze on her face," he commanded.

One of the guards backed the clip up, played with it a few moments until he could freeze on the woman's face. The shot was grainy, too blurry to see any of the features clearly.

"Can you enhance it at all?" Kai asked, leaning forward, pulse quickening.

"Some." He tapped some keys, zoomed in and tightened the focus.

The woman's features became clearer. More distinct.

Kai cursed silently, dread and recognition exploding inside him. "That's her," he grated out. "How long ago was this?"

"Eighteen minutes."

Fuck. More than enough time to disappear somewhere on the resort. Why was she here? For him? Did she have someone working with her? "Follow her after this clip. Where does she go?"

Two of the guards began checking various feeds, searching for her. "Here, got her," one said a minute later.

The blood rushed in Kai's ears as he watched the woman walk out of the lobby, heading to the right. Past placards flanking the start of a long hallway that led off the lobby.

Placards listing events for the pharmaceutical conference. His eyes stopped on the left one, scanning the words.

An event hosted by NextGen Pharmaceuticals. Abby's company.

His gut constricted, foreboding rocketing up his spine in a cold wave. "Where does this hallway lead?" he demanded.

The head of security glanced over his shoulder at him. "The conference rooms."

Jesus Christ. *Abby.*

"Get up there now and call the cops for backup," he said, yanking his phone out of his pocket as he bolted for the door.

****

In her spot against the wall at the rear of the ballroom, Diane's entire body vibrated with pent-up nerves as she listened to the man on stage giving the closing remarks for the conference. Walter Ling, CEO of NextGen Pharmaceuticals. The rich, arrogant asshole who'd become a millionaire tens of times over by profiting from other people's misery once they got addicted to the shit his company made.

The blonde pixie who worked for him sat up front, watching her boss with a disgustingly pleased expression. The same woman Diane had seen here the other night
with Hani and that dirty DEA agent, Kai. She was sure they were together.

Ling carried on with his speech, going on about how his company was making a difference in the world, spinning his lies about how the poison they manufactured and pedaled were improving the quality of life of so many suffering people throughout the world. And worse, how their latest drug was *safe*.

Diane clenched her jaw as she stared at him. He had power, money and prestige, the admiration of almost everyone in this room. But not her. And he was about to get a firsthand lesson in just how fragile and fleeting life could be. Him and that blonde bimbo.

She cast a furtive glance around the room. Her wig made her look a good ten years older, but she wasn't supposed to be here. A composite sketch with an uncanny likeness to her was all over the news and social media. She hoped her disguise would buy her the time she needed to pull this off.

Yet that wasn't the most important reason why she shouldn't be here.

The man who had surprised her at the motel last night had texted her about an hour ago, saying she was being watched. She hadn't given him her number, so the fact that he'd contacted her scared her. He'd made it clear that she was being watched. That she was to await details about the location of the dirty DEA agent, Kai. She didn't much care why the man wanted the agent dead. Once she got her next two victims, she was to find and kill him too.

Well, too fucking bad for her mysterious shadow. Instead of following his instructions, she'd come here instead because this was about *her* mission, and she was determined to take out Ling and the woman. They were softer targets than the DEA agent, likely without any training, giving her a higher chance of success.

Killing the DEA agent wasn't her priority, and it likely wouldn't happen anyway. As soon as she pulled her weapon and fired at Ling and the woman, it was all over. She would never make it out of the hotel before they captured her. Or if she did, she wouldn't get far.

Diane accepted that, and was willing to pay the price. There was no way she would be able to pull off a murder here and walk away, not even with an accomplice helping her. As long as she could shoot both NextGen targets, she was willing to go to prison now, and live the rest of her life with the vindication of knowing she'd made at least a few key people pay for Bailey's death. At least then she would be able to sleep better at night.

And if she was killed, well... Then her agony would be over for good.

She jolted when her phone buzzed in her purse. Several people around her gave her disapproving looks, then went right back to watching Ling. Releasing a quiet breath, she opened her purse and peered at her phone, skimming the text there.

Target is at Grand Wailea. Find him and report back after. We're watching you.

She snapped her purse shut, surprised and jarred by the news. The DEA agent was here? Probably coming to see the blonde bitch. Well, if so, he was about to watch her die, and then Diane would shoot him too.

She looked back up. The audience was still listening attentively to Ling's speech. All the tables were full, and it was standing room only around the sides and back of the expansive room.

Ling made his closing remarks, finished with a few words that he no doubt saw as rousing, then gave a nod and a smile that set Diane's teeth on edge. To her disgust, the room erupted into a cacophony of applause. People even stood while they did it.

Tears burned her eyes. A standing ovation for a

monster like him?

God *dammit* she wanted him dead. For what he'd done to her and her daughter. For what he'd done and would continue to do to his nameless victims, all in the name of money. For deceiving all of these so-called intelligent and respected physicians and industry insiders. Fuck them all.

Moving fast, she blinked away the tears and ducked out the side door into the hallway just as people began to spill out of the room, focused on tracking Ling and the woman. She stayed against the hallway wall, watching both doors anxiously. Hundreds of people streamed out, soon blocking her view.

Her heart began to pound, sweat dampening her palms. She couldn't miss them. Not now. This was her only chance to do what she'd come here to do.

Just when she'd begun to despair that she'd lost them, a flash of platinum blonde hair caught her eye through the crowd. Diane pushed her way toward it through the crowd, a bolt of relief surging through her when she spotted the woman's lavender dress.

She was talking to someone. A man. He moved aside a moment later, and Ling appeared in Diane's field of vision.

She stayed where she was, watching them both while people flowed around her, heading for the lobby or out the doors that led to the grounds.

Come on, come on, she urged them silently, impatience making her jittery. The longer she stood out here in the open, the higher the chance that someone would recognize her or hotel security cameras would give her away.

To do this she needed to corner her targets in at least a semi-private place. It was the only way she'd have a chance to pull it off. She had to be even quicker this time than last night, or when she'd killed Bradshaw. Her weapon had a full mag in it, and she had an extra one tucked inside her purse just in case.

Finally, when increasing anxiety and doubt threatened to erode her courage, Ling started for the exterior door, the woman beside him. Diane hurried after them, leaving a good distance between them so as not to arouse suspicion.

Pushing open the door, she stepped outside into the balmy tropical twilight. Her gaze immediately found her two targets walking together down the sidewalk, heading toward the pool area.

Diane's pulse tripped, her breathing speeding up. Taking a deep, bracing breath, she followed them, reaching her right hand into her purse to curl her fingers around the grip of her pistol.

Chapter Nineteen

———◇◇◇◇◇———

"**Y**ou did really well this week," Walter said to Abby as they strolled down the lit walkway toward the main pool area. She tossed him a smile, filled with a sense of relief and pride. It had been a long week. Even longer because she'd been away from Kai far more often than she wanted to be, especially over the last twenty-four hours.

Now her work here was all done. The conference had gone better than she'd expected. She'd made personal connections with many of their best clients, along with other company executives and experts within the industry. Her chance of promotion looked good, her future bright.

A future she hoped would include the extraordinary man who had completely won her heart and made her realize that she didn't want to keep her walls up any longer. Not with him.

"Thanks. And thanks for asking me to come," she added, giving him a playful nudge in the ribs with her elbow.

"You were the logical choice. Don't tell anybody back at the office, but you were a shoe in. Dan and I both decided on you weeks ago."

She raised her eyebrows. "And you let me sweat it out all that time because why?"

He shrugged. "It's good for you. Didn't want you to get all full of yourself," he said with a smile playing around the edges of his mouth.

She snorted. "I'll remember that."

"Oh, I know you will." He glanced at her. "You got time for a quick drink before you meet your *friend*?"

Abby wasn't telling him anything more about Kai than she already had. She felt crazy protective of him, even though he was huge and badass and could more than look out for himself. "If it's a really quick one. I've made us dinner reservations."

"Something romantic, I hope?"

She hid a smile. He was a nice man and a great boss, even if he could be a little arrogant at times. Spending this week with him had shown her a far more human side of him than most people ever got to see, and he'd also gotten to know her on a more personal basis. For those things, she was grateful. "You can keep trying, Walter, but I'm not giving you anything more."

He sighed. "All right, be that way." He took her elbow gently, gestured with his free hand to a path on the left. "Just through here there's a little tiki bar by the pool. Sound good?"

"Sure." Abby went with him, her high heels clicking on the stamped concrete path. Her phone was in her purse. She'd text Kai from the bar and let him know where she was. He was really social and outgoing, so she was sure he wouldn't mind having a drink with her boss before their private dinner.

"So am I going to get to meet this guy, or what?" Walter asked as they neared the pool. The underwater lights made it glow a beautiful bright turquoise in the darkening twilight.

"You might, if you behave."

"Good. I need to make sure he's worthy of you," he teased.

She smiled. "Oh, he is." Kai was…incredible. Already familiar to her in so many ways from the start of this trip, but now he meant so much more to her than ever before.

Over the time they'd spent together here they'd not only solidified their bond, but she'd seen so many sides of him that she hadn't before. The dominant, skilled lover who made her insides quiver with a single look. The trusted friend who cared about her and went out of his way to do things that made her feel special. Even the tender, vulnerable part of him that she bet he'd only ever let a handful of people see.

Strong as he was, watching his cousin die in front of him in such a horrific way had shaken him to the core. It didn't matter how strong he appeared, or how well he seemed to be handling the loss, Abby knew he was reeling.

She'd hated being away from him today, but he'd had so much to deal with, and it made tonight even more special. Tonight, they could simply relax and be together. She could be there for him without time constraints or schedules, hopefully take his mind off everything else for a few hours.

Right after she got through this drink with Walter.

"I'm glad to hear it," her boss said, guiding her to the right, toward the well-lit tiki bar set up next to the pool. Three other people were seated around it, talking amongst themselves. "But I'll be the judge of that when I meet him. You change your flight home yet?"

"Yes. I'll be staying until after the funeral, and flying home the next day."

Walter nodded and slid out a stool for her at the bar. "What'll you have?"

"Lava flow, please." A piña colada swirled with strawberry syrup, served with a fresh wedge of pineapple here. Work was done, so she was officially off the clock and ready to make the most of her remaining time here.

She settled onto the stool, crossing her ankles and resting the platform portion of her high heels on the foot rung. While Walter ordered their drinks, she reached into her purse for her phone. She'd missed three calls from Kai several minutes ago. Silently laughing at his over-eagerness, she typed out a quick text, alerting him to their slight change of plans.

At tiki bar beside main pool. Come meet boss and me for quick drink before reso.

"I asked him to meet us here," she said to Walter, who had his back to her as he took her drink from the bartender.

"Good. So what do you have planned for—" His

words cut off and he sucked in a sharp breath.

Abby's head snapped up, her thumb still touching the send button. Walter was staring at something to her left, his face frozen, body tense.

Alarmed, she jerked her head around to see a woman standing twenty feet away from them. Her gaze was fixed on Abby and Walter, her preternatural stillness making Abby's nape prickle in warning.

As she gaped at the woman, a sudden flash of recognition blasted through her.

The woman who had shot Hani. An image of her had been all over the news.

Now she wore a grayed wig, but there was no mistaking that face…or the deadly intent in her eyes as she stared at them.

The thought had no sooner flashed through Abby's brain than the woman's hand emerged from her purse…with a pistol in it.

Abby's spine jerked taut, her eyes glued to the weapon as it swung toward them. Disbelief hit her, then fear.

A scream locked in her throat, her hands automatically coming up to shield herself.

Walter grabbed her by the arm and yanked her off the stool. Her high heel caught on the foot rung. She threw her hands out to catch herself as she tumbled to the stamped concrete just as gunshots exploded in the night.

Abby scrambled around the edge of the bar, curling into as small a target as possible. People all around them screamed and dove for cover, but the shots kept coming.

One bullet slammed into the edge of the bar,

sending up a spray of bamboo shards. Another hit the ground near her, sending chunks of concrete into the air.

Then Walter grunted and dropped to his side with a strangled cry.

Oh, God, he was hit.

Terrified, Abby grabbed the edge of a nearby table and toppled it over, trying to give them more cover. Glass shattered as a shot hit it.

Walter groaned and tried to roll over. The front of his shirt was soaked with blood over his lower belly. Abby reached for him, trying to keep as low as possible, cringing at the helpless feeling of exposure. His eyes were wide, his face pale as he pressed his hands to his front.

Shit, oh, shit…

She grabbed his shoulders, shoved him flat beneath her as more bullets slammed into the table. Two punched through it. Sharp bites of pain peppered her right calf. Abby bit back a cry and tucked her leg in tight, curling into a ball on her side.

The firing abruptly stopped.

Heart lodged in her throat, Abby waited a second, then risked a peek around the edge of the downed table when she heard the distinct sound of people in some kind of a scuffle. A security guard had one arm clamped around the shooter's waist, his free hand twisting the wrist holding the pistol. The woman was snarling at him, an animal sound of rage as she struggled in his grip, teeth bared.

No one was helping him. Abby lurched to her knees, her legs wobbling. Afraid or not, she would help him take that bitch down.

"I'll be right back," she blurted to Walter, kicking off her heels before getting up and running toward the security guard, ready to help him wrestle the woman to the ground so she couldn't hurt anyone else.

The woman screamed as the guard twisted her wrist. A loud bang rent the air as the gun went off. Abby gasped and jerked to a halt, ducking on instinct.

The guard grimaced and slumped, turning as he fell to his knees, and the pistol went flying. It hit the stamped concrete with a clatter and skittered out of sight to Abby's right. But even disarmed, the shooter continued to fight the wounded guard.

Rage and determination swept through Abby in a burning wave. *Now or never.* Gritting her teeth, she started running toward them.

In that instant the woman fought free of the man's hold, shoved him to his back and clambered to her feet.

Abby skidded to a stop, her bare feet slipping out from under her. She threw out a hand to catch herself as the woman tore toward her with an expression of absolute murder.

Skin crawling, terror bursting inside her, Abby lunged to her feet and took a running step back toward the bar. She scanned for something to grab and throw at the woman. People there were cowering in fear behind whatever cover they could find. Walter lay flat on his back, blood pooling around him. His head was turned toward her, his face full of pain and dread.

The running footsteps behind Abby seemed to be

getting closer, sending a bolt of fear through her.

She'd only made it a few steps before a hard weight hit her in the back. Abby gave a stifled cry a second before slamming into the unforgiving concrete, the woman's weight landing on top of her.

Pain radiated through Abby's ribs and pelvis, her forearms where she'd tried to catch herself. Her chin struck the ground, skin scraping as they skidded along the surface.

Within a few heartbeats, the pain and shock of it flipped the internal switch inside her from flight to fight.

With a feral snarl, Abby flipped over, throwing the woman off balance. Jumping to her feet, Abby assumed her fighting stance without thinking, fists raised. Before the woman could stand, Abby twisted and lashed out in a left roundhouse kick. Her shin smashed into the woman's ribs as she tried to rise.

Pain streaked along her shinbone as the shooter screeched and grabbed her side, but the insane woman wasn't down yet. Immediately Abby stepped back and did another left roundhouse, aiming for her opponent's head. The skirt of her dress restricted her movement. She missed her target by inches, yelped in surprise when the woman caught her ankle in both hands and pulled.

Abby barely managed to wrench her foot free in time to stumble back and regain her footing. The woman pushed to her feet, her expression set. She was way too close for Abby to risk turning and running.

Fight. You have to take her down.

Abby wound up, lunged forward and swung out

with a right cross. Pain shot through her hand as her knuckles plowed into the woman's jaw. The shooter's head snapped back and she began to fall backward.

Abby whirled to flee. A foot flashed out, tripping her.

Once more she crashed to the concrete, on her hands and knees this time. *Get up. Quick.*

She flipped over onto her back just in time to put her hands up as the woman launched herself at Abby in a flying tackle. Down they went in a tangle of limbs, rolling, flailing. A streak of agony shot through Abby's head as the back of her skull bounced off the concrete.

They rolled once more, Abby coming up on top, scrambling to her knees, disoriented. But the woman heaved and twisted, sending them both tumbling over the edge of the pool.

The shock of plunging into the water knocked the breath from her. It closed over her head, the woman's weight shoving her down, down. She flailed, kicking out with her arms and legs, couldn't reach the bottom.

Hands tangled in her hair. Locked there and shoved down. Abby twisted her head, reached up blindly to rip at the restraining hands.

Legs wound around her ribs, squeezing. Forcing her little remaining air from her lungs.

Abby thrashed, both hands clawing at the restraining wrists. Her lungs burned, her heart seeming three times its normal size as the panic burned through her. She yanked hard against the seemingly unbreakable grip, finally freed her hands and used the woman's shoulders for leverage to push up and kick toward the surface.

Her head broke through the water. She dragged in a desperate gulp of air, then those frantic hands locked around her shoulders and dragged her back under again.

Panic turned to rage. Abby was all instinct, lashing out with her legs, her fingers curled into claws as she raked at the woman's face. Anything and everything to get free. To get air.

Someone plunged into the water close to them. Abby didn't look, too focused on fighting her way free. The breath of air she'd sucked in was almost gone now, her entire chest on fire, eyes about to pop out of her skull from the strain.

Help me. Oh, God, help me…

A powerful arm wrapped around her ribs, tearing her from the woman's grasp.

Using her final burst of strength, Abby kicked and headed upward, that strong arm propelling her toward the surface.

OVERCOME WITH FEAR and fury, Kai ripped Abby free of the woman's grasp and hauled her to the surface.

"Get out and get behind cover," he ordered as soon as she'd cleared the water and dragged in a heaving breath. He gave her a hard shove toward the side of the pool to make sure she was clear, then turned back to deal with her attacker.

The woman's head broke the surface a few yards away, her furious gaze narrowed on him. She made an unintelligible sound of rage and took a stroke toward him.

Before she'd made it a single yard, Kai lunged, locking an arm around her throat, his other hand flashing out to catch her right wrist in a punishing grip that squeezed her bones together.

Ignoring her screech of outrage and pain, he pinned her to the front of his body, applying just enough pressure with his forearm to cut off her air. She made a choking sound, grabbed at his arm with her free hand and went rigid.

"Don't fucking move," he snarled in her ear, and began dragging her in a rescue swimmer's hold toward the pool's edge, adrenaline screaming through his veins.

He'd been in dozens of firefights. Faced overwhelming enemy fire with a calm determination drilled into him by his instructors in the Corps and the experience that came with enduring combat. He was steady under pressure. Calm.

But the moment he'd heard those gunshots off in the distance as he'd raced toward the pool to meet Abby, his heart had stopped. He'd never known fear like that, the kind that iced his blood and froze his muscles. And when he'd veered around the corner to find Abby underwater, the woman trying to drown her, a red-hot, primal wrath had overtaken him.

Without conscious thought he'd sprinted full out to the pool and dived headlong into the deep end, his only thought to save Abby. Now that she was safe, the bitch who'd attacked her would fucking pay for what she'd done to Abby and Hani.

"Let me go, you corrupt *bastard*," the woman gritted out, raking her nails over his forearms.

Kai barely felt the sting, his body in combat mode. "Shut up." He squeezed her throat tighter, and the garbled words stopped.

From the corner of his eye he saw Abby scramble up over the edge of the pool and stay there on her hands and knees. Fuck, he wanted to go to her so badly, see if she was hurt. And he would in a few minutes.

But first, he had to deal with this murderer.

None too gently, he towed the woman the last few feet to the side of the pool. The water here was just shallow enough for him to be able to stand as he wrenched the woman's arms behind her back and hefted her out of the water, dumping her onto the deck on her stomach like a landed fish.

She twisted and tried to sit up but he was faster, using the side of the pool as a springboard as he leapt out of the water and seized both her forearms, dragging them behind her back to pin them in place.

"I said, don't fucking *move*," he growled, shoving her arms higher, enough to make her cry out and arch from the pressure against her shoulders. She was goddamn lucky he had enough restraint to stop from breaking both her damn arms.

Three security guys rushed over to take her into custody. Kai kept a firm hold on her wrists until they cuffed her, then shoved to his feet, water sluicing off him onto the pool deck.

"Get her out of here," he rasped out, half-afraid of what he might do to her if they didn't get her out of his sight right fucking now. Because God knew he was amped up and ready to kill, but he wanted answers more. And by God, he'd get them.

A shrill scream behind him split the air. "Look out!"

Kai's heart rocketed into his throat and he whipped around. *Abby.*

She was still on her hands and knees at the edge of the pool, but she wasn't looking at him. He followed her gaze to a man who had appeared near a pathway leading to the pool. He was in silhouette, backlit against the shot-up tiki bar.

But Kai clearly saw his arms rise, along with the pistol in his hands. It was aimed directly at Kai's chest.

Muttering a curse, Kai dove for the ground just as a shot shattered the taut silence.

Chapter Twenty

Abby jolted as the shot cracked through the air, ice congealing in her veins.

People were screaming again. Running from this new threat.

Through the chaos she cast a frantic glance at Kai, a sob catching in her chest. He was down. She couldn't see him clearly because of all the people running around. Was he hit?

Trembling from shock and exhaustion, she swung her head back around to look at the shooter. He was still there, weapon pointed at Kai.

He fired again.

"No!" Abby screamed, the word torn from the deepest part of her, but it was drowned out beneath the noise of the panicked people trapped between the shooter and Kai.

The man must have heard her though, because he

whirled to face her, weapon aimed. And everything stopped as her gaze locked on the muzzle of the pistol in his hand. Her heart lurched. Time froze.

Blood roared in her ears in deafening waves, heavy as a bass drum, raw terror flooding her body. Lurching to her feet, she took a running step just as a shot detonated behind her.

She flinched, cried out as a concrete planter exploded inches beside her. Desperate to find cover, she ducked behind a huge rectangular-shaped planter filled with tropical plants.

More screaming around her. Two more shots hit the planter, raining bits of plant and ceramic down on her.

Jesus. She huddled there, trapped and helpless. There was nowhere else to go. And he was coming for her.

She cast a frantic glance around, looking for something she could defend herself with.

Her gaze snagged on a dark shape lying on the ground a few feet away. The woman's fallen pistol.

Stretching out on her stomach, Abby flung out an arm and snatched it just as another bullet smashed into the planter. Shards flew out, nicking her left forearm.

She flipped onto her back, raised the pistol in her shaking hands and braced herself. She'd never fired a gun, didn't know what the hell else to do, but if he kept coming at her then she had no choice but to shoot. Kai might be bleeding to death right now. Abby had to end this if she could. At least had to try.

Battling the shaking in her arms and hands, she crept to the edge of the planter, risked a peek through the foliage. The man was coming toward her, a dozen yards or so away.

She had to do this. She had to do it *now*.

Praying she wouldn't hit an innocent bystander by mistake, she took aim and fired. The gun bucked in her hand, jerking both arms upward. The man flinched but didn't stop.

Dammit! She'd missed him.

He adjusted his aim to fire at her, his expression set. Promising death.

Lower, quick! Adjusting her aim, she fired again. Again. He grunted and lurched forward. The hand holding his gun dropped a few inches.

Again. Locking the muscles in her arms to counteract the recoil, she pulled the trigger once more. This time he fell to his knees. His pistol dropped to the concrete.

Abby fired again. Her weapon clicked. She squeezed the trigger. Another click.

Shit. Empty.

Trembling all over, Abby scrambled to her knees, gun still in her hands as she peered over the edge of the planter. The man was on his knees, one hand holding him up.

Then a human blur streaked through the darkness and plowed into the man's side. Abby swallowed a cry. *Kai.*

He took the shooter down in a flying tackle, both of them slamming into the ground with a bone-jarring thud that wrenched a bellow of pain from the wounded shooter.

Shaking, queasy, Abby struggled to her feet and took a step toward them, the empty pistol still frozen in her grip.

Kai eased off the guy and got to his knees, both hands pinning the man's wrists behind his back. His head snapped toward her and their gazes met, his chest heaving, stark relief on his face as he stared at her.

He's okay.

Her heart started beating again. Hard, bruising thuds against her ribs. She stopped walking, lowered her arm.

Her hand was numb. The gun fell from her fingers. Clattered on the concrete.

Was it over? Were there any more shooters? She darted glances around her, looking for more threats. The woman was gone, and Kai had the man pinned. Security and cops were rushing toward them.

A strangled groan sounded from behind her. She whipped around. Walter was watching her from over behind the tiki bar, eyes glazed. "Ab-Abby," he wheezed out.

On wobbly legs Abby rushed to him, dropped to her knees at his side. There was so much blood. His hands, belly and lap were covered in it, and a pool had formed around him. Two people were cautiously crawling toward them, now that the danger was over.

"Call 911," she choked out. "Now." God, she hoped somebody else already had.

Her boss gave a low, guttural moan, his legs moving restlessly. In agony.

"Walter," she said, her voice hoarse and breathy. God, she was freezing. Shaking, her teeth chattering. But she had to stop the bleeding somehow.

"You...okay?" he managed. His face was pale,

shiny with sweat.

"Fine," she said, forcing a reassuring smile that fell way short of the mark. Her whole body trembled, her breaths coming in shallow gasps.

Someone handed her a shirt. Her hands shook as she wadded it up and pressed it to Walter's belly. He cried out and arched, his expression twisting with pain.

"I'm sorry, I'm sorry," she whispered, leaning into her hands to apply pressure. She didn't know how else to help him. "G-get a blanket," she said to the man nearest her.

They had to keep him warm. Keep him alert until they could take him to the hospital. She blocked everything else out, afraid to lose focus for even a moment, or she might fall apart.

A solid hand landed on her shoulder. "Ma'am. Ma'am, you can move back."

She glanced up into the concerned face of a security guard. Blinked at him.

The man nodded once. "I'll take over now. The paramedics are on the way."

Reluctantly, Abby lifted her hands and eased away. She gripped one of Walter's hands instead, squeezed tight. "I c-can't leave him."

"I understand."

The guard ripped open a bag and began pulling out bandages. Holding Walter's cold hand, Abby looked up, scanned for Kai.

She couldn't see him. Everyone who had been trapped on the pool deck and pathways were now rushing away, back into the hotel, obscuring her view. And the man she'd shot…

A hard lump formed in her throat. The scent of Walter's blood filled her nose, meaty and nauseating.

She swallowed, trying to force the prickly obstruction down, but it wouldn't budge. Instead it grew, filling her windpipe until she could barely breathe, the memory of the gun kicking in her hand so vivid it was as though it was happening all over again.

Had she killed him? Hit someone else by mistake?

Her stomach twisted, bile rushing up her throat. The shaking got worse, an uncontrollable tremor that rolled through her in waves. She shut her eyes, tried to block everything out.

Kai. She wanted Kai.

"Ma'am?" the security guard said.

Abby didn't respond, just squeezed her eyes shut and struggled to hang on to the last shred of her control.

"Somebody bring her a blanket," he called out.

She barely heard him, fighting the sobs that burned in her chest. Everything faded out. Sounds around her blurred, voices became indistinct. She couldn't even feel her fingers clutching Walter's hand anymore.

"Abby."

That deep, familiar voice penetrated the thick fog she was in.

"Hey. Shortcake, look at me."

She opened her eyes, raised her head. Searching for the source of that voice.

Warm fingers grasped her chin gently, tipping her face up to meet concerned dark brown eyes.

Kai. He was kneeling in front of her, a worried

frown puckering his brow. "Abby, say something. Are you hurt?" His voice was urgent as he swept his hands over her arms, her sides. Checking for injuries.

The knot in her throat burst free. A hard, dry sob ripped out of her. Releasing Walter's hand, she reached for Kai.

Kai cursed under his breath and caught her to him, his big, strong arms locking around her back. "Sweetheart, are you hurt anywhere?"

She shook her head and buried her face into his shoulder, her bloody hands clutching fistfuls of his shirt. God, they'd almost died tonight.

"Okay, it's all right," he soothed, one big hand coming up to cradle the back of her head. Protecting her, sheltering her.

But he couldn't take away what had happened. Or what she'd had to do.

"Is he...d-dead?" she ground out between chattering teeth. God, she was shaking apart, her bones aching.

The hand on her hair tightened, pressing her face harder into the wet fabric stretched across his chest, the warm muscle beneath it. "Yes."

Her face scrunched up as another sob tore loose.

He made a soothing sound. "I've got you, shortcake. Just hold on tight." Scooping her up into his arms, he got to his feet.

"No—" Abby lifted her head and twisted around to see Walter. "I can't l-leave him."

"The paramedics are taking care of him. See?"

Her blurry gaze found the uniformed men loading her boss onto a stretcher. "But—"

"Where are you taking him?" Kai called out to

them, correctly guessing what she'd been about to ask.

"Memorial," one of them answered, and went back to tending Walter.

Kai carried her over to another paramedic. He pronounced her banged and scraped up, in shock, but otherwise uninjured.

"She should probably go to the hospital and get checked out, just in case," the paramedic said.

"No," Abby said, adamant. "I just want to go to my room." She gave Kai a pleading look. She just wanted to get away from all of this and be alone with him to get her bearings.

"I'll take you up as soon as we give our initial statements," he promised, squeezing her tight.

He held her to him while the police questioned them, warming her with his big body. It seemed to take forever, but finally they finished and were allowed to go—and only because he was DEA.

Kai started carrying her from the scene with rapid strides. "We'll get an update once your boss is out of surgery. For now, I'm getting you the hell out of here."

Abby nodded, glad to be leaving.

Several people came up to them as Kai carried her from the pool area. Security guards. Police officers. Kai snapped at them that they'd have to wait, and walked faster.

Guests and staff all moved out of their way as he headed for the main building, shock on their faces. Abby hid her face in Kai's broad shoulder again and curled into his chest. She hated the stares, the horrified eyes on her. She wanted to be alone with

Kai.

She didn't know how long it took to get up to her room, but finally they were there. A staff member ran ahead and unlocked her door for them. Kai gave him instructions to tell the police and security services he would call them up to the room to answer more questions when she was settled, and not until. Then the door closed behind them, locking out the rest of the world.

Abby expected him to set her on the bed but he walked straight through to the bathroom, shifting her in his arms so he could reach out and start the shower. She didn't move, needing the comfort of his hold almost as much as she needed air to breathe.

He seemed to understand that, because he waited a minute, then walked straight in with her, both of them fully dressed. She gasped as the warm water hit her chilled skin.

"I can't—s-seem to—catch m-my—breath," she said between gasps.

"It's shock," he answered in a low voice. "Totally normal. Just let the shakes roll through you. Don't fight 'em. Slow your breathing. In, out, one at a time."

She tried to do as he said, but the hitching in her chest made it hard to control her breaths. "C-cold," she whispered.

"I know. I'm gonna get you warmed up right now."

Kai set her down on the small bench seat built into the shower wall, adjusted the spray so that the water sluiced over her body, then hunkered down in front of her to take her face in his hands. He scanned her face, settled his gaze on hers, then lowered his hands to grasp hers.

Abby looked down. They were covered in dried blood. Walter's blood.

She shuddered, sucked in a breath and forced it out slowly.

Kai squeezed her hands. "That's good, sweetheart. Nice and slow. Let your muscles relax."

Focusing on his calm, steady presence, she willed her body to go lax. She was safe now. Kai had her, wouldn't let anything else happen to her.

"Good girl." Reaching up beside him for the soap set into a nook in the wall, he washed Walter's blood from her skin. By the time he was done her breathing was more even, but she was still cold, occasional shivers wracking her.

He set her clean hands in her lap. "Let me get a better look at you," he murmured, reaching for the sodden hem of her lavender dress. The soaked fabric clung to her skin as he gently peeled it up her body. "Lift your arms." He eased it over her shoulders and head, tossed it aside before stripping off his own shirt.

Abby sat there, docile as a doll as he undid her bra and dropped it. His hands were warm and sure as they stroked over her shoulders and arms, her ribs. The scrapes and bruises all over her throbbed, but the cuts on her legs stung the worst.

He grasped one ankle and raised her leg, watching her face. She couldn't quite control her flinch and looked down at where his fingers were probing. Thin trickles of blood ran down her calf to her ankle, turning to pinkish rivulets that dripped off her foot and swirled down the shower drain.

Raising her calf slightly, Kai angled her leg and squeezed two fingers on either side of a cut. She bit the inside of her lip at the swelling burn, hands gripping the edge of the bench.

Easing back on his haunches, he raised his hand to show her the tiny ceramic fragment he held between his thumb and forefinger. "All done. They're not too deep. I'll clean them and get a bandage after you're dried off. I don't think you'll need stitches, except maybe for this one. We'll see how it goes." He stroked his thumb along the cut he'd just pulled the debris from, his touch gentle, soothing. "Can you shift around for me?"

"I'm fine."

"Then turn around and let me see for myself."

Abby turned a little, giving him her back. Every bruise and scrape throbbed and stung now that the adrenaline rush had disappeared. "That woman killed Hani?" she asked softly.

His hands stilled on her back. "Yes." He smoothed his palm over her spine in a soothing caress, pressed a kiss to the top of her right shoulder. "I stopped at security to update them about everything when I got here. I was on my way to meet you when they called me back to look at some surveillance footage. It was her. Heading for the conference rooms."

So she'd followed Abby and her boss outside from there. "Who is she?"

"Don't know yet. But we will soon enough." There was a dark edge to his voice she'd never heard before.

Abby wrapped her arms around herself, bowed her head and closed her eyes. "And the man? Who was he?"

"My guess is somebody working for Juan Montoya."

She peered over her shoulder at him. "Who's that?"

"Head enforcer for a new lieutenant with the *Venenos*."

Abby faced the wall again, shock welling inside her. The bounty. He'd come here to kill Kai. "I thought he shot you," she rasped out, shuddering.

Kai made a low sound and wound both arms around her ribs, pulling her off the bench. "He tried. Might have hit me if it hadn't been for you." He scooted back against the wall and slid her into his lap, one hand on the back of her head as he held her to his bare chest, his other arm wrapped securely around her waist.

He held her tight, the steady thud of his heartbeat beneath her cheek helping to soothe her. "And I thought he shot *you*. Jesus Christ, I swear my heart stopped."

Another shudder sped through her as those terrifying moments replayed in her mind, but at least now her teeth weren't chattering and she didn't feel like she was going to throw up anymore. "I saw the gun lying there. Never fired one before. I was scared I might hit someone else by accident, but it was the only thing I could do to stop him, so I had to try."

"God, you were so damn brave, Abby." He buried his face in the side of her neck, his breath warm against her skin. "I'm so fucking proud of you, and sorry as hell you were forced to make that decision in the first place."

Proud of her? She'd killed a man. Now they wouldn't get any information out of him. She wouldn't face criminal charges because she'd acted in self-defense, but it was still something she was going to have to grapple with. Tonight would haunt her for a long time.

"But mostly—" He drew in a deep breath. "I'm just glad you're okay."

She nodded. "Me too." He felt so good against her. A solid wall of warm muscle for her to lean on and cling to. An anchor and safe haven in the storm. His arms held her tight, protecting and sheltering her. She sighed, let out a shuddering breath and leaned against him, her rigid muscles finally relaxing.

They were quiet for a few minutes, both of them savoring the closeness, the soothing rhythm of the warm water as it flowed over them. She wasn't cold anymore. Just sore and exhausted. "So what happens now?"

He stroked a hand up and down her back. "When you're ready we'll call the cops and security up, so they can finish questioning us both. Then we'll get a status update on your boss."

"And after all that." Her fingers dug deeper into the muscles of his back, a scary vulnerability taking hold. She didn't know how to process all this. Didn't know what to do. "You'll stay with me?"

Kai groaned and pulled her head away from his chest to frame her face between his hands, his expression so tender and sincere it brought a sheen of tears to her eyes. "I'll be right next to you through all of it. *All* of it, I swear." And he sealed the vow with a long, possessive kiss.

Chapter Twenty-One

On Wednesday afternoon Kai stood at the edge of Hani's grave as they lowered his casket into the hole.

Around him, nearly a hundred people crowded around the gravestones to offer their support to him and his *tutu*. Mostly people from his old village, but also law enforcement members, and Hamilton and Taggart, who had flown in for the funeral. That meant a lot to Kai.

Almost as much as the presence of the two women on either side of him.

Kai wrapped his arm tighter around his *tutu's* frail shoulders as she leaned into him, silent sobs shaking her slight frame. Losing Hani cut deep for him, so he could only imagine how much worse it was for her.

On his other side Abby held tight to his free hand, her thumb stroking over his knuckles in wordless comfort. Even after the terrifying ordeal she'd been through Sunday night and the long hours of interviews over the next two days, she'd put aside her own troubles and done everything she could to be there for him. While he'd kept his promise and stayed by her side through it all.

Diane Whitehead was in jail awaiting a hearing. She'd lost her daughter to opioid abuse she blamed on the medical and pharmaceutical systems. Killing Bradshaw had been step one of her plan for revenge, taking out the man who had prescribed her daughter the final dose of drugs that had sent her back on the tailspin that ended in a heroin overdose.

Taking out Hani eliminated someone higher up the drug trade supply chain than just a low-level dealer. Abby and her boss had represented the pharmaceutical aspect, presenting as suitable targets.

Apparently, Diane had seen Hani meeting with Kai and Abby at the hotel that night. In her grief-ravaged mind, because he and Hani were cousins, they were all in league together in some dirty deal—the cartel, NextGen and Kai, who she'd seen as a dirty DEA agent.

As for the man Abby had been forced to kill, he was an up-and-coming hitter for Juan Montoya and the *Venenos*. And Abby had been right—she *had* been watched, maybe even followed about a week before she'd run into Shelley. The cartel had been keeping tabs on his old building, hoping to get a lead on him. Not surprisingly, after the botched attempt to kill Kai and collect the bounty last night, Montoya had apparently left Maui sometime overnight without a trace. No doubt heading back to Mexico and whatever rock he'd crawled out from under.

Kai set his jaw as he stared down at the lid of his cousin's coffin. God, what he wouldn't give for the chance to go back and somehow force Hani to go straight. He should have done something more, should have tried harder. Now he was gone, cut down in his prime when he might have turned his life around with the right help and encouragement.

In the background beneath the pastor's voice, the muted crash of the waves hitting the beach behind him was a bittersweet requiem. Within sight of this very cemetery, he and Hani had spent countless hours at their favorite beach spot swimming, surfing, and of course fishing together. It was fitting that his cousin be laid to rest here, within a stone's throw of the ocean he'd loved so much.

The casket made a thudding noise as it hit bottom.

He hid a flinch, stared down at the polished surface of it while the pastor continued with his prayer in Hawaiian, offering words of comfort. They didn't comfort Kai much. The only thing that helped was knowing Hani was in a better place now. No more suffering, no more fear. The only pain now was for the living.

His grandmother pulled away to gather a handful of earth from the pile beside the grave. She stood at the opening for a long moment, staring down at the casket, then tossed it in, her lips trembling. Kai went next, murmuring a prayer in Hawaiian to his cousin.

Soon after that it was over. People moved out of their way as Kai led his *tutu* and Abby through the cemetery and back to the parking lot.

She glanced up at him, gave him a sad little smile of understanding. She was beautiful in her cobalt blue dress, the color a few shades darker than her eyes, making her fair skin almost glow in the late afternoon sunlight. The scrapes on her chin were healing, along with the rest of her cuts and bruises.

At first, she'd been shocked at the thought of wearing such a bright color to a funeral, but he'd assured her that's how they did things here. They were focused on celebrating Hani and his life today, rather than on mourning his loss.

A few dozen people came back to his *tutu's* place for the reception. Mostly his and Hani's old friends, and Hamilton and Taggart, who stood out like sore thumbs in their somber, dark suits.

Abby booted everyone out of the kitchen to visit and mingle while she bustled around readying the food the three of them had prepared the day before. Hani's favorites.

Out on the lanai and in the back garden, everyone gathered to eat and share stories about Hani. There was a lot of laughter, a lot of reminiscing about the good times they'd shared over the years.

The gigantic knot in the center of Kai's chest eased as the hours passed. All he wanted now was to be alone with Abby.

He caught her around the waist as she bustled past with a tray of appetizers, and pulled her close to kiss her. "You don't have to serve us," he murmured against her mouth. "Everyone can help themselves. Come out and visit for a while."

"I will when everyone's fed," she said, kissing him lightly before sauntering off, tossing him a half-smile over her shoulder.

Hamilton stepped up next to him, his gaze trailing

after Abby. "Seems like a keeper to me, man."

"Yeah, she definitely is." He'd thought she was strong before, but her actions the other night had completely stunned him. And she'd done it to protect him as much as herself. He wasn't sure how much longer he could contain his feelings for her.

"What's happening? What'd I miss?" Taggart asked, stopping beside them with a fresh beer in his hand. He'd cut his red-gold hair short for the trip, but at least had ditched the somber suit jacket and tie for the reception.

"Just admiring the view," Hamilton said with a smirk.

Kai ignored them both, his gaze stuck on Abby as she bent slightly at the waist to offer one of his oldest friends something from the tray. Whatever he said to her must have been funny as hell, because she laughed, and in that moment she was so beautiful— inside and out—it made him ache. Their time together here on Maui hadn't been at all what he'd imagined or hoped it would be.

And yet…everything that had happened, including the bad things, had only brought them closer and intensified his feelings for her.

Someone nudged him in the ribs. He tore his gaze away from Abby, blinked at Taggart. "Sorry?"

His commander chuckled. "She's got you twisted around her finger already, huh?"

"More like welded, I think."

He took them both around, introducing them to various people, and stopped finally at his *tutu*, who was seated on the padded bench in the corner of the garden, holding court like a Hawaiian queen of old, no less than a dozen men surrounding her, hanging on her every word.

As the conversation flowed around him, Kai's gaze drifted back to find Abby, who was near the kitchen talking with two women. She was watching him.

The instant their gazes met, she smiled, a private smile just for him. And the open admiration and reverence on her face was so powerful it hit every last undefended piece of his heart.

She was *proud* of him.

For a moment, Kai couldn't breathe. No one had ever looked at him like that before. Not even his *tutu*, who loved him to death and was proud of him in her own way. But not like this.

Because Abby looked at him with total pride—as though she was honored to call him her man.

Heart thudding hard against his ribs, Kai set his beer down on a nearby table without even looking, unable to tear his gaze away from hers, and closed the distance between them. He needed to tell her. *Now*.

She stood and met him partway, her eyes searching his anxiously. "You okay?" she murmured, cupping the side of his face with her hand.

Her concern and touch almost undid him. Kai curled his fingers around hers, his heart about to burst. "Come with me." Holding her hand tight, he started for the front door.

"Where are we going?" she asked, trailing after him.

He didn't answer, too overcome with emotion to

speak yet. He had to tell her now or he'd explode. Couldn't keep it in a second longer.

Outside the house, he turned right and headed to a secluded spot in a grove of palm trees where a hammock hung between two gracefully bending trunks. He stopped there, turned her so that her back was against one and took her face in his hands, a burning knot of emotion lodged in the center of his chest.

She studied him for a moment, then a soft smile curved her lips and she mirrored his move, cupping his face in return. She shook her head a little, almost in amazement. "You're the most incredible man I've ever known, Kai Maka. I swear you take my breath away every time I look at you."

Kai exhaled in a rush, his heart splitting wide open, his throat tight as he searched for the right words. Tracing his thumbs over her cheeks, he savored the silky softness of her skin. He didn't know the exact words he wanted to say, hadn't planned on telling her like this. But life was too damn short, so he needed to do this right now or he would regret it.

Damn, his heart was racing, and she was staring up at him with those big blue eyes, waiting.

He found his voice. "Until you, I didn't know what I was missing." He paused, drew in a breath. "I've been looking for you my whole life, and it turns out you were right there across the hall from me for the past two years." He shook his head, awestruck all over again at how blind he'd been. "I didn't *see* you. But I see you now, and I can't look away. Abby...*aloha au ia oe*." It felt right to say it in his language.

Her eyebrows drew together as she frowned at him in confusion. "Hello and…something?"

He huffed out a laugh. *Real romantic, Kai.* "I said, I love you."

Her face lit up with joy, making her eyes glow. "Oh, thank God. Because I love you too."

Kai groaned and crushed her to him, one hand on the back of her head to hold her cheek against his heart. He thought he'd been in love before? No way. Nothing had ever felt like this. Nothing had ever felt this right. Not until Abby. She was a piece of him now, and always would be.

"How do I say it in Hawaiian?" she asked, peering up at him.

He smiled, his hands at her lower back, holding her close. "*Aloha au ia oe*," he said slowly.

She repeated the first bit, got stuck at the end and made a frustrated sound.

"*Ia oe*," he finished.

Wrapping her arms around his neck, she gazed deep into his eyes. "*Aloha au ia oe*, Kai," she said.

Her pronunciation was all wrong, but the effort was adorable and heartfelt, and hearing that declaration from her in his language made it ten times as powerful. "You're mine, shortcake." His voice was a low rumble, edged with a possessive growl.

She hugged him tight in return, pressing her delectable body into him in an effort to get closer. "Yes, I sure am. And that makes me the luckiest woman in the world."

EPILOGUE

Five weeks later

When Kai pulled up in front of his building and saw none of the lights in his place were on, he frowned, surprised at how disappointed he was. "I thought the girls were supposed to meet us here when we got back?"

It was his birthday. The whole team had gone to grab a quick beer after their long day of meetings at headquarters before coming back here to Kai's place for a barbecue.

In the weeks since returning home from Maui, Abby had already formed a bond with all the significant others. She had been cooking for two nights in a row to get everything ready for his party, and he'd helped as much as she would let him. Which hadn't been much, but at least he'd been willing and made the effort.

"They were," Colebrook said from the back seat of Kai's truck. "Hang on. Let me text Piper and see where they are."

"Maybe they're watching a movie or something," Kai muttered. He drove around the corner and turned into the gated underground parking garage.

"Yeah, she says they're here," Colebrook said.

"Jaliya's here too," Khan said from the back.

"And Charlie and Tess," Prentiss added. "Rest of the guys are already on their way up the elevator."

"So everybody's here except Taylor. Where's she at, Granger?" Kai said with a wry grin, already knowing the answer.

"Home with her cat and a pint of ice cream," said Granger, also in the back. "She loves the other women and she's getting better about coming out to social events, but this was way too many people in a confined space for her comfort level. Too 'people-y' for her, as she put it."

Kai chuckled. "Gotta love her."

"Yeah, you'd better," Granger said. "Otherwise I'll pound your smirking face in, birthday boy or not."

Kai didn't respond to the little jab, still grinning.

Abby's car was parked in her usual spot next to Kai's. He pulled in beside her and shut off the engine. They all climbed out, and the cab raised several inches without the burden of their combined weight.

Stepping out of the elevator on the top floor a minute later, Kai spotted his other four teammates standing outside his door, all grinning like idiots. "What?" he asked. "What's going on?"

"Wait'll you see this," Rodriguez whispered with

a laugh, his hand on the doorknob.

See what? Curious, Kai stepped up next to him, craned his neck to see as his teammate pushed the door open. It was almost pitch dark inside his loft, but the unmistakable sound of feminine giggling came from the back area where the master bedroom was located.

"Hello?" he called out, walking in. Smelled freaking amazing in here, all kinds of tantalizing aromas coming from the kitchen.

Along with a faint glow from there, too.

A half-smile curved his mouth when he rounded the corner and spotted what was on the kitchen island. The girls had been busy over the past couple hours. Half a dozen jack o' lanterns carved out of pineapples sat there—he'd told her they carved those instead of pumpkins at Halloween, and she must have liked the idea. Their little triangular eyes, noses and grinning mouths glowed from the candles inside them, illuminating what looked like an equal number of wine bottles lined up on the counter.

"Anyone here?" he joked as the others came in behind him. It was way too quiet now. That spelled trouble. He put his hands on his hips. "Hey, if you guys are having a naked pillow fight back there, we want in on that action."

A chorus of enthusiastic affirmations from his teammates backed up his statement.

The words had no sooner left his mouth when a barrage of foam darts streaked out of the darkness, pelting him from every angle. He threw up a hand to shield his face, took a stumbling step back and slammed into Prentiss. "Hey!"

Yells and war whoops erupted from the darkness as the unseen attackers rushed them, peppering them with a continuous barrage of foam ammo.

Stifling a laugh, Kai lunged over and hit the nearest light switch. The firing stopped.

When he turned around, what he saw made his eyes widen.

Abby, Charlie, Piper, Tess and Jaliya stood before them, fanned out in a semi-circle, all of them wearing helmets and NVGs. All of them pushed the NVGs up onto the mounts. The brim of Abby's helmet dipped almost over her eyes. Her face was covered in camo paint.

"Hi," she said with a saucy grin that told him she was adorably tipsy, and popped one more round at him. It hit him dead center in his chest and bounced off, and she looked so pleased with herself he had to smother a laugh. "Welcome home, birthday boy."

"Hi. Been busy, I see."

"Oh, yeah." Another cocky grin, and she pushed the helmet up. "Your present's ready. Wanna see it?"

"I dunno, do I?" Since he'd come home to a bunch of pineapple jack o' lanterns and a barrage of foam darts, he wasn't sure what kind of present she'd got him.

"Yeah, I think you do." She laid his specialized Nerf gun over her shoulder and sauntered out of view, those sexy hips swaying.

Kai shared a grin with his teammates. As far as birthdays went, this one was pretty memorable already.

"Okay, here it is."

He looked over as Abby emerged from around the

corner with someone behind her. Shorter than her, dressed all in black, face covered by one of his black balaclavas. As Abby stepped aside, the smaller figure pulled off the balaclava.

The air rushed from Kai's lungs. "*Tutu*."

His grandmother broke into a wide smile and held her arms out. "Surprise."

Kai rushed over to scoop her up in a hug that lifted her from the ground. She was so damn small, but she hugged him so hard with her frail little arms. He buried his nose in her hair, breathing in the sweet, familiar scent of her plumeria perfume. "When did you get here?"

"About two hours ago. Abby picked me up at the airport."

Still holding her off the ground, he swung his gaze to Abby. She was watching him with such love, her expression soft, and damned if he didn't fall in love with her all over again right then and there. "You set this up?" He already knew the answer. No one else would have done this for him.

"Yep. Happy birthday."

Kai set his *tutu* down and carefully set her aside, his gaze on Abby. He stood there staring at her until her smile slipped, and a flicker of doubt entered her eyes.

Hiding a smile, Kai rushed her.

Her blue eyes, twice as vivid with the dark camo paint surrounding them, widened. She let out a squeak of alarm and whirled to flee, but she had no chance. He was on her in a heartbeat, grabbing her around the hips to hoist her over his shoulder. She laughed and grabbed the back of his shirt to hold on as he ran straight around the corner of the brick wall and into the master bedroom, where he kicked the door shut with one foot.

"Kai, are you serious? Your *tutu* just flew for like, fourteen hours straight to get here. Put me down."

"I'll put you down when I'm good and ready to put you down," he answered.

Without slowing, he went straight to the bed and tossed her onto it. She landed on her back with a little "oof" and scrambled up onto her elbows, pushing the helmet up so she could see him. Kai pounced, caging her beneath him.

Her delighted giggle made his heart turn over, and it turned into a soft shriek when he buried his face in her throat and blew a big raspberry against the sensitive skin there, grazing her with his stubble. "Kai!" she warned, weak with laughter, her hands pushing at his shoulders.

Raising his head, he peered down at her. "This is a new look for you."

She waggled her camouflaged eyebrows. "Yeah. You like?"

"I do." Grinning, he kissed her. "You missed a spot though," he said, nibbling on first her lower lip, then her upper one. She tasted like her favorite red wine.

"I know. I didn't want to spoil the taste of the wine with camo paint."

He shook his head at her. She was so adorable. "Do you have any idea how much I love you?"

She frowned, considering it. "No. Remind me."

He glowered playfully and smacked her hip with his palm, earning a yelp of outrage. She knew damn good and well that she meant the whole world to him. "What the heck did you guys get up to while we were gone?"

"Training."

"Training?" he echoed. She was a hell of a lot more than tipsy. If it wasn't for his *tutu* being here, he would have told the others to go the hell away now so he could enjoy Abby's current state to the fullest. "What kind of training?"

She traced his mouth with a fingertip, her teeth dug into her plump lower lip. "CQB."

He laughed. Close quarters combat? "Really. And who was teaching you?"

"Charlie. She's badass."

Colebrook's sister, who was also Rodriguez's other half. "Yeah, she is." Came from a whole family of Marines, and she could handle herself. "So…I'm confused. Why were you guys practicing CQB in my loft?"

"So we'd be ready to ambush you. And we totally did. You weren't expecting it at *all*."

So damn cute. "No, I wasn't." He rubbed the tip of his nose against hers. "What else did you do?"

"We practiced room clearing."

His eyebrows went up. "Did you? With my Nerf guns?"

"Well, not at first. At first we used those." She gestured lazily to the floor beside her.

He glanced over, smothered a snort at the objects strewn across the rug. "Those are coat hangers."

She shrugged. "I can do a perfect buttonhook now. Wait 'til I show you."

A slow grin curved his mouth at the pride in her

voice. "Can't wait to see that later."

She leaned up to nip at his lower lip, stroked her tongue across it. "I got some other moves you haven't seen yet either."

He swallowed a groan at her suggestive tone, the way she snaked one hand down the length of his back to grip his ass and squeeze. Damn, he still had to go out there and play host, because it was his damn birthday and everyone was here to spend time with him. If he didn't love them all so much, he'd be damned annoyed right now. "You did this to torture me," he accused.

"Mmmm. Would I do that?"

Yeah, she would. Because she loved pushing him until he reached his limit, then stripped her naked before pinning her to the nearest flat surface where he could have his way with her.

Her eyes sparkled naughtily up at him, her hips lifting to press against his erection. "So I guess the camo paint works for you then, huh?"

"On you it does." He kissed her, pushing his tongue into her mouth to claim her in the only way he could for now. "I've got a surprise for you too," he murmured.

She stilled, that seductive sparkle leaving her eyes, replaced by curiosity. "You do?"

"Mmhmm. In my pocket." He nudged his hips into her, rubbing his erection against her.

She wedged a hand between them and turned it over to cup him through his jeans. He growled low in his throat. "That's not my pocket."

"No?" She squeezed him, adding to his torment, making him reconsider his decision to wait until

290

later. "Just checking." Her palm slid over him with firm pressure, dragging a groan out of him as her hand dipped into the front pocket of his jeans. She stopped when she grasped what he'd tucked in there, her eyes searching his in silent question.

"Pull it out," he murmured.

She withdrew her hand, holding the blue satin ribbon tied to the Maui keychain he'd bought for her. It held a single key, decorated with palm trees. A knowing smile transformed her expression. "Are you asking me to move in with you, Agent Maka?"

"Yes, ma'am. As soon as fucking possible." She stayed over a few times a week, but it wasn't enough. He wanted her here permanently, so that he could always come home to her. And before he and the team deployed to Afghanistan in a couple months, he was putting a diamond ring on her finger.

She wrapped her arms around his neck, arching her sexy body beneath him. "Is tomorrow too soon?"

His heart turned to mush in his chest. "Tomorrow works perfectly for me. But you're staying here tonight."

"Only if you make it worth my while," she teased.

"Oh, shortcake, you know I will." Gripping her head in his hands, he kissed her with all the hunger burning inside him. Abby drove him out of his skull just by being near him. And the way she accepted and loved him made him feel like he could do anything.

"Hey!" A heavy fist pounded on the closed door just as things were escalating to the next level. "Maka, get your ass out here, *brah*. You promised us all food. It's your birthday, for Chrissake. Get out here and do your hosting duties, asshole."

Kai paused, his hands in the process of working Abby's shirt up. "Get lost, Granger," he called back. "There's all kinds of food in there ready to be heated up. Figure it out."

Muffled male laughter came from outside the door, and this time his *tutu's* adorable voice spoke. "But I came all this way to see you. Abby promised me steak and a baked potato with all the fixings. And a pineapple cake. Pretty sure she mentioned my pineapple cake, too."

Kai growled and lowered his forehead to Abby's while she shook with silent laughter. "Damn, they stooped to using my own *tutu* against me."

"Because everyone knows you can't say no to her."

He couldn't say no to Abby either, but was smart enough not to tell her so.

Pushing up onto his knees, he grasped her hand and hauled her upright. "Come on, shortcake. The sooner we get out there and feed everybody, the sooner we can come back in here and finish this."

"Oh, all right," she grumbled, shooting a glare at him when he swatted her playfully on the butt as she climbed off the bed.

With his lady at his side, he walked out of the bedroom to spend the rest of the night with the people he loved the most, all of them gathered here to help him celebrate his birthday.

Because of Abby, his heart had never been so full.

—The End—

Thank you for reading FAST FURY. I really hope you enjoyed it and that you'll consider leaving a review at one of your favorite online retailers. It's a great way to help other readers discover new books.

If you liked FAST FURY and would like to read more, turn the page for a list of my other books. And if you don't want to miss any future releases, please feel free to join my newsletter:

http://kayleacross.com/v2/newsletter/

Complete Booklist

ROMANTIC SUSPENSE

DEA FAST Series
Falling Fast
Fast Kill
Stand Fast
Strike Fast
Fast Fury

Colebrook Siblings Trilogy
Brody's Vow
Wyatt's Stand
Easton's Claim

Hostage Rescue Team Series
Marked
Targeted
Hunted
Disavowed
Avenged
Exposed
Seized
Wanted
Betrayed
Reclaimed
Shattered

Titanium Security Series
Ignited
Singed
Burned
Extinguished
Rekindled

Blindsided: A Titanium Christmas novella

Bagram Special Ops Series
Deadly Descent
Tactical Strike
Lethal Pursuit
Danger Close
Collateral Damage
Never Surrender (a MacKenzie Family novella)

Suspense Series
Out of Her League
Cover of Darkness
No Turning Back
Relentless
Absolution

PARANORMAL ROMANCE
Empowered Series
Darkest Caress

HISTORICAL ROMANCE
The Vacant Chair

EROTIC ROMANCE (writing as *Callie Croix*)
Deacon's Touch
Dillon's Claim
No Holds Barred
Touch Me
Let Me In
Covert Seduction

About the Author

NY Times and USA Today Bestselling author Kaylea Cross writes edge-of-your-seat military romantic suspense. Her work has won many awards and has been nominated for both the Daphne du Maurier and the National Readers' Choice Awards. A Registered Massage Therapist by trade, Kaylea is also an avid gardener, artist, Civil War buff, Special Ops aficionado, belly dance enthusiast and former nationally-carded softball pitcher. She lives in Vancouver, BC with her husband and family.

You can visit Kaylea at www.kayleacross.com. If you would like to be notified of future releases, please join her newsletter: http://kayleacross.com/v2/newsletter/

Made in the USA
Columbia, SC
11 January 2018